I0691939

A Magic Redemption

by

Tena Stetler

A Demon's Witch Series, Book 5

This is a work of fiction. Names, characters, places, and incidents are either the product of the author's imagination or are used fictitiously, and any resemblance to actual persons living or dead, business establishments, events, or locales, is entirely coincidental.

A Magic Redemption

COPYRIGHT © 2018 by Tena Stetler

Cover Art by *Kristian Norris*

The Wild Rose Press, Inc.
PO Box 708
Adams Basin, NY 14410-0708
Visit us at www.thewildrosepress.com

Publishing History
First Black Rose Edition, 2018
Print ISBN 978-1-5092-2342-8
Digital ISBN 978-1-5092-2343-5

A Demon's Witch Series, Book 5
Published in the United States of America

Time seemed to go on forever as she slowed and walked backward for a while, her foot steps in the sand filling with water as she traveled along the shoreline, as if nature erased her intrusion. She turned around and continued her trek. Unaware of how long or how far she'd walked, the sudden outline of a figure, cloaked in the fog, jogging toward her caused panic to set in. Her heart pounded rapidly in her chest, she swallowed hard, adrenalin pumping through her veins as flight or fight response kicked in. Digging her good foot into the sand, she prepared to attempt a sprint…to where. Where the hell am I? A quick glance around, she spied a light from a familiar building far off on the bluffs as the figure burst from the fog. A tall, wide-shouldered male with long muscular legs came closer. She froze.

Once lithe, strong, and agile in her former life, a boss's retaliation had taken a toll on her body. Because she was tired, her gait was uneven and unsteady, even a slow sprint would likely end with her face planted in the sand.

Praise for Tena Stetler and…

A VAMPIRE'S UNLIKELY ALLIANCE, which was voted Best Romance Novel 2017 by Critters/Preditors & Editors Readers Poll.

~*~

A WARLOCK'S SECRETS: "Thank you, Ms. Stetler, for creating a phenomenal world! It's one where I fell in love with a Warlock and believed in the beauty of a gryphon."

~Author Mary Morgan

~*~

AN ANGEL'S UNINTENTIONAL ENTANGLEMENT: "I wasn't prepared for how much I would grow attached to both Mystic and Caden. I'm always impressed when any author can create such a bond between her characters and the readers. Tena Stetler has an immense talent for that and more."

~ Reviewer: Mrs. N. Book Heaven

~*~

"What a nice surprise to discover a well written paranormal romance with a touch of fantasy. [*A WITCH'S JOURNEY* is] a story of witchcraft, dark secrets and second chances. Blended with Magic and Romance, a fun read."

~Books & Benches

Dedication

To my family and friends
for their continued unwavering support.

~

To my husband
for his dedication and encouragement.

~

To my editor extraordinaire, Lill.
You make my words shine.

~

To The Wild Rose Press, a fantastic publishing house.

~

To my fellow authors at the Wild Rose,
who are always ready to lend a hand.
What a great team!

~

Most of all to my READERS,
for whom I write the stories!

Chapter One
Is Freedom a Choice? A Responsibility? A Way of
Life—She Didn't Know

Synn lounged in the front window seat of her
cottage, one leg tucked under her, the other dangling,
bouncing a stream of gold magic current between her
thumb and fingertips. *What am I doing here?*
The voices in her head had been silent since
defecting to the side of the Demon Overlord of the
Western Hemisphere. *It was the right thing to do.* Her
reward for a job well done, "freedom with a few
conditions" to quote the Overlord's words. *But am I
really free?* She scrunched up her face and pursed her
lips.
A question she still didn't know what to do with.
Impatiently, she pushed her long hair over her
shoulders, tucking a few shorter wisps around her face
and behind her ears. Tobi, a hairdresser at The Wycked
Hair Salon had tamed her tresses before she'd
accompanied Bruce and Angie to Ireland, giving her a
short-layered look around her "pixie-like" face—Tobi's
words not hers—and leaving the back long.
Tobi claimed it softened her sharp features and
made her look cute. Back then she didn't want cute, she
was a warrior, wounded—but warrior still the same.
Tobi insisted cute could give her the drop on an enemy.
Now, she wasn't sure what she was, and that was

1

disconcerting.

Staring out the window at the mist thick as pea soup, she couldn't see the ocean. But the constant beat of waves crashing against the shore made her restless. She uncurled her legs and stood, padding over to the door and opened it. A cold wind made her eyes water and whipped her hair around her face in stinging tendrils.

The door slipped out of her hand and crashed against the wall with a bang. Sucking in a breath, she shrugged into her coat, pulled a red, yellow, and orange knitted hat over her unruly raven hair, tugged gloves out of her coat pockets, and slipped them on.

She shivered zipping her coat up, tucked her feet into the warm boots Gavin had given her, all the while telling her the north wind off the coast could be bitter. *He was right—about a lot of things. Most of all that she needed her own space.* She wrestled the door closed behind her and locked it, pocketing the keys.

As she picked her way down the trail, the wind died down to a friendly breeze heavy with brine except for an occasional brutal gust. Screaming sea birds swooped and dived into the white capped waves hunting for food. Wrapping her arms around her body more for a sense of security than for warmth, she continued down the path to the ocean shoreline.

She breathed in the crisp air and skipped along the beach, skirting the incoming waves and chasing them out. Her limp was barely noticeable. A calm replaced her restlessness. *Is this what it's like to be free? Make your own decisions, take action without permission? It's nice, but lonely in a way.*

Time seemed to go on forever as she slowed and

walked backward for a while. Her footsteps in the sand filled with water as she traveled along the shoreline as if nature erased her intrusion. She turned around and continued her trek. Unaware of how long or how far she'd walked, the sudden outline of a figure, cloaked in the fog, jogging toward her caused panic to set in.

Her heart pounded rapidly in her chest, she swallowed hard, adrenalin pumping through her veins as flight or fight response kicked in. Digging her good foot into the sand, she prepared to attempt a sprint…to where. *Where the hell am I?* A quick glance around and she spied a familiar building far off on the bluffs as the figure burst from the fog. A tall, wide-shouldered male with long muscular legs. She froze.

Once lithe, strong, and agile, her former life, and boss had taken a toll on her body. Because she was tired, her gait was uneven and unsteady. Even a slow sprint would likely end with her face planted in the sand.

"Synn, are you all right? You're a long way from the cottage," a male voice called to her.

A familiar male voice. She blew out a breath as her heartbeat slowed a bit. "Am I?"

"Aye, it's bitter out here. The pub's only over the ridge. Want to get something hot to eat and drink?" With a gentle brush of his fingers over her cheeks, he said, "You're freezing." Gathering her into his arms, Gavin held her tightly for a moment before loosening his hold. "Let's get you to Shaughnessy's where there's a roaring fire. You'll be warm in no time."

"I'm okay—just out for a walk. The walls were closing in." She stomped her feet. They were so cold there wasn't any feeling.

He narrowed his eyes. "How long you been out walking?"

"A while." She pushed his arms away and trudged toward the lights of the pub.

He grabbed her by the shoulders and whirled her around to face him. "You promised to call me when things got too difficult."

She tried to shrug out of his hold, but his hands were so warm. "You also said I need to learn to stand on my own two feet. Discover who I really am in this new world I've been thrust into."

"Okay, I'll admit those words were said in frustration."

"Anger." She shot back, giving him a defiant stare.

"Aye. You're right." He scooped her up and sprinted for the pub ignoring her objections and flailing limbs. "We can argue in the warm pub."

He was right—again. Relaxing against his muscular body sent spikes of desire through her. Feelings she had no business acting on. At least until she could hold her own without leaning on anyone for anything. She needed to earn his family's respect—his respect. The fact she was a demon with a terrible history that everyone was aware of was an obstacle she might never overcome. At least the townspeople were oblivious. That was a start.

The heavy wooden door to the pub groaned as he kicked it open. Warmth and laughter spilled out into the frosty night along with the mouthwatering aroma of Mulligan stew and yeasty scent of the establishment. All the tables in the center of the floor were full as were most the booths along the wall.

"Put me down. Don't embarrass me by carrying me

into the bar like a medieval knight with his conquest."

"Where the hell did you come up with that?" His lips twitched as he set her on her feet and steadied her. Grasping her gloved hand, he strode toward two empty chairs at the bar and motioned for her to sit.

She straightened her shoulders and remained standing though she was starting to shiver.

"I'm going to go in the back and get a couple of extra chairs and put them by the fire." His da, Tim and ma, Mary sidled over to where they stood. Mary touched her cheek. "She's chilled to the bone."

Gavin grabbed her around the waist and thrust her into the last chair at the end of the bar. "Be right back." He sent a significant glance to his ma and da. Mary nodded and bustled into the kitchen. Before he returned, Mary emerged with a mug and teapot on a tray. She set the tray down and shoved up the pass through at the opposite end of the bar.

"Darlin', you look frozen," Mary murmured. "What were you doing out on an evening like this?" She poured the steaming dark brew into the mug. "Cream or sugar?"

"A little of both. I can do it myself." She picked up the spoon, added sugar, and poured cream into the mug. "Thanks. I lost track of time. Sorry. Needed to get out of the cottage for a bit."

"Gavin saw you walking along the shore. After a while when you didn't turn back, he got worried." Mary shook her head. "We were talking about…" Then she reached out and touched her hat. "Glad you like the hat I made. Looks great on you."

"I like it a lot. Makes me feel cheery when it's gloomy outside." She smiled. "Thank you."

"You're welcome." Mary smiled and returned to take orders at the bar. "Check on you later."

Tim came up behind his wife with a bowl, spoon, and large piece of bread on a plate. "Thought you could use a bowl of stew and freshly baked soda bread." He set the bowl and plate on the bar in front of her.

Gavin swung out of the back room with two chairs and set them in front of the fireplace, then arranged a small table in front. "Now Kevin, and Will, don't you think these are for you." He winked at two men ambling toward him. "My lass and me be occupying these for a bit of a while. Go on with you."

They gave a hearty laugh and returned to the bar with their half empty pints.

She scooped up a spoonful of stew, slipped it in her mouth, and swallowed. "Mmm, this is delicious. Thank you." She took a couple more spoonfuls and bit into the bread, chewing slowly.

He sauntered up behind her. "Want to move over by the fire?"

"Sure." She could tell from his smile the argument was far from his mind, and that was fine with her. She picked up the deliciously warm mug and wrapped both hands around it. He carried the bowl and plate of bread to the little table, waited for her to take a seat, then eased down in the chair next to her.

Finishing the stew, she licked the spoon. "That was wonderful." She nibbled on the bread.

His face grew serious. "I have an idea. Hear me out before you answer. Okay?"

She hesitated for a moment, hoping he wasn't going to bring up…

"It's been a couple months since you moved into

the cottage. I've given you space as we agreed. You're comfortable there?"

"Yes, it's quite cozy. I love the ocean so close. Somehow, the crashing of the waves is comforting."

"Maybe it's time for you to move forward. By that I mean, think about getting a job, meeting people. Making this your home."

"Who's going to hire me? The skills I have are not what most people are looking for." She lowered her voice, "Demon warrior or assassin for hire."

"Well about that. Ma and Da want to hire a couple people during the upcoming tourist season."

"Stop right there." She held her hand out in front of her. "I'll not take any more charity from your ma and da."

"It's not charity. Bridget will be happy to train you. A dependable employee is what we need, and they think you would fit right in. April, May, and early June we'll be swamped, then again in October. Ma wants to help Brandy plan the wedding. Especially since Brandy and Stefan had to postpone the wedding for nearly a year due to Randy's fall."

Synn shook her head slowly, what an unfortunate turn of events. Brandy, Gavin's sister was engaged to Stefan, a vampire. They'd planned a big wedding in Ireland the first of the year, but their plans were derailed due to her boss's accident.

Brandy worked as a park ranger in Glacier National Park. During an inspection trip, her boss Randy lost his footing on a steep trail and tumbled down the side of a mountain. Due to complications, his injuries had taken longer to heal than anticipated, putting their plans on hold indefinitely.

"Yeah, what a freak accident. Lucky he only sustained a few broken bones. Messed up Brandy's plans." She shrugged. "I could help. If Brandy would let me."

"I imagine Ma's going to need it." He paused a beat. "What Brandy doesn't know won't... Anyway— according to Ma, Brandy's leave has now been approved for mid to late December. It got pushed back again. Stefan's radio station is more flexible, he's free to leave anytime, but they want remotes once a week. That should be a bugger."

"A remote?"

"Yeah, he'll broadcast from here to his station at a certain time. Don't have any idea how he'll pull that off." He waved his hand dismissively. "Not my problem. The wedding is set for the end of December now. It's off-season, but prep in October or November is going to drive Ma nuts. Especially with Christmas festivities and the wedding celebration all taking place in the pub. Bridget will cover for Ma, but someone has to cover for Bridget." He stood and brushed the wrinkles out of his pants. "I'll be right back."

"Brandy won't be here until maybe December, and the wedding is scheduled for the end of the month?" Her eyes widened. "That's not much time for final details."

"Nope. Possibly mid-December," he called over his shoulder. After making his way to the bar, he said a couple of words to his da before his ma joined the conversation. Tim turned, drew a pint, and handed it to his son.

When Gavin returned, a smile brightened his face. "All we ask is that you think about the offer."

Staying cooped up in the cottage wasn't doing her any good. As a teen, she hadn't been idle after Baltizar murdered her family and forced her to do his bidding. As she grew up, her parents were proud of her many talents. If they'd kept that information to themselves, they might still be alive and her life oh so different. She sighed.

"Hey, how about it?"

His voice brought her back to the present. The music, laughter, chatter, she could—would enjoy—but what if someone found out? "I don't know. I'm a stranger and a yank to boot." She unzipped her coat, tucked her hat and gloves in the pockets, glad she'd worn new black jeans and a turquoise sweater today.

He grinned. "Oh, you're more than a yank... That's why you're so damn attractive." He leaned over and kissed her on the cheek.

"I'm anything but." She put her hands to her cheeks as they warmed. "Don't do that in public."

Ignoring her comment, he continued. "So you say. Don't over think it. You're brilliant. You'll learn the duties in no time. Bridget isn't much older than you, might enjoy the company. Da, Ma, and I will always have your back. You'll be great."

With a mischievous twinkle in his eyes, he grinned wider. She should have anticipated what came next. That Irishman had an ornery streak a mile wide.

Quick as a wink, he bent over and brushed his lips over hers murmuring, "Don't want any of these lads trying to steal me girl."

Her lips parted to object. He covered her mouth with his and his tongue swept inside. Her traitorous body responded before she could think, arms wrapping around his neck, and her lips responding to his kiss. Hell, her body had a mind of its own. *He felt so good.* Desire spiraled through her body warming her lower regions as he eased away stroking her lips with the tip of his tongue.

"Way to go, laddie. Kiss her again," demanded the crowd through whistles and friendly shouts.

Her hands flew to her face, and she rushed into the ladies' room. *How could I ever face anyone again? Let alone work here?*

After a couple of minutes, Bridget bounced in face flushed and laughing. "Looks like you've taken the most eligible bachelor out of circulation." She patted her back. "Well done."

"What? I'm sure I don't know what you're talking about."

"Lass, I've never seen him kiss a woman like that in all my life. And I've known him since he was in nappies." She lowered her voice. "There was a time I yearned for him to kiss me like that." Bridget's expression went dreamy for a second, then she waved her hand dismissively. "Those times are long gone since I met me Quinn." Bridget fanned herself with a paper towel. "That man's got moves. Know what I mean?"

She had no idea how to react. Giving a quick nod, she shoved her sweaty hands in her pockets and stood there.

Without missing a beat, Bridget said, "Mary tells me you might be helping out around here while she plans Brandy's wedding." She snickered. "Says she's gonna help her plan the wedding, but we all know the truth." Bridget cackled again grabbing her by the arm.

"Come on, let's get out of here. 'Tis early and Gavin has the night off. He'll be waiting on you." She waggled her eyebrows. "And Tim will take me to task for disappearing during my shift."

Stumbling as Bridget dragged her out of the ladies' room, she regained her footing but couldn't avoid bumping into Bridget when she stopped short. "See, what'd I tell you." Pointing to Gavin waiting outside the doorway, she gave her a little shove and winked at him. "Best keep track of your lass, boyo, less other lads get ideas."

Bridget sashayed through the crowd, batted a couple men's wandering hands away from her ass. She stopped at the bar, picked up a tray of pints, and delivered them to a table in the center of the room. On her way back, she thrust a piece of paper in her hand. "Give me a call. We'll get together on my day off and have some fun."

When she unfolded the paper, Bridget's name and phone number were scribbled inside.

"Well looks like you've met Bridget. Making friends already, are ya?" He glanced toward the fireplace. "We seemed to have lost our seats. How about a dance?"

She shook her head. Even as he swung her into a jig, the band played a lively tune.

She tried to keep up, but her bum leg kept her off balance at times. No one seemed to notice. At the end of the dance, he put his hands around her waist, picked her up, whirled her around, and kissed her again before setting her on her feet. Quick and flirty, not like the soul-searing kiss he'd planted on her earlier. Still he left her tingling to her toes. She smiled. *This was fun.*

He grabbed a couple of pints, handed one to her, and introduced her around the pub. It was well past midnight when he swung his arm around her shoulders and pulled her to him. "Ready to get out of here? You can talk with Ma tomorrow about a job."

"Back to my cottage?"

"Of course. Unless you want to come home with me?" he teased.

Eyes wide, she stared at him too tired to come up with a witty answer.

"Only kidding." He paused his expression turned serious. "But one day I won't be." He helped her on with her coat and waited for her to put on her hat and gloves.

When they reached the car, he turned her to face him and pressed her against the passenger door with the length of his body. His mouth took hers with heated passion. She was shocked at her own eager response to his lips. Her body melted into him. Through their winter attire, she could feel his heat.

With hesitation he lifted his mouth from hers and trailed kisses down her neck. His hand slid up her side then he raised his head pursing his lips. "I think we better get you home, before I…"

The last thing she wanted to do was return to her empty cottage. But the alternative was even more scary—or was it?

Chapter Two
First it was the Challenge, then the Allure of Synn

Gavin closed the door to his home with a bang and kicked off his shoes. After starting a fire in the stone hearth, he grabbed a glass from the kitchen cupboard and poured two fingers of whiskey. Taking a swig, he hissed as it slid down his throat. Picking up the bottle, he ambled to the living room careful not to spill his drink. He plopped down on the comfortable couch. In his opinion, furniture was to be used, not admired. He set the bottle on the wooden table beside the sofa.

This house had been his ma and da's first home. Sometimes he imagined the laughter and fun they'd shared as a family inside these walls. Family meetings were always held in the kitchen around a large wooden table. Good news or bad it was shared as they all sat around the worn piece of furniture. Idly he wondered whatever happened to it.

His parents had built a bigger house designed to keep his sisters from killing each other as they reached their teenage years. Their fights were epic, but you wouldn't know it now. Living across the pond, they'd grown closer than they'd ever been. Sometimes he felt like the odd man out, but when they came home, it was grand. After college, they'd decided to remain in America. He'd moved in to claim the family's first home for his own, after the last set of renters left.

His feet ached. It had been a long day when he'd glanced out the pub windows and seen Synn wandering aimlessly on the beach. Plain and simple, he'd panicked, afraid she'd given up or retreated into the dark secrets she refused to talk about. She'd revealed none of her life before her contact with Bruce, claiming it was too horrible to relive. Someday, sooner than later, he'd get her to trust him and confide in him. Until then, he'd wait.

Dropping Synn off at her cottage, he'd sensed she didn't want him to leave. But their agreement, when she decided to stay in Ireland, was that she had to find her own way before they could resume any kind of intimate relationship.

It had been several months since his sister, Brandy, caught him and Synn in the kitchen at the pub. Brandy had thrown a conniption fit. She dragged Synn out of the kitchen, shoving her at Bruce, the Demon Overlord, and Angie, his mate, who had been seated at the table with friends and family.

Brandy issued an ultimatum that couldn't stand. Stefan, her fiancé, had talked her down and made her see that Gavin had the right to make his own choices. It was a good thing the pub was closed at the time. He grinned. After all who was she to say who he could date? She was engaged to a vampire.

None of them had remained true to their gryphon roots. He shook his head. *Funny how that happens.* Hannah the oldest, married a powerful warlock, who served at the pleasure of the Demon Overlord as his assassin. Now Tristian managed his teams that made sure the laws of creatures were observed. Justice was swift and deadly for those outside the law.

Brandy would soon wed a vampire, Stefan, whose previous history included a stint as assassin for The Vampire Council. He'd traded his weapons for a microphone and was a DJ for a radio station in a tiny town in Montana. What a strange turn of events. But Stefan was a good man.

His thoughts wandered back to that day in the pub. At the time the whole thing had been innocent. Synn had been helping him rinse and stack the dirty dishes in the washer. But from the moment he'd seen her, his attraction was undeniable. Eventually, they'd become friends with benefits. Her assistance to Bruce was invaluable in helping to locate a missing Book of Shadows and stop the migration of the dark demons in a world already on a destructive course.

Eventually, Brandy and her soon to be husband, along with Hannah, Gavin's other sister, and her husband, Tristian; and Angie and Bruce had combined magic and woven spells to seal the portals to Hell restoring the balance of magic.

For her efforts, Bruce had given Synn her freedom with a couple conditions. She'd decided to stay in Ireland and try to make a life here. He wanted to believe part of the reason she remained was because of him. But who knows?

He'd had his fair share of women, none holding his interest for very long. Most he'd known the majority of his life. Settling down with a wife and children was not on his radar, though his parents thought it was time. Ma and Da were talking retirement, and Ma wanted to travel the world. Da not so much, but he would follow his bride of over forty years anywhere she wanted to go. He smiled. When that happened, he'd take over the family pub and enjoy the life.

Pushing up from the couch, he walked to the windows that overlooked the moody sea and pushed one open a crack. The waves crashed against the shore, scent of the brine and the ocean washed over him cleansing his melancholy mood. He showered and fell into bed. Disturbing dreams awakened him in the middle of the night. The foreboding feeling that had plagued him on and off over the last week was back with a vengeance. He reached for the phone and tapped in Synn's number. She answered on the first ring.

"Gavin. I'm so glad it's you." She was out a breath.

He sat up in bed. "What's wrong?"

"Nothing that I know of, but I can't get to sleep. When I do, it's only for a few minutes, and Baltizar is controlling me again. I relive the horror over and over." Her voice trembled.

"When he injured you?" She'd told him a bit of what had happened. Brandy had filled him in on the rest, probably to discourage him from seeing Synn, and partly because Brandy really felt sorry for her. At least that's what he liked to think.

"Yes. It was…"

"I'm coming over."

"No, no that's not necessary. I know you have to work the early shift. I feel better hearing your voice. I'll be fine."

"Bollocks to that. I know better. I can… I'll be over shortly." He hopped out of bed, stripped his pajama bottoms off inside the front door. Stuffed jeans, a sweater, and boots in his go bag, then he yanked open the door and shifted into his gryphon form. The door banged shut. He picked up the bag in his beak, unfurled his wings, and pushed off into the moonless night.

Over the tree tops he soared loving the freedom of flight. The wind lifted him higher and higher as he dipped, caught the air currents, and banked left. It had been too long since he'd enjoyed the experience. His job, keeping an eye on Synn, and family obligations had kept him grounded. Fun and pleasure were in short supply. *It's about time for a change.*

Quietly landing among the trees a few yards from her porch, he shifted into human form. He yanked on his jeans, pulled the sweater over his head, and slid his feet into his scuffed, brown boots.

When he looked up, she stood in the open doorway dressed in only one of his black T-shirts. She'd apparently absconded with it after one of their trysts months ago. The shirt engulfed her. But he loved the fact that she wore it to bed. At least part of him was in bed with her. *How pathetic.* She'd fanned his flame into a raging bonfire and sated it. Oh God had she sated it. *Shit. I'm hard just thinking about it—her. But those days were over—for now. Maybe forever.*

She bounced on her toes as he approached. "You didn't need to come. I've got to learn to handle this on my own. Remember our agreement." Yet she slithered against him, wrapping her arms around his neck pressing into him. Resting her cheek on his chest, she closed her eyes.

Talk about mixed messages. *Her words say one thing. Her body is saying something entirely different.* He slid his arms around her, allowed them to slip to the small of her back, and brushed his lips over her cheek when she turned to him. "Synn, maybe living alone wasn't the best idea for you, yet," he murmured against her face.

"Okay, if not now—when?" she demanded. "Is it me—or the sex you miss?" Her mouth formed a thin line, but her eyes glittered for only a moment with what appeared to be unshed tears. She took a deep breath.

"Both," he shot back before he thought.

A single tear rolled down her cheek. She buried her face in his chest. "Will it always be this way? As long as he's out there I'll never be completely free."

"Not true. You're a captive of your own memories, fears, and feelings. You can't just walk away from something like you've endured most of your adult life and expect it not to leave scars. I can help you heal those scars. If you let me in. Trust me or someone enough to share those…" His voice trailed off, and he eased away from her. "Let's go into the house, fix tea, or something stronger, and talk about what's spooked you tonight."

Turning in the doorway, she stepped inside the sparsely furnished front room. She padded across the hardwood floor to the kitchen, where a small table and two chairs occupied the majority of the space in the tiny area. Placing the kettle on the stove, she flipped on the burner and turned to him. "That night when he punished me for losing Brandy and Stefan keeps playing in my head like a horror movie when I try to sleep, rest, or even close my eyes. It's getting worse, not better."

"You're dwelling on your past too much. Need something to keep you busy and your mind occupied. For now, take the job at the pub. You'll be surrounded by people that know and understand you. Learning the job will take your mind off of that situation. At the end of the day, you will be so tired, chances are you'll fall into bed and not wake till the next morning."

"I don't know." She hesitated a couple beats and shook her head. "What if I can't do it?"

"Don't be ridiculous." He softened his tone. "Bridget can teach anyone." He bit his lip and back peddled. "What I meant to say was, if I understand part of your previous situation—the reason Baltizar took you was your keen intelligence and many talents." He reached out and caressed her shoulder. "Waitressing isn't complicated. It will be a snap for you." He grinned. "Don't tell Bridget what I said. She'll skin me alive."

She scrubbed her hand over her face and straightened her shoulders. "You're right. But I don't want your family's charity. I'll earn my way. Thank you." The kettle whistled. Taking it off the stove, she poured the steaming water over a tea infuser in both mugs and handed one to Gavin.

He grabbed her hand. "Got anything a bit stronger, lass?"

She sniffed and smiled. "I think you've had enough for tonight."

They walked into the front room. He started a fire in the hearth, then settled down beside her. She snuggled into him and sipped her tea. After only a few minutes, her mug slipped from her hand. In one swift movement, he caught it without spilling a drop, leaned over, and set it on the floor. Her breath slowed to an even rhythm. She was asleep. Shifting a little in an effort to get comfortable, he rested his head against the back of the couch. *Tomorrow—scratch that—today will be another long day.*

A bright, Irish jig playing on his phone woke him.

She shot out of his arms and landed in the middle of the floor in a crouched position. She wiped her face, eyes wide and gaze darting from side to side. Her cheeks flushed bright red.

"'Tis all right, lass. 'Tis only my phone." He waggled the offending device back and forth in his hand then peered at the screen. Grimacing, he put the cell to his ear. "Hi Da, I know—I'm late. Be there shortly." He disconnected the call and scrubbed his hand over the scruff of his beard. "I gotta get cleaned up and head to work. I'll tell Ma you'll be at the pub by noon to help her with the dinner menu. Tonight, Bridget will show you the secrets of waitressing. You okay with all that?"

She blinked, yawned wide, and nodded. "Guess so." Straightening, she took a more relaxed stance, picked up the mugs, turned, and started toward the kitchen.

"Yep, me too. But if I gotta work, with so little sleep—so do you." He tousled her hair with his fingertips. "Better get moving." He knew better but couldn't help himself as he swatted her firm round butt hesitating only a beat to feel the warm female flesh. A beat too long.

She whirled around, the mugs crashed to the floor, and she planted her tiny fist in his gut.

He bent over at the waist. "What the hell was that for?" He wheezed trying to catch his breath.

Chapter Three
A New Job, a Fresh Start, no Punching the Customers

"I'm so sorry." She patted his back. "Lately, it's an automatic response. Been on edge and I don't know why."

"I strongly suggest you get a grip on that response before working with the customers tonight." He paused and straightened. "They can be a bit grabby after a few pints."

"And you think that's all right?" she asked hands fisted on her hips trying to keep her temper from spiking.

"No, it's not all right. But Bridget knows how to handle the unruly ones without knocking the air out of them. Most don't mean anything, it's the alcohol. No excuses. The ones who persist, we toss out with a warning not to return. The lessor offenders we threaten to inform their wives." He shrugged one shoulder.

A retort popped in her mind, but she didn't let it slip through her lips. She ambled into the bathroom and returned with a small leather bag. "You left this when we decided I should have my own place. Never had an opportunity to return it." Her gaze wandered over him. "Your clothes are clean. A shower and shave should get you on your way quickly rather than returning to your place."

He took the bag, unzipped it, and peered inside. "Yep, razor, shave cream, toothbrush, toothpaste, deodorant, and aftershave. I'm set. Thanks." Taking a couple long strides, he lurched to a stop. "You don't mind if I use your bathroom?"

"Of course not. Otherwise, I wouldn't have offered your bag." She bit her lip having said too much.

"I thought you hadn't had a chance to return it to me?"

"Oh…that too." Grinning, she felt the heat rise in her cheeks. Pivoting around, she bent to pick up the bigger mug pieces, dropped them in the trash, then grabbed the broom. She swept the shards of glass into a dust pan. After dumping them into the kitchen rubbish bin, she washed her hands and poured another cup of tea. Wrapping her hands around the warm mug, she waited.

Steam whooshed out of the bathroom as Gavin opened the door wide. "Thanks." He winked, grabbed her mug, and took a swig. "I'll be on my way. See you around noon."

"Yep." Shoulder resting on the door jam, she watched him sprint down the path and wished the warning bells would stop going off in her head. There hadn't been any visible signs of danger for months, even as she wandered alone on the beach at twilight last night. So why the constant flight or fight response welling up in her? Was something coming? She gave herself a shake and backed into the room. "Nonsense." The word echoed in the empty area and she closed the door.

A half smile turned the corner of her mouth. He was right. She couldn't haul off and slug a customer on her first day on the job. Standing in her closet, she sorted through her clothes. She slipped into a teal blouse and tugged on snug black jeans. Ignoring a pair of black leather over the knee boots, she toed on a pair of black comfortable shoes and opened her small wooden jewelry box. It was one of a few possessions she'd been able to secret away. A pair of onyx and silver drop earrings glittered under the lighting. She fingered the matching bracelet, then encircled it around her wrist. Her mother had given the jewelry to her for a birthday years ago. Somehow, it seemed right to wear them for the first time today.

Arranging her hair in one long braid, she flipped it over her shoulder, added lipstick, a touch of eye makeup, and glanced in the mirror smiling. *It's now or never.* Two of her warm coats hung on the pegs next to the door. She grabbed the heaviest one and bolted out the door, closing and locking it behind her. The walk to the pub cleared her head and left her with a surprising discovery. She was actually looking forward to working there. Mary and Tim had been supportive when Brandy had thrown that conniption fit and when Gavin announced she'd be staying in Ireland.

When she reached Shaughnessy's, she paused. Should she use the front door or the back? Gavin's car was parked in the lot along with only a couple others. Surmising the pub was closed, she ambled to the back door and pulled it open. Her senses were assaulted by the most delicious aroma, and warmth flooded around her.

"Hey Synn, we're about to send someone to find you. Figured you'd chickened out," Gavin teased.

"We were not," Mary said bustling over to give her

a hug as he took her coat. "Hurry, lass, we've got to get the specials cooked."

"What are we making?" she asked.

"Tonight's specials are colcannon with corned beef brisket, shepherd's pie, and salmon with whiskey cream sauce. Soda bread and the brown bread are about ready to come out of the oven. Grab a mitt and take 'em out."

"Smells wonderful." She donned oven mitts and scooted over to the stove. He hovered a few feet behind her. A quick glance at his sly grin made her wonder what he was up to.

"Gavin Amos Shaughnessy. Don't you dare take off with one of those loaves." Mary grabbed him by the shirt sleeve and laughed. "Yours are in the warmer. I made extra. Now shoo. Your da needs you behind the bar to stock the shelves. He said something about the distributor shorted him the good stuff."

She set the bread on the counter watching Mary hustle around the kitchen. It seemed like Mary was everywhere all the time. A couple of hours passed as she fetched ingredients, washed dishes, and followed Mary's instructions. Surprised, she actually enjoyed mixing the ingredients and inhaling the delicious aromas as she created the dishes from the recipes Mary handed her. When she had finished, Mary taste tested the dishes that she'd prepared.

"Wow, you are a natural." Mary smiled and got out a clean spoon and offered her a bite of salmon with whiskey cream sauce. She started to wave Mary off, but the tantalizing scent had her reaching for the spoon and tasting it. "Mmm…this is really good." The approach of quick footsteps had her whirling around as she dropped the spoon in the sink.

The kitchen door swung open. Bridget rushed in, tugging at the apron ties behind her back. "Time to open. You're with me."

She brushed her hands together over the sink, took off her flour smudged apron, then washed her hands thoroughly. "What do you want me to do?"

"Take orders of course." Bridgett snickered. She handed her an order pad, pen, and a list of items and prices. "I was going to have you follow me for an hour or so, but Callie called in sick, so it's just you and me tonight."

"You can't expect her to…" Mary started to untie her apron." I'll help you."

"No…you've got your hands full. Let her try. Best way to learn this job is on your feet." Bridget winked at her. "Take the order down. Everything is on the list. You can price it at the bar. If it's for food, walk into the kitchen. Mary or I will help you." She caught the little black apron Bridget tossed her way.

She slowly put it on and tied it in the back, slipping the pad and pen in one pocket, and the price list in the other as she'd seen Bridget do.

Bridget gave her a quick pat on the back and shoved her out the swinging door. "You'll do fine."

Gavin caught the door and held it open. "If you need anything, I'll…" He stopped mid-sentence at the glare his mom gave him and Bridget's finger waggle in front of his face.

She raised her hand to her mouth to hide a snicker, then waved him off. "I can handle it." *I hope. How hard can it be?*

Pasting a smile on her face, she pushed through the door into the main pub area. Several customers were seated at the bar and more trickled in. Gavin finished stocking the shelves while taking orders and building pints. All the while, he chatted with customers and gave others a hard time. *How could he do everything at once?* She watched for a second more before Bridget came up behind her. "He's been doing this all his life. Born to it."

She sucked in a breath and sauntered up to the first table. "What can I get you?"

At the table sat two burley men laughing and joking with an older man. In a loud rough voice, the younger of the two men said, "Lass, pints all around. We'll have the salmon too. Got any pan boxty?"

She paused for a moment. "I'll check." She hurried over to Gavin at the bar. "Do we have pan boxty?"

"Always."

When she returned to the table the older man grinned. "You're new here. I'm Burt. These are my two son's Ian and Patrick."

Inclining her head, she smiled. "Nice to meet you. Yes, I'm new, and we do have pan boxty."

"We'll have the pan boxty and bread comes with it. Right?"

Scribbling fast on her pad, Synn stopped. "That's three orders of salmon with pan boxty and I'll have to check…" She bit her bottom lip and glanced around.

Bridget slipped up behind her and shot the guys a warning glance. "Of course it does. You know that. Now quit giving Synn a hard time," Bridget scolded, yanking a towel from her apron and flipping it at the youngest.

"Her name is—" Burt paused a sly grin turned up a corner of his mouth. "Synn?"

"Yes. And any bad behavior from any of you and I'll tell Maggie. Understood?" Bridget raised an eyebrow then patted Burt on the shoulder.

"Yes, ma'am," the men said simultaneously.

She again read back the order, and the three men nodded. She smiled and hurried to the kitchen. Once the door swung shut, she handed the order to Mary with a shaking hand. Straightening her shoulders, she pushed though the swinging doors and into the main pub. Bridget was behind the bar pulling pints beside Gavin. There was no way she was going to try that. So she leaned on the bar close to Gavin and said hesitantly, "I need three pints."

He winked at her. "Be with you in a moment." He reached under the bar and slid a round tray in front of her.

Bridget finished her pints. "Go ahead and take a couple more orders, by then we'll have your pints. Mary will call your name when the order's ready. Looks like we are going to be slammed tonight." She jerked her chin toward main room and glanced at Gavin. "When is Katie coming in?"

"She should be here by now." A cold breeze blew through the pub as the door burst open. A short plump woman with bright blue eyes and auburn hair cut in a bob rushed in

"Sorry I'm late. Sean was late getting home. Had to feed the kids. Lord knows I can't leave that task to my ol' man." She waved a hand dismissively. "We'll get into a routine now that I'm workin' again." Grabbing an apron, she tied it on and grinned at her. "Who's the new girl?"

"That's Synn. She's a friend of the Shaughnessys."

Bridget motioned toward the shorter woman. "This is Katie. She fills in for us during the busy season."

"Nice to meet you," Katie said shifting her gaze from Synn to Gavin who was staring intently at them. Katie laughed. "I see."

"It's not like that." Bridget snorted. "Now go on with ya."

There wasn't an empty seat in the place when she turned around to survey the crowd. Where had all the people come from while she'd been in the kitchen? Making her way through the crowd, she took orders from the people seated in the booths on the far wall. "Need twelve more pints," she said in passing on her way to the kitchen.

"Your first order's up." Mary pointed to the tray on the counter and returned her attention to the stove where sauces simmered and Tim flipped the sizzling pan boxty.

She picked up the order, bumped the kitchen door open with her backside, and carried the meals to Burt and his sons. The pints were ready when she returned to the bar. Picking up the tray, she served them to the men. Weaving her way past a group seated near the bar, a thin woman stood at the end of the table. She laughed at something her companions said. The sound was so engaging that Synn smiled. *Not a bad way to make a living.* The night passed quickly. Most of the patrons wanted to converse with her after she'd taken their orders, slowing her down. Bridget and Katie teased and talked to the customers while taking orders and delivering pints much faster.

As the door closed behind the last customer, Gavin locked the door, and the staff gathered around the bar.

She plopped onto a stool, kicked her shoes off, and leaned her arms on the bar. Her feet hurt from being on them all night. Her arms hurt from carrying the large trays, but she'd not spilled a meal or drink all night. She smiled to herself. *Not bad for my first time. A little slow.*

Bridget sidled up behind her and patted her on the back. "Great job. You sure you've never waitressed before?"

She shook her head. "I was a lot slower than you or Katie."

Bridget snorted a laugh. "That's because the customers wanted to listen to you talk. So they asked all kinds of questions to hear that yank accent sprinkled with the soft southern drawl of yours."

Katie snickered.

The heat rose in her cheeks. She'd picked up the drawl to blend in when she'd been on assignment in Kentucky for Baltizar. When she was nervous it seemed to surface making her stand out in this crowd. "Oh. I noticed you didn't stop and talk as much as I did."

"Of course not. No one wanted to listen to me or Katie talk." She cackled.

Gavin glared at the two women. Tim slapped him on the back. "Leave 'em be."

"Hey Brig, we still going shopping next week on your day off? If we give them enough notice, Colleen and Gale may still be able to join us." Katie glanced over her shoulder to a thin woman with wire rimmed glasses, reddish brown hair waiting by the door.

Following her gaze, she recognized the woman as the one she'd passed by earlier with an infectious laugh.

"Planning on it. Colleen's your ride home tonight.

Right?"

Katie nodded. "Sean kept the car. I'll ring Gale too. She'd like to join us, since she missed the last one. Sick as a dog she was."

"Great. I'll check back with you when I get my schedule. We'll make a day of it. I'll pick everyone up bright and early." Bridget paused for a beat and turned to Synn. "Hey, wanna come along?" Bridget pointed the Synn's stocking feet. "You need some different shoes and layered clothes if you're going to stick around."

"Oh...I don't want to intrude on your—"

"Don't be silly. The more the merrier." Katie leaned over and whispered, "We're going to visit the lingerie shop. The one Bridget spends all her tips at in order to entertain her man."

"I heard that." Bridget giggled. "Quinn has nothing to do with it. I like soft things next to—"

"That's a different tune than last week—you like it hard." Katie leaned back on her stool laughing outrageously and nearly toppled over.

"I know several tunes, and it depends what we are..." Bridget shot back.

"That's enough ladies." Tim interrupted chuckling as his cheeks blushed. "Go on home with you." He made shooing motions with his hands. "Synn, great job tonight. See you tomorrow, same time."

"Synn, could I see you for a moment." Gavin nodded toward the kitchen.

Mary pushed out through the swinging doors. "Gavin leave her be." She walked to Synn, put an arm around her shoulders. "What'd you think? Can you put up with us?"

"Yes, of course. I had fun." She rubbed her aching foot then eased off the barstool eying Gavin. "Mostly."

He held one door open to the kitchen.

She ambled through the door Gavin held for her. The doors swung shut.

Chapter Four
A Disagreement

Gavin shrugged into his jacket then helped Synn on with her coat. When he pulled the back door open, the frigid north wind stung his face as they stepped outside. Once outside the pub, he turned Synn to face him. "I'm not sure it's a good idea to spend the day with Bridget and her friends, so soon."

"I'm not asking." She shot back wriggling out of his hold. "I'm a big girl. I can take care of myself."

"Sure you can. You could have been in serious trouble, had I not seen you at the water's edge." He snatched at her arm. She dodged him.

"I was fine." She huffed out wrapping her arms around herself.

"Bloody hell—you weren't even aware how far you'd wandered." He raked his fingers through his hair. "Synn, I care for you."

"Then trust me to make my own decisions."

"What if—I mean—"

"What if Baltizar returns and tries to regain influence over my being?" Her huge aqua eyes watched his face intently. "Then I'll be beyond anyone's help. He'll kill me."

She said it so nonchalantly it worried him. "So that's it?" He ground out.

Quizzically she glanced at him, one eyebrow

raised. "No. But it's a hell of a lot better than having him defile me again as he did when he murdered my family and forced me—I don't want to talk about this anymore. I'm going with Bridget and her friends next week. We'll be fine. You wanted me to make friends— yet when I try—" She raised her arm waving it around in frustration. "You can't have it both ways." She whirled around and marched down the street in the direction of her cottage.

"Wait—" He bellowed.

She stopped, turned, and glared at him. "You have no idea the things that have happened to me, and I survived. I put it all behind me when Bruce gave me my freedom. At least I tried. But they will always be a part of me. Before there can be you and me, there has to be a me, without you hovering and being overprotective. What you don't understand—if he returns—" She emphasized each word. "There is nothing you can do."

Her voice returned to normal. "Learn to live with it, or—" Sucking in a breath, she blew it out slowly, shrugged one shoulder. "There can't be an us." She paused as if letting her words sink in.

He rubbed the back of his neck and lowered his voice. "Okay—let's take a step back. Maybe I was a little overbearing."

"Ya think?"

"But the other night, you weren't—"

"You're right. I wandered into that dark place. But with Bridget and the girls, that won't happen. Only happens when I'm by myself. I have to learn to control it. As far as Baltizar is concerned, I trust Bruce and Tristian to keep him at bay. They'll know the minute he sets foot in the mortal world. That has to be good enough." Her voice gentled. "You worry too much." Rising up on her tiptoes, she kissed him softly on the lips. "I'll check in with you during the day. Okay?"

He sighed. "No, you don't have to. I trust you'll be fine. But if you run into a problem…"

"You'll be the first to know."

He reached for her hand. "Mind if I walk you home?"

"I'd like that."

He sprinted back to the pub, yanked open the door, and grabbed his coat. His da was wiping down the bar. "I'm going to walk Synn home. I'll clean up when I get back. You and Ma go on home." The door banged shut behind him.

It was an amicable silence as they walked hand and hand, under the cover of darkness, though the streets to her cottage. The breeze tousled his hair and sent a cold chill down his spine. The moon almost full, washed everything to a silvery gray. A contrast to the yellow pool of light cast on the ground from her outside lamp. On her porch, he took her in his arms and covered her cold lips with his mouth his tongue traced the full softness of her lips.

A quiet sigh escaped her lips. His tongue slipped inside teasing, tasting, and dancing with hers. He hoped to convey what his words had failed to do. Wrapping her arms around his neck, she leaned into him. He reveled in her curves pressed against him. Slowly, he released her and backed away. "I'll wait as long as it takes."

"Thank you." She took the keys from her pocket and unlocked the door. "See you tomorrow."

He waited for her to turn on the lights and close the

door before he trudged down the streets to the pub. He started to insert the key into the lock. The door flew open and his best friend, Quinn, stood in the entrance.

"You look like you could use a friend. You know, if you keep hanging around that girl, people are going to talk." Quinn joked. "You haven't fallen—" He glanced at his friend again. "Oh, no the ranks of the eligible men have decreased by one tonight. 'Tis a sad day for womankind," Quinn quipped following him to the bar. "Hey, can a guy get a pint around here?"

"No…we're closed." He punched his friend's shoulder as he swung up the pass through. "I've no idea what you'd be talking about. Too much of the drink tonight?" He picked up the bucket, filled it with hot water, and plopped the mop in it. Water splashed all over the floor.

"Naw, it's written all over your face. What's the matter? This one won't succumb to the Shaughnessy charms, laddie?" Quinn leaned his elbows on the bar and watched as Gavin mopped the floor behind the bar.

"They've never failed me, yet." He shot back wringing the mop out, pouring the dirty water out, and filling the bucket again. "What brings you around here so late? Bridget kick your sorry arse out again?"

"Oh, that'll be the day. My woman loves my arse." He jumped off the bar stool, did a little jig, and sat down again. "She's all excited about going shopping with the girls next week. Chattering on the phone with Katie. You know—girl stuff. But the way you were working that muscle in your jaw all evening, thought something was bothering you."

"Bollocks to that. I'm fine."

Quinn leveled his gaze at his friend. "Sure you are.

Don't want to talk about it, all right. Tell me it's none of my business. But don't lie to me. We've been friends way too long for that."

"Okay. It's none of your business," Gavin said sharply.

Both hands in the air, Quinn leaned back. "Okay boyo, whatever you say. You know where to find me." He backed off the bar stool and started toward the door.

Water sloshed over the rim, when he shoved the mop into the bucket. He tossed the pass through up and walked to his friend. "Quinn, sorry. I've a lot of things on my mind tonight. When I get them all sorted out, maybe I'll bend your ear a bit."

"No worries." He gestured dismissively. "Don't want to keep my lass waiting too long." He waggled his eyebrows. "See ya later."

"Okay." Finished cleaning the pub, he loaded the glasses in the dishwasher and turned it on. He paused for a beat, then poured a pint, flipped the lights out, and walked to the kitchen. Kicking the chair out from under the table, he plopped down in the seat, leaned back, and stretched out his legs beneath the table.

Taking a sip of his beer, he licked the foam off his upper lip. *What a mess. Why did I ever agree to those bloody terms of Synn's.* He knew why. But he wasn't ready to admit it to himself or anyone else. Water sloshed inside the dishwasher as it ran through its cycles, and he nursed his pint—thinking. Finally, he heard the dishwasher click off. He finished his pint, considered building another, and decided against it. Ambling over to the sink, he washed and dried his mug, turned out the lights, closed and locked the door.

Arriving home, he kicked off his boots and

moseyed over to the hearth. He'd banked the fire before leaving this morning. Taking a poker from the stand, he jabbed at the ash. Nothing. He walked to the neatly stacked wood, yanked a couple logs from the pile, and tossed them in the fireplace. A fine plumb of ash rose and scattered over the hearth. Crumpling up paper, he lit the corner before throwing it onto the logs. A tiny spark flamed and died. *Aw hell.* He flipped the heater on and stomped up the stairs to bed.

Sleep was elusive. He tossed and turned until the wee hours of the morning. When he finally fell into a troubled slumber, he had nightmares of Baltizar kidnapping Synn as he stood paralyzed unable to help. Her terrible screams sent shivers down his spine as she begged Baltizar to let her die. When he awoke, his pajamas were soaked with sweat, his heart felt like it would beat out of his chest. A bead of sweat trickled down the side of his face. He wiped it away with the back of his hand.

The clock read four in the morning as he grabbed his phone off the nightstand. When his feet touched the cold floor, he winced, then leaned over and felt under the bed for his slippers. He wiggled his feet into them, wanting so bad to hear her voice. Know she was all right. But she wouldn't be happy if he called her now. Besides, how could he explain why he called at this ungodly hour?

He padded to the bathroom, turned on the shower, let the room fill with steam, undressed, and stepped inside. The warm water cascading over his body relaxed his bunched muscles, cleared his mind from adrenalin overload caused by the nightmares. *I need to have a conversation with Bruce or Tristian—Find out exactly... Not a good idea. I'm not on the best terms with either and Tristian is plain scary. Need another avenue of information. Angie?*

Flight always had a way of settling his nerves. He picked up a small bundle of clothes and stepped out the door. The edges of his human form blurred like a trick of light, and his gryphon took over. One push up from the ground and he was soaring. Midway to his destination, he hovered and dropped the bundle of clothes in a clump of trees.

With every beat of his wings, he flew higher and higher. Sometimes, he never wanted to return to land. So much easier to glide along in the dusky sky, but the sun rose and the chance of him being spotted grew. The warmth of the sun on his wings as it peeked over the horizon improved his mood exponentially. He banked left over Ballycotton Cliff Walk. Not a soul to be found. Freedom of soaring above the sea and land made him forget his earthbound problems. With reluctance and several back beats of his tawny wings, he landed on the sandy beach as pinks, oranges, and reds blended together spreading across the horizon.

With what would appear to most as a shimmer of light, he quickly transformed to human once again. Sprinting to where he left his bundle of clothes, he stopped and dressed quickly. The beach was still deserted as he set out for home.

She danced inside the fringe of his conscious as he increased his pace, inhaling deeply the fresh sea air, and pushed her to the corner of his mind to be dealt with later. The memory of last night's kiss seared across his mind. The warmth of her gentle curves pressed against him. *Aww shit.* His body reacted to the memory. Lost in his thoughts, he'd covered more ground than intended.

Looking up just in time, he avoided a collision with a couple walking along the beach in front of him. He swerved, lost his footing, and crashed down on the rocky beach, striking his knee on a sharp stone ripping a large hole in his new jeans. Blood poured from the jagged cut soaking his pants and dotting the golden sand with red. Pain ripped through him.

"You're injured." The man reached down grasped a hold of Gavin's arm, helping him to his feet.

Brushing the sand from his jeans, he said, "It's only a scrape. I'm fine."

The man slung off his backpack and pulled a first aid kit out. "No, you're going to need stitches. Can we give you a ride to the hospital?"

"Not necessary, my house is right up there." He pointed to the home rising from the rocky coast.

"Then let me clean and bandage the wound. It'll only take a minute."

"Are you a doctor?"

"Yes." He glanced at the woman standing beside him. "We decided to visit Ireland for our tenth anniversary celebration."

"And he never goes anywhere without at least a first aid kit." She laughed sliding a loving glance toward her husband. "It served him well and you too, this time."

He limped over to a rock outcropping, eased down, and winced as the doctor dabbed antiseptic on his knee then bandaged it.

The doctor patted his arm. "That should hold you until you get home." He stuck out his hand. "Roger Neal and this is my wife, Tara."

He clasped the man's hand smiling. "Nice to meet you. I'm Gavin Shaughnessy. Thanks for patching me up. Sorry I almost mowed you down. My mind was a million miles away from here."

"We could tell. That's why we slowed our pace. You might want to pay more attention while you run." Roger grinned.

"Will do. Hey if you get a chance, stop by Shaughnessy's Pub." He reached in his pocket, drew out a card, and handed it to Roger. "It's not far from here. Pints on the house. It's the least I can do after you kept me from bleeding to death." He chuckled, glancing down at the wound, a speck of blood seeped through the gauze bandage.

The doctor took the card. "We might take you up on that tonight." He turned, waved, and ambled down the beach hand and hand with his wife.

He stretched his leg and flexed the knee back and forth. The skin around the wound was tender, but it tightened as the healing process had already began. He blew out a breath, relieved the doctor left before an explanation became necessary. Walking up the path to his house, he paused and turned to survey the area. For several moments, he was unable to shake the feeling of being watched.

Chapter Five
A Girl's Day Out

Synn groaned and rolled over opening one eye. The bright sunlight made her squint. She flexed her arms. They were slow to obey her commands, and the muscles were taut like rubber bands stretched too far. Gingerly, she touched her fingers to her temples massaging in a circular motion to ease the pounding in her head. The disagreements with Gavin over the past week must have caused subconscious thoughts of Baltizar to surface.

Each nightmare seemed so real. When she woke up, she was damp from sweat, and tears dried on her face. Several times she'd reached for her phone to call Gavin in the wee hours of the morning and thought better of it. Though nightmares had decreased in intensity, getting up and going to work had been difficult with little sleep, but she'd done it.

The upside was that her arms were starting to get used to hoisting the heavy trays but being on her feet all night…not so much. She'd hope for a good night's sleep since she had the day off and was going shopping with Bridget and the girls.

No such luck, the nightmares had returned with a vengeance. She'd gotten up in the middle of the night, fixed herself a cup of the herbal tea that Angie gave her before she and the overlord returned to DC. Whatever was in that concoction always soothed her nerves and let her get back to sleep.

But this morning—wow. The tea had never had this effect on her before. She suspected hefting the heavy trays nonstop all night at the pub had strained the muscles in her neck and arms. Hesitating for only a beat, she swung her legs off the bed, touched her feet on the floor, and scooted to the bathroom to stand on the comfy bath mat. At least it had a little warmth to it.

A glance in the mirror and she winced. Her huge aqua eyes were puffy, and dark circles curved under them. She reached for a washcloth, turned on the shower, and waited for the water to get warm. Holding the cloth under the stream, she wrung it out then placed the cloth on her face leaning into its warmth while the water cascaded over her body easing her aching muscles.

Jeez she was out of shape. The pounding in her head lessened. She washed her hair, lathered, and rinsed off, then stepped out of the shower and toweled off. When she wiped the steam from the mirror, her reflection hadn't improved. *This would never do.*

In the bedroom, she glanced at the clock on the wall. The girls would be here in less than an hour. She couldn't go out looking like this. What would her new friends think? There was only one choice she'd have to use a glamour. She rubbed her hands together. A soft violet glow passed between her fingers. Her forehead creased. She touched her hands to her face and closed her eyes. Sucking in a breath at the sting of the spell, she slowly opened them and released a breath.

Another glance in the mirror, her eyes sparkled, the swelling and dark circles were gone. She smiled. This was the first time she'd used magic in several months and hoped it didn't draw attention to her. A swipe of green eyeshadow, a touch of pink lipstick and she was all set. Now what to wear? With no experience to draw on for a girl's day out, she swallowed hard and looked at the clock on the nightstand. *What if they've changed their mind?*

****

Half an hour later she was ready. Dressed in a purple V-neck sweater that hung to her hips, blue jeans, and black boots, she blew out a breath and hoped her attire was appropriate. There was a soft knock on the door. "Synn, you ready?" Bridget called out in a cheerful voice. "We're going to paint the town red."

"I'll be right there!" She rushed to the door, swung it open, and grinned. "Why would we do that? Won't the shopkeepers be displeased? I don't have any paint. Do I need some?"

"Don't be silly. Have you spent most your life under a rock? It's an expression. We're going to have a grand time."

"Oh." She slung her tan bag over her shoulder, locked the door, and dropped the keys in her bag. Bridget grabbed her arm and towed her toward the car where Katie and Colleen were waiting seated in the back seat, grinning like Cheshire cats. Squished between them was an unfamiliar face. She slid into the passenger's seat, giving a fleeting glance at the new face as Bridget got behind the wheel.

"Synn, this is Gale Boohar. She was able to get away from her shop and join us today. She owns Pixie Magic a couple of blocks from the pub. Best lotions and herbal remedies in all of Ireland."

"Oh, I wouldn't go that far. Its secrets have been in my family for centuries. Nice to meet you, Synn." The tiny woman with bright red hair, freckles, and blue eyes that sparkled with mischief offered her hand.

A bit unsure, Synn shook it, trying to place the subtle magic signature she detected. It had to be coming from either Colleen or Gale, since it wasn't apparent at the pub when she'd worked with Bridget. For that matter she'd didn't notice anything when she'd passed by Colleen that night in the pub. Though she was busy, and the pub had its own aromatic atmosphere, there wasn't any type of magic signature in the pub that night. She stole another glance at Gale who smiled amicably.

"First stop, get Synn a pair of comfortable shoes and maybe a few accessories to spice up her wardrobe." Bridget cackled.

"My clothes are fine. Aren't they?" She smoothed the wrinkles in her jeans. *Maybe this whole trip was a mistake.*

"Oh, you look great, I love your jumper. Bridget just wants a reason to stop at the lingerie shop in Galway." Katie snickered.

"I don't need any—lingerie," Synn said uncertainty creeping into her voice.

Bridget reached over and patted her shoulder. "Oh honey, we all need lingerie to keep those men in our lives interested and wrapped around our fingers."

"I don't have a man in my life. And that works for me," she said.

"You couldn't be more wrong," Katie piped up from the back seat. "The way Gavin looks at you, it's a wonder your clothes don't go up in flames."

"I don't know what you're talking about. We're just friends. The whole family has been kind to me." She shifted in her seat, slinging her arm over the back to join in the conversation with Colleen and Katie.

Colleen shook her head. "In denial that one is." She jerked her thumb toward Synn.

Bridget smiled in agreement and continued. "Oh that may be true of Mary and Tim. They are the sweetest people—unless you cross 'em."

"Or mess with their family." Colleen added. "Remember that time you—"

"Hush Colleen. Don't go there. Gavin and I weren't meant to be."

"But you sure had the hots for him." Katie laughed fanning her face.

"Here we are," Bridget announced her face flushed. "And none too soon."

The women piled out of the car. She hung back watching where the women were headed first.

"Come on." Katie gave her a little nudge. "The sooner we get your shoes and a few outfits for the pub the sooner we get to the lingerie shop. Then to lunch and wine." Katie licked her lips.

"I knew there was a reason I came along." Gale snickered miming sipping wine.

Forty-five minutes later, Synn had new sweaters, three pairs of jeans, and two pair of shoes. They were so comfy, she left a pair on and shoved her boots in the box.

As they walked down the street, Collen asked, "So really Synn, is Gavin off the market?"

"I already told you—"

"No, you skirted the issue. Just friends my foot,"

Katie scoffed. "Your longing glances at him, when you think no one is looking, tells a different story than you're trying to feed us. With that bod, he's gotta be great in bed." She looked expectantly at her.

Shit. How am I going to answer that? The heat crept up from her neck to her cheeks, which she covered with her hands.

"Now that's enough. We don't know her well enough to be askin' those questions. Katie is there a problem with you and Sean? Not getting the job done?"

"Oh, no…we're just fine. You know all the rumors about Gavin's prowess—curious that's all—" She shrugged. "Never mind, you're right." Katie pushed the door open to the Soft & Silky Lingerie shop and held it for the others.

She enjoyed the light fragrance of perfumes wafting through the air as she and her friends entered the door. With a whoosh and bells tinkling, the door closed behind them.

"Back again?" The dark-haired saleswoman teased, grinning at Bridget.

"Of course. Bridget just got paid. What else is she going to spend her money on? Food? A roof over her head? Silly things like that?" Katie giggled.

"No, Quinn has those covered," Bridget said smugly with a flip of her hand. "Gotta keep him happy and coming back for more."

"And you want something to keep Quinn covering you," Colleen said barely holding a giggle in. "When are you and Quinn going to make it legal?"

Scalpel sharp, Bridget's gaze leveled Colleen. "When I'm ready. It's a big step. Especially with our family's history of failed relationships. Marriage is forever, not something to take lightly."

She glanced from Colleen to Bridget hoping to avoid being drawn into the conversation.

Chastised, Colleen shrugged. "Sorry. I didn't mean anything, only teasing."

"No…it's me that's sorry. Didn't mean to go off on you. It's a touchy subject. Quinn is anxious to make it official, me—not so much."

"You don't think he's the one?" Katie asked in hushed tones.

"Yeah, I think so. We'll probably elope, so neither family will have an opportunity to cause embarrassment."

"Oh… I remember the scene your brother, Kevin, caused at the Ceilidh Mary and Tim held for Brandy and Hannah and their lads?"

"How can I ever forget?" Bridget rolled her eyes. "Still, there was something weird about Brandy's beau. Never saw a man set Kevin back on his heels that easily. Strength of ten men, I tell ya. Anyway, you'll be the first to know when I decide."

"We could have an impromptu celebration at the Shaughnessy's on a Sunday. Since the pub is closed. That way your families couldn't interfere and your friends would get a chance to wish you well and celebrate your happiness," Katie suggested.

Bridget put her finger to her lips in a thoughtful expression. "That could work. I'll talk it over with Mary. I'm about ready to tell Quinn yes."

"I don't remember you ever mentioning telling him no." Katie roared with laughter.

"Depends on what we're talking about." Bridget said.

She stared, as the friends bantered back and forth, still she couldn't think of anything to say. Her cheeks were on fire, and this conversation wasn't helping matters any. *Would Gavin like me in something like this?* She touched the red silk panties on the counter a matching bra hung next to them. *It shouldn't matter...but it does.*

"Would you like to try those on?" the sales woman asked.

Relief flooded though Bridget's voice at the change of subject. "Gavin would love those on that cute figure of yours." She nodded at her.

The clerk winked at her. "Don't let the girls get to you. They're only having a bit of fun. Is there something I could show you?"

She shook her head. "No...no...I'm just looking." Her gaze wandered to the floor.

Bridget waggled her finger in front of Synn's face. "I don't think so."

"This lass doesn't own one set of sexy lingerie. It's our duty to—"

"I have one," she protested. "A lot of my clothes were lost in transit between the US and Ireland."

"If that was the case, Gavin would be doing more than undressing you with his eyes," Colleen snarked.

"He has—I mean—we used—things are different—" Unable to control her emotions and fearing a magic episode, she rushed out of the store and down the street, her bags banging against her legs making her limp more pronounced. Tears threatened, and she blinked them back. *Why can't I get my footing here? I used to be a feared warrior. Now...I can't even negotiate a girl's day out.* She leaned her hot forehead

48

on the cold window of a store front and wished she were back at her cottage.

Suddenly she felt herself floating. *No…no…no.* She willed herself back to the storefront and looked around franticly. She breathed a sigh of relief when there was no one in sight. The light bounced off the glass as Bridget shoved out the door of the lingerie shop and sprinted toward her.

"Synn! I'm so sorry. We be only kidding around." Bridget rushed to her friend's side. "Mary said you'd had a rough life…but…I…" She slapped her hand over her mouth and her face fell. "I thought getting you out with us girls for a fun time would do you good. I guess we went about it all wrong. Sorry."

"Do the other girls know?" Synn asked accusingly.

"No. I didn't say a word, and that's all Mary told me." She paused. "You don't hate us, do you?"

She shook her head. "No… It's all so different. I've never—had friends—I mean like this."

"Why don't you come back to Soft and Silky while we pick out some things. You don't have to buy. We won't put you on the spot. Then it's off to lunch. Okay?" She looked at her watch. "And we still have appointments for mannies and peddies."

"And wine?" She straightened her shoulders determined to fit in.

Bridget snorted a laugh and reached for her arm. "Of course. A day out wouldn't be complete without wine."

"Sure. I'd like to look around." She grinned.

Inside the shop, she tried on a couple of matching pantie and bra sets and decided on the red silk, black lace, and an aqua set, because the girls said it accentuated her eyes. *This was fun.*

Finished shopping, they dropped their packages off at the car and walked a couple blocks to a pizza place. Colleen yanked the door open and sashayed over to a large table in the corner of the room. She and the other girls followed slipping into the corner booth. The atmosphere reminded her of America. The booths and chairs were upholstered in red with red and white checked table cloths and matching curtains at the windows. After much discussion, Bridget ordered a pizza with everything, extra cheese and sauce, plus a bottle of Albarino wine. At lunch the conversation was light.

"It sure is nice to be waited on rather than doing the waiting," Bridget said quietly. The corners of her mouth turned up in a wide smile.

The establishment wasn't busy, and she was surprised how quickly the waitress brought the extra-large pizza along with plates, a bottle of wine, and five glasses. Katie poured the wine, and Colleen placed slices of pizza on plates and passed them around. Gale picked up her wine and drank deeply, nearly emptying the glass. At the other woman's surprised expressions, she shrugged. "What? I was thirsty."

"Guess we better order another bottle." Bridget teased, pouring more wine into Gale's glass then motioned to the waitress.

Colleen took a bite of pizza and blurted, "Synn is there any truth to the tales that Brandy and Stefan had something to do with breaking the curse and allowing Tiarnan, King of Faeries', wife, Erin to walk with him at dawn in the sunlight? Have you ever seen Tiarnan or Erin?"

"Colleen!" Bridget scolded, dropping her piece of pizza onto the plate. "We agreed not to put Synn on the spot."

"I wasn't—" Colleen argued taking another bite, "—just making conversation. The Shaughnessys know." A hush fell on the table.

She nearly choked on her bite of pizza and set her fork down. Glancing from one face to the other, her lips set in a thin line she waited a beat, eyed her pizza, and burst out laughing. In a conspiratorial tone, she said, "I have no frigging idea. I wasn't privy to that information, but something sure happened that night. Have any of you seen Erin walking the beaches in the sunlight with Tiarnan? It's not just folk lore, is it?"

Relief flooded over the faces of her new friends as she grinned holding up her wine glass. *We're going to need more than two bottles.* She swirled the light amber liquid in the glass, sniffed, and closed her eyes. The wine had a bouquet of lilies and orange blossoms. Taking a sip, she let it grace her tongue with a flavor of bone-dry limes and peaches. She took another sip and sighed, opening her eyes to find the others staring at her. "What?"

"You ask questions like that then appear to enjoy your wine waaay to much," Bridget squeaked. "I think we need another bottle of wine." She waved to the waitress and pointed to the bottle.

"It's been a long time since I've had a great light wine. Sorry. If my questions are out of line? I apologize." The corners of her mouth turned up in an uncertain smile.

"No, not out of line, but you act as if it's normal everyday conversation, faeries, witches, magic, curses."

51

The error of her ways became immediately apparent. Pausing she said, "We are in Ireland, right? Land of the magic, folk lore, myths, and legends galore?"

"Oh sure to hear Brandy, Mary, or Tim tell it. The Shaughnessys are full of blarney."

"Are you sure… now?" She grinned mischievously and sighed at being able to tease her new friends. *So this was what it was like on a girl's day or night out. Not so bad. Maybe Gavin was right.* The thought surprised her. *Perhaps things weren't as dire as I envisioned after all. Still I need to find out about Gale.* She'd noticed Gale had remained quiet during the conversation involving magic.

"Come on, girls, we don't want to miss our nail appointment." Bridget smiled, collected the check from the waiter, and held out a credit card.

The waitress took the card. "I'll be back in a moment."

"What do I owe you?" Synn asked pulling out her wallet.

"Nothing, our treat," Bridget said.

"No. I pay my own way," she insisted. "You don't even know…"

"We all agreed on the way to your house. Our treat for the new lass," Gale piped up.

She shook her head. "I'd really rather—"

"Call it our way of making up for being so pushy in Soft and Silky." Bridget waved her hand at the other women. "We've been friends for so long—"

Katie chimed in interrupting, "Yeah, since we were in nappies. Anything kinda goes with us."

Bridget glared at her for a beat then continued.

"We didn't consider you don't know us well enough to tell when we're kidding. Now unless you want to make us late arguing a point you won't win. Let's get a wiggle on." She led the way out of the pizza place, rushing down the sidewalk. "Good thing it's only half a block down."

"Thank you!" she said following as fast as possible behind the others.

"We'll let you pay next time." Katie winked at her. "Only kidding. Hey Bridg…slow down. We've time." Katie and Gale kept pace with her.

"I've never had a mannie or a—peddie. I think I'll pass."

"Oh no you don't. It will be fun. You can pick out your polish and nail art," Katie said. "I go to this place all the time. We'll get our hair fixed too."

"I'm not sure we have time for all that. Synn and I have to work tonight."

Relief flooded over her, until—

Katie piped up, "A trim and blow dry won't take long." She pointedly rolled her eyes toward Synn.

"I like my hair the way it is. Tobi at the Wycked Hair Salon styled it for me before we returned to Ireland."

"Ooooo… I've heard of that salon—it's in one of the fancy style magazines I have. Caters to the rich and famous in America," Colleen said. "How'd you manage to get an appointment there? Somethin' you not telling us?" She raised her eyebrow in question.

"Friends in high places?" Katie teased.

"That's enough." Bridget said shoving the glass door open to the salon. "We really don't have time. Besides I'm not going to pay to look good for only a couple hours. It'll be busy in the pub tonight. By night's end I'll need… I'd rather wait till I have a couple days off. You know what I mean."

"Yeah, yeah, yeah, we know—" Katie grinned at Colleen then they chorused "—to look good for Quinn."

Gale dissolved into a fit of giggles.

Bridget narrowed her eyes at Katie, who waved her off. "Next time." She turned her attention to the red-haired woman who greeted them. "Hi, Rita."

"Ready for you." Rita pointed to four empty chairs. "Who's the new girl?

"Our new friend from across the pond, Synn."

Rita's eyebrows rose nearly to her hairline before she smoothed her expression.

Katie continued. "You know the Yanks revel in strange names. Anyway, she's settled in Ballycotton. Works at Shaughnessy's with Bridg."

"Oh she does—does she?" Rita looked thoughtful. "You know Gavin?"

She sucked in a breath. *Everyone seems to know him.* That thought made her a little uncomfortable.

Chapter Six
A Surprise Rescue in the Pouring Rain

After his escapades on the beach, Gavin returned home, showered, and glanced at the clock. Three hours until Synn's shift began at the pub. He needed to talk to her about his dream, hell, nightmare, about the feeling of being watched. Warn her to be on the lookout. He shoved an arm though his shirt with more force than necessary tearing the cloth. A large rip with frayed edges spread across the arm hole and stretched across the shoulder seam. *That's a bloody shame*. Wadding the shirt up in a ball, he threw it violently across the floor.

Catching a glance in the mirror, his face reddened, and he kicked the ruined shirt. Bad temper seemed to follow him around of late. He had no idea why. Taking a deep breath, he picked up the material and shoved it into the trash. Yanking open his closet, he searched for something else to wear. Deciding it would be best to walk off this mood before reporting for work, he donned a pair of sweats and pulled on his sneakers.

He bent and touched his toes, then leaned from side to side before jogging down the path and along the beach keeping an eye on the building clouds across what was a blue sky this morning. Turning around and heading for home, he'd only gotten about half way there when large rain drops splashed on his face and body. He quickened his pace.

Thunder shook the foundation and lightning followed him as he jerked open the door to his home. *Shit. Didn't realize I'd been gone so long. Felt good though. Better take the truck to the pub.* He glanced out the window. "Looks like it's going to be an all-nighter." His concern for Synn ratcheted up another notch. Was she all right? What if something happened...because the women were with her? They had no idea... "Oh for god sakes. Stop it," he growled out loud climbing up the stairs to take a shower.

A few minutes later, he jumped into the truck and slammed the door. He'd seen the clouds building this morning. *It's nothing more than a thunder storm.* Torrents of rain streamed down his windshield as he turned the wipers on, to no avail, they couldn't keep up with the torrential downpour. Pounding the heel of his hands on the steering wheel impatiently did nothing. He was forced to wait out the storm.

Forty-five minutes later, his truck bumped down the dirt road throwing rooster tails of mud and water in its wake. He took the long route to work, driving by Synn's cottage. It was dark. They evidentially weren't back yet. The knot in his stomach tightened. Did the storm impede their way home? Why did he encourage her to make friends, get out and enjoy life? *Because it was the right thing to do.*

As he arrived at the pub, the rain had slackened up a bit. Bridget's car was already there. A knot of people were gathered in the pouring rain outside the pub door. Synn was on her knees in the middle of the group. He slammed on his brakes in the middle of the road and jumped out rushing toward her. "What's going on? Are you all right?" he bellowed shoving his way through the people. He reached for her arm, started to pull her up—she twisted away from him and hunkered over something. Leaning in to get a better look, he saw a wet ball of fur.

"I'm fine. That's more than I can say for this poor little soaking wet mop of a puppy." She got up from her knees holding the tawny colored ball of fur close to her chest. "Can we get a blanket or towel, please?" Synn started to pull the door to the pub open.

"You can't bring—that inside." No sooner than those words flew from his mouth, he regretted them. The door banged closed.

She whirled on him, her eyes blazed with anger. "You expect me to leave this poor creature out here where it'll surely die?" Her voice stung as she continued glaring at him.

"Animals are not allowed in the pub. Health regulations. Not mine."

The door creaked open. Mary stood in the door way, one hand fisted on her hip, the other holding the door open. "What's all the commotion out here?"

"He wants me to leave this helpless creature out here to die." Synn accused staring pointedly at him.

"Drama queen," he said under his breath but held his hands out in front of him in a gesture of surrender as the rest of the crowd looked from him to Synn then to Mary. "Not true." Gavin knew the soft heart of his mother and the trouble he was already in. "I merely stated that she couldn't take that creature inside the pub."

"Awww—" Mary untied her apron and wrapped it around the shivering bundle of fur, handing it back to Synn. "Take it around back. I'll unlock the storeroom.

Sure we got a box for a bed, blankets to warm the pup and dry her off. Then we'll see what we see. But it can't stay here." She looked over the crowd. "Anyone know where this poor puppy belongs?"

Several heads shook back and forth. "No. Maybe a stray," a gruff man's voice said.

"Too young for a stray. Why it's no more than a few weeks old." Mary glanced at Synn holding the pup and clicked her tongue. "You're going to need a change of clothes too."

She looked down at her soaking wet shirt streaked with muddy paw prints and hugged the pup. "I'll take it home,"

He grunted. "What do you know about raising a puppy?" Again, his damn mouth opened before engaging his brain. Water trickled off his hair and ran down inside his collar. He wiped his face with his hand. "Com'on. I'll show you around back where we can put the puppy and get out of this rain." His voice had an edge to it, and his ma glared at him.

"I'll meet you two in the storage room. The rest of you quit standing around." She held the door open, motioning them in. "You're gonna catch ya death of cold. We'll open the pub early." Shaking her finger at some of the regulars, she said, "Don't you be expecting to be served right away."

"Aye…" Several men said in unison.

He blew out a breath and escorted Synn behind the pub, pulled out his keys, and unlocked the storeroom. His ma bustled in with an arm full of blankets and towels.

She held out a t-shirt to Synn. "Might be a wee bit big, but it's dry and clean. Should do you for tonight."

His da followed close behind carrying a huge box with a slotted lid. Tim glanced at him and shrugged. He nodded. His ma was a force to be reckoned with when she set her mind to something. Wise men didn't stand in her way.

Synn toweled the pup as dry as she could. The pup whined and poked his nose in the air sniffing.

"Poor thing is probably starved." Mary looked up as Quinn appeared in the door way of the store room. "Be a good lad and run over to the market. See if they have puppy food. A bag of dry kibble and a couple cans of wet. Then bring them around to the storeroom. You can pour a little kibble in the bowl we'll have set out for it."

Decked out in his rain gear, Quinn nodded. "Stopped by for a pint and see how Bridg's shopping trip went. Saw all of you headed back here so I followed." He glanced around. "Where's Bridget?"

Tim jerked his chin toward the other entry into the pub. "She's inside." He put down the box. "Mary, we may have some of that Mulligan stew left over. I can fix him up a bowl."

"Aye and you can clean up after the pup gets the runs from the rich meat. It's too young to eat that kind of food. Remember the last stray you fed stew to?"

He took off his hat, rubbed his head, and grimaced. Wrinkling his nose, he replaced the hat. "Aye. 'Twas a god-awful mess."

"Hey Gavin, we need a cook. Customers are hungry, and Dan isn't due in for a couple hours." Bridget stuck her head in the door from the pub.

He cursed under his breath, allowed a quick glance in Synn's direction, and bolted for the door.

"Today's specials are simmering on the stove, and loaves of bread are in the warmer." Mary looked at her watch. "Made fresh cinnamon rolls for dessert. They're still in the oven. Check 'em. Should be done about half past four. Anything else will have to be made from scratch."

He nodded and started through the door.

"Son, did you confirm the band for tonight?" Tim asked helping Mary arrange a couple blankets in the box.

"Aye. And Cori is joining the band tonight. Should be a lively set with her on fiddle." He closed the door behind him before anyone else wanted his time and set to work on the orders stacking up. All though he barely noticed when the others returned to the pub, he was ecstatic to see Dan walk into the kitchen thirty minutes early. "You're a welcome sight."

Dan washed his hands and tied his apron on. "Heavens lad, why didn't you call me in? Your da is three deep at the bar."

"I've barely had time to think let alone make a phone call. It's only going to get worse. We've a popular band tonight, and Cori is joining them." He took off his apron, washed up, and gave Dan a thumbs up sign. He swung through the kitchen doors to help at the bar.

Bridget had called in the whole regular staff plus part-timers. He stopped to admire Synn as she flew around the tables carrying a tray full of drinks on her shoulder like she was born to it. She delivered the drinks and returned for another tray his da had ready for her. Bridg and Katie were taking and delivering food orders, their motions a blur. An elbow gouged him in the ribs.

"Quit gawking at the lass and cover your end of the bar. Boyo," his da instructed glancing toward the stage where the band was setting up.

Quinn rushed through the door. He waved to Bridget, strode toward the storeroom a bag of puppy food slung over his shoulder and a paper bag in his hand.

Synn sprinted after Quinn. She held up five fingers and mouthed "Be back. Checking on Storm."

He nodded. *Apparently the pup had a name.* Pinching the bridge of his nose, he closed his eyes for a moment, opened them, then rubbed his temples. The headache didn't abate. *I need a break.* Traffic at the bar slowed down, and he glanced around but his da was nowhere in sight. *Damnit.*

"Hey, Gavin," a male voice called in greeting. He swiveled around to see Roger and Tara Neal, the doctor and wife he'd seen on the beach this morning. They were standing at the end of the bar. Roger held a menu in his hand. He waved and scooted over to them. "What you havin'?"

"A couple pints and two plates of your salmon," Roger said.

"Coming right up," he said cheerfully despite the pounding in his head.

"Wow, you have quite a crowd. Is it always like this?" Tara motioned to the crowd.

"Saturday nights are busy, but it's crazy tonight. Popular band is here, and a talented local fiddle player will be joining in. Makes for an explosive evening." At the expression on the doctor's face, Gavin clarified his statement. "In a good way." He slid the pints across the bar to the doctor and his wife. "Your food will be up shortly. Thanks for coming in."

"Oh, it's our pleasure." He raised his mug as his wife ducked under his arm and scurried through the crowd to stake a claim at a just vacated booth. Roger took a drink, licked the froth from his lips. "Stout ale as good as promised." The doctor plopped down cash.

He pushed the money back. "Of course, but it's on the house. You saved my life." He laughed. "I'll have the waitress bring your dinner to your booth."

"I'm paying for the food," Roger said in a determined voice, then picked up Tara's glass and made his way to the table she was guarding, turned, and waved.

A few minutes later, Tim threw up the pass through, ducked in, caught it with one hand, and lowered it in place without a sound. "Your turn."

Eager to get fresh air and a couple moments to himself, he slipped under the counter and nearly collided with Katie at the kitchen entrance. "Sorry." He grabbed a bottle of water from the fridge, and he exited out the back door. Leaning his back against the building's exterior, he inhaled deeply of the cool evening air and took a gulp of his water. What a night. He looked forward to Sunday.

He'd amble over to his parent's house, enjoy his ma's cooking, and relax for a bit. *I should invite Synn— and the pup. Can't leave it alone and she won't come without it.* Pleased at his plan, he walked around to the front of the pub and talked with customers who'd stepped out for a breath of fresh air after dancing. The door groaned as he pulled it open and held it for a couple just arriving. Warm fragrant air whooshed out of the pub, along with happy voices and lively music.

Skirting the dance floor, he saw Synn serve the drinks on her tray and start back to the bar. A man grabbed her arm, and she bent down to talk to him. His mouth was way too close to her ear. Gavin's hands fisted. She shook her head and straightened. The man's grip appeared to tighten on her wrist. Jerking her arm out of the man's hand, she flashed him a triumphant smile and flounced away.

On a whim, Gavin strode across the floor, playfully grabbed her arm, and took the tray. He handed it to one of the men seated at a close table. Synn peered up at him, her eyes big as saucers.

"What are you doing?" she hissed.

"Snatching a quick dance with my girl. Get the blood pumping. It's good for the heart," he whispered letting his lips caress the soft outer shell of her ear. At his signal the band segued from a lively jig to a sweet ballad and lowered the lights. He wrapped his arm around her waist and pulled her close. To his surprise, she rested her head against his chest and curved into him moving with the music. Her long dark eyelashes brushed her cheeks as she closed her eyes. He savored the unexpected moment, then leaned down. "Thought you could use a break."

"Thoughtful of you. Now if only I could give my poor feet a rest," she replied.

With little effort he lifted her a few inches off the ground and held her to him, still swaying to the music.

She gave a quiet squeal in surprise. "Gavin. Put me down." But there was no heat or insistence in her request.

"After the song." He lightly brushed his lips over

her hair then rested his cheek on the top of her head. The last notes of the song hung in the air a few moments, as if refusing to let go of the mood, then the lights flickered back up.

He lowered her to her feet and brushed a kiss across her cheek. Wanting more, much more, he sighed, released her, and returned to the bar. In a way he hoped his actions had not gone unnoticed by the men in the crowd, especially Mr. Grabby Hands.

Chapter Seven
Another Day Another Adventure—Did She Bite off more than She Could Chew?

Once again behind the bar, his ma poked him in the side, a sparkle in her eye. "Way to go, boyo." She slipped out the pass through and returned to the kitchen.

Finally, the last patrons of the pub said their goodbyes. The band packed up their stuff and carried it out to their vehicle. Mary and Tim talked with Cori for a bit as she set her fiddle in its case before he joined them and tucked a generous amount of money into her case. He thanked her for spending the evening with them.

"Thank you so much." She leaned over, kissed him on the cheek and winked. "Looks like you found what you were searching for. Wish you happiness. Enjoyed the evening." She motioned toward the stage. "A talented, fun bunch of guys to play with." Mirth shone in her eyes as her grin widened.

"Not saying a thing to that double entendre." He snickered and gave her hug. "How about we schedule you for a mid-week gig? Give the customers a pleasant surprise." He paused. "Say a week from this coming Wednesday night?

"Sounds good. I'll add it to my calendar. Nite."

Picking up her case, he turned and winked at Synn. "I'll be right back." He pushed through the door carrying Cori's instrument out to her car.

When he returned, Synn stood next to Mary who was whispering something to her. Synn brightened considerably. Tim looked on, leaning against the bar a slight smile on his lips. He reached for Synn's hand and leaned into her. "How about joining us for Sunday dinner tomorrow?"

"Oh, I don't want to impose," she said pulling away.

"No imposition," Mary said. "Love to have you. Bring your little pup with you."

"I couldn't. She'll tear up your house."

Mary hooted. "We've raised two wild girls, pets of all kinds, and Gavin. The house survived it all. I don't think a wee pup will be a problem. Besides, we've a huge crate for her and a fenced back yard. She'll be fine, dear," Mary said.

"Used to use it for Gavin," Tim said his eyes twinkling.

When Synn's eyes rounded and her mouth dropped open, Tim roared with laughter. Wiping his eyes, he gulped in air in an attempt to catch his breath and patted her arm. "Only kidding, lassie."

Red patches bloomed on Synn's cheeks as she continued to stare at Tim. "If you're sure."

"We're sure," Tim and Mary chorused.

Gavin slung an arm around her shoulder. "Tell you what. It's late. Let me drive you and Storm home. Tomorrow, I'll pick you two up mid-morning. We can take a walk and enjoy a relaxing day." *Together.* He dare not say that out loud, not yet.

Mary smiled knowingly while Tim wrapped his arm around her shoulder. "Nite," they chorused again.

Gavin and Synn walked through the pub pausing at the inside entrance to the storeroom. "I'll lock the outside door after we get the pup," Gavin called over his shoulder.

"Thanks." An answer came from the kitchen where he assumed his parents were locking up for the night then would head home.

A few minutes later, they opened the storeroom door and a bundle of matted fur with a wiggling tail greeted them.

"How'd she get out?" Synn asked flipping on the light and picking Storm up. She was wiggling so much that Synn had trouble holding on to her. "Well, you don't act like you're sick."

The answer was apparent as soon as light flooded the room. The box that had been made into a bed for her had a large hole chewed in the bottom corner.

"Why would you think she was sick?"

Synn turned the squirming creature to face him. "Because, look her tongue is black or—" She switched the angle of the pup around. "Purple? It couldn't be good."

He chuckled. "It's the breed. I've not seen one of these in a long time." He reached over and scratched the pup's belly. "Chows were bred as guard dogs to the Chinese royalty. Don't know of anyone that owns or breeds—" he scratched the side of his face "—them around here. But someone must have had a litter of pups. Strange." Pausing, he shook his head and shrugged, glanced at the box. "Appears she broke out of bed. Want to stop at the house and pick up the crate Ma was talking about? Otherwise, Storm could make a helluva mess of your cottage by morn." He picked up the box and carried it out to the truck, tossed it in the bed.

"No… I can handle it. I don't want to bother Mary any more tonight." She picked up the old leather belt Mary had given Storm to chew on. It was covered with teeth marks. "Besides she'll have nowhere to stay at Mary and Tim's house tomorrow."

He took the toy from her. "Guess we better get some chew toys and things in the morning—like a leash—after I pick you up." Glancing around the storeroom, he reached up, grasped a coil of rope, and held it up. "This will make a temporary leash."

Synn nodded in agreement. "It'll do for tonight."

"Okaay. Don't say I didn't warn you. By the way, how'd shopping go today?" Opening the vehicle door, he held the pup while Synn climbed inside. He handed the dog back to her. "Make sure you hold on to her tight. Don't want teeth marks in the upholstery—unless it's mine."

"You don't—oh, it's a joke. I get it. I've got her." She paused as he started the engine. "I won't lie to you. It was a rough start. But the shopping turned out to be really fun. We had a great time—stopped for pizza and wine. There was a lot of girl talk. I was uncomfortable at first. After a while it was easier for me to join in the conversation." She grinned, and a mischievous sparkle shown in her eye. "There was some talk as to your prowess in the bedroom."

He felt his eyebrows shoot up nearly to his hair line. "What?"

"Well, one of the girls wanted to know if the rumors where true." She turned her head to look out the window.

"What did you say?"

"Nothing, I changed the subject." She paused shifting in her seat. "I'm not comfortable discussing those kind of things. Besides, I'm not going to confirm or deny that we were intimate."

He laughed turning onto the road to her cottage before glancing over at her. "Smart girl. So this shopping…did it involve lingerie of any kind?" A deliberate seductive smile curved his lips.

"You've been talking to Quinn," she accused.

Gavin slowed the truck then stopped in front of her cabin. "Maybe. I saw him earlier."

"Well, you'll never know." She pushed the truck door open without waiting for him and flounced out of the truck. Storm almost wiggled out of her arms. By the time he reached the passenger side of the truck, his outstretched hands caught the puppy as it jumped out of her arms. "Synn, you gotta be careful. She's only a baby and has no fear."

The horror on her face had him rethinking the rest of his lecture.

"I'm sorry. She's so wiggly." She reached for Storm. He took the pup and put her in the back of the pickup.

"What possessed you to volunteer to take the pup home? You have no idea what it takes to raise a puppy. Heck, you are…" he stopped right there.

A single tear rolled down her cheek. "She was so scared, cold, wet and needed a home. Someone to love and care for her. I know what that feels like…"

He reached up cupped her chin and wiped the tear away with his thumb. "Okay. But tomorrow we're going to get a book on raising a puppy in addition to all the necessities, like a bowl, brush, real bed, and a puppy pen. It will keep her safe and your cottage in one piece. Fair enough?" He took her in his arms and held her against him for a couple beats, then brushed his lips over hers backing her up against the side of his vehicle.

She leaned into the kiss, nibbling on his lips before he covered her mouth hungrily. She moaned and parted her lips for him. He thrust his tongue inside her mouth, stroked, teased, and tasted. She felt so good in his arms, but it was too soon. Her emotions were all over the place, and he didn't want to push her to do something she'd later regret.

Slow, steady, and dependable was what she needed right now. As he started to pull away, Storm jumped up, paws on the side of the pickup bed and snagged Synn's braid with her teeth, barking, growling, and tugging.

She grabbed hold of her braid while Gavin disengaged the puppy's paws and teeth. "You're sure you don't want me to stay tonight?"

"I'm sure. We'd..." She blew out a breath. "Not a good idea." She reached in the bed and scratched the pup's head.

"You could model the lingerie you bought—make sure it fits," he teased.

She slapped at him. "I already tried it on. It fits fine."

He couldn't hold back the wide grin and smug expression. She hauled off and smacked him.

He grabbed her arms and kissed the tip of her nose. "I knew it."

Her expression changed from frustration to thoughtful in a blink of an eye. "Do you know Gale Boohar? She came along with Bridget, Colleen, and

Katie."

"Of course. Her family has been here for centuries. She took over the family apothecary business last year when her ma and da retired to travel the world. Why?"

"Just wondered."

Tilting his head, he raised an eyebrow. "Picked up the magic signature—did you? She wouldn't try to hide it from you."

Synn's eyes widened, and she sucked in a breath. "Would she know what I am?"

Chapter Eight

When You Know What is Possible, Seeing a Myth can be Disconcerting. Talking with One May Cause You to Question Your Sanity

"No doubt." He moved closer, took her chin with his thumb and forefinger, and tipped it up. Leaning down, he gazed into her eyes.

She couldn't breathe. He was too close. She could feel his heat. Putting her hands on his broad, muscular chest, she meant to push him away. Instead she traced the outlines of the contours of his muscles with her fingertips. Before she realized, her hands had slid around his neck, pulling his full lips to hers.

The tip of his tongue traced her lips, teased them apart, and slipped inside for moment. Then he eased away, taking her hands from around his neck. "Don't misunderstand, I want you as much as I ever did, but I don't think you're ready. I'm not going to put either one of us through this unless we are ready to commit to each other and this relationship." He held her hands a minute longer then released her. "I've been meaning to talk to you about something. The other night— No, let me start over. Are you still having nightmares? Could you be broadcasting those?"

She worried her bottom lip with her front teeth and gave a slight nod of her head. *No use lying to him.* "Yes, still having nightmares. The other night it was bad."

"Yeah." He described the dream in every graphic detail.

"That was exactly like mine. I almost called you. Just to talk," she clarified. "But didn't want to wake you at that hour. You had to be at work early the next morning."

He sighed. "You should have. I was up anyway. I have to wonder if these nightmares are of your own making or if somehow he's still able to control your dreams and subconscious. Whether unintentional or intentional it's serious enough that I'd like to talk with Bruce or Tristian. See if there's been any chatter. Would you have a problem with that?"

She stared at the ground for a long time. When she raised her eyes to meet his, in a quiet voice she said, "I've been thinking the same thing. I don't want to bother either of them, but the last nightmare wasn't like the others I had when I first came here. It was a feeling…"

"Want me to stay in the cottage with you?" He offered reaching out, stroking her hair, twisting a curl around his finger, then letting it spring free.

"That's not in our agreement."

"Neither are the terrifying nightmares we seem to be sharing. Makes it damn hard to get up early in the morning after a night of those." He paced along the fence like a caged animal.

Her gazed followed him until Storm begin chewing on her shoe. "Leave it," she commanded, pushing the pup away with her shoe. Storm blinked up at her and barked. Ready to pounce at any moment, her butt was in the air, tail wiggling, and front end on the ground.

"She wants you to play." He stomped on the ground close to the puppy. Storm took off barking, circled, and came back to nip at his booted foot. "Best not get her wound up, if you want to go to bed."

"Oh yeah, I'm the one stomping my foot at her." She sighed. "Our little conversation isn't good for my psyche. Now I'll have more nightmares." She threw up her arms in frustration.

"Sorry. As long as we brought this out in the open, I might as well tell you…"

She held her hand up." No. Nothing more tonight. It's late. I'll see you tomorrow." She glanced up at the clear sky. The rain-washed air was warmer than previous evenings. *Maybe summer was on the way.*

He nodded, kissed her on the cheek, and walked to the truck. Pausing before he stepped into the truck, he turned toward her. "Listen for her whines and let her out right away or you'll have a mess to clean up." Chuckling, he climbed into his vehicle, rolled the window down, and waved as he drove away.

She looped the rope leash around Storm and tugged in an attempt to get the pup to follow along. The fur ball had other ideas. She chewed on the leash, rolled over on her back, took the leash in her mouth, and tugged in the opposite direction that Synn was trying to get her to go. Finally, too tired to fight her any more, Synn scooped the pup up, hugged her, then returned to the cottage. "We're going to be best friends." Storm looked up and licked her face. Synn giggled. "Tomorrow we get you a proper leash, and you'll learn to walk on it… I hope."

Once inside, she put the pup on the floor, picked up the cardboard box, and examined it. *Pretty flimsy.* First, she touched the corners. A blue glow came from her hands as she reinforced the box with a little magic. She hoped it wouldn't draw attention to her from the magic community. Nor did she want to break the conditions Bruce had imposed when he'd given her freedom, but…maybe Gavin was right.

She straightened out the blankets in Storm's box, put the container at the foot of her bed, and placed the pup inside. At first Storm cried, scratched, and whined. Sitting on the edge of the bed, she ignored her. Soon snoring came from the makeshift cardboard crate. A sigh of relief escaped her lips, and her body slumped.

Leaving her clothes in a heap on the floor, she trudged to the bathroom, closed the door, and turned on the shower. Inside the warm water cascaded over her tired body easing the aches and pains created by hefting the heavy trays. Her muscles weren't used to that type of work anymore. But she liked talking to customers and her co-workers. Each day was easier. Lathering up the nylon scrubby she'd bought during her outing with the girls, she washed and rinsed.

When she pushed aside the shower curtain, steam bellowed out into the tiny room. She dried off, then used the towel to wipe the moisture from the mirror and paused a couple of beats. Even without the glamour, the woman in the mirror looked better. *Now, if I can only get some sleep.*

Padding into the kitchen, she opened the shopping bags she'd dropped off before going to work and put her purchases away except the red bra and panty set. Those she held up to admire. She would wear the red set tomorrow. A smile crossed her lips, and she fell into bed.

Moonlight flooded through the window in her cottage when something woke her. The trees outside swayed in the breeze casting moving shadows on a silvery background against the walls. She rolled over and wondered at the whining noises coming from the bottom of her bed. The whines evolved into cries then barks. Her brain fuzzy from sleep, it took several minutes before she finally recalled the events of last night, and the poor little puppy she'd taken home.

With the magic reinforcement, no way that pup would be able to get out on her own. She rubbed her eyes, leaned up on her elbow, and looked at the clock. Four in the morning. She flopped back down on the bed. Gavin's warning had her bolting upright and pulling on a robe and slippers.

Flicking on the light, she reached in the box and picked up the wriggling ball of motion. Hugging Storm, she hurried to the back door. "Just hold on a minute more." There were no close neighbors, so she put the rope leash on the pup and shuffled outside in her robe. The minute she put the pup down Storm squatted. *Whew. That was close.* After several additional minutes of sniffing around, she insisted that Storm come back inside. Taking her off lead, she put the creature back in the box, and crawled into bed pulling the covers over her head.

When she opened her eyes again, an orange glow shown through the space where the curtains didn't quite come together. A thin orange line peeked across the horizon. Maybe it would be a nice day. Ireland's spring was colder than she'd expected. After the recent rains, she'd noticed green sprouts poking out of the ground in what she'd assumed was a flower garden in front of her cottage. The brown grass had green blades mixed in now. Hopefully the world wouldn't seem so dreary.

Slipping on her silky, red bra and panties, she wondered what Gavin's hands would feel like caressing… *Stop it.* She yanked on her black jeans and pulled a new light blue sweater over her head. The girls said the color accentuated her aqua eyes. Now looking in the mirror, she would have to agree with them. She brushed her hair and braided it, then let the pup out of the box. "Come on, girl; let's go for a walk."

Storm charged out the door and down the path. She ran to keep up with her, snatched her up, and put the rope leash on the pup. *Lesson number one, don't open the door before leashing the pup.* She was glad Gavin hadn't been around to see that mistake. Rather than take the path to the beach, the pup paused at the fork in the path then bounced up the rocky trail to the cliffs, nose high in the air.

She saw a couple meandering along the cliffs as the sunrise spread across the sky in fingers of orange, red and yellow. Idly she thought about Colleen's questions yesterday. She considered how terrible it would be never to walk in the sun or enjoy a spectacular sunrise or set. If you believed the folk tale, Erin had given it all up because her family didn't like that the witch had fallen in love with a faery.

She took a moment to appreciate this sunrise, thinking about other's she'd seen over the years but hadn't given a second thought. The beauty of the world was lost on the young warrior programed only to do her master's bidding. Storm tugged at the leash and yipped. She shook her head in an attempt to displace the thoughts of her early capture at Baltizar's hands. His brutal domination of the child she was and forcing her into submission of his every desire—she wouldn't go there.

Letting the full length of the rope out allowed Storm to explore the area. She eased down on a rock out cropping and watched the colors fade into the cerulean sky as the sun rose higher. A rustling sound in the brush startled her. She jerked her head around. Standing behind her stood a tall willowy woman with auburn hair flowing to her waist and misty blue eyes. She had a wistful smile.

"'Tis not so bad, when you have the love of a man you desired more than life itself," the woman said.

"Who are— How do you— What are—" she spluttered, tugging the rope in and bringing Storm to her without taking her eyes off the woman. Small gold sparks flickered at the ends of her fingertips. She closed her fists in an effort to hide her magic.

The woman tilted her head. "Lass, do you ever finish a sentence?" A melodic laugh burbled up from her throat. "So you are Gavin's heart? Wasn't sure that lad would ever settle down," the woman mused moving closer to her. "But that's neither here nor there. You've nothing to fear from me." The woman held out her petite hand. "I'm Erin, and you are?"

"Synn," she said in a wavering voice and clasping the woman's hand. "So it's true. They broke the curse. You're— Your husband is—" She blew out a breath and gathered her thoughts. Sounding like an idiot wasn't to her benefit. She could finish sentences.

"Her husband be Tiarnan, King of the faeries." His voice boomed off the rock faces.

She jumped then blinked, shading her eyes against

the sun. *This was not happening.* She blinked again. Still a man several inches taller than Erin, with long tresses the color of straw, dressed in jeans, and a shimmering multicolored sweater stood before her. "Who might you be?"

"Synn." She twisted around to face him.

"Oh the demon warrior that lent a hand to Bruce and his group. Correct? Nice job."

She narrowed her eyes and stared suspiciously from one to the other. Gathering Storm up in her lap, she held her tight. The pup covered her face with kisses. "What do you two want with me?"

Erin rested her hand on Tiarnan's arm. "Dear, you're making her nervous. Could you give us a few minutes?"

"Of course." He leaned down and kissed his wife. "I'll not be far, should you have need of me." The mist thickened where he stood then disappeared on the breeze leaving only a wisp floating along the ground.

Her eyes widened, and she stared at Erin.

"Oh don't mind him. He loves to make an entrance and exit especially around those who aren't sure what they're seeing." She waved her hand dismissively.

"'Tis true witch, vampire, demon, and gryphon broke the curse when Brandy began weaving her spell." A far-away look clouded Erin's eyes, and she sighed. "Bruce stood beside Angelique, Hannah by Tristian, as they joined her, each murmuring different incantations. The three Books of Shadows lay open on hallowed ground glowing as they turned into soft, rich liquid gold, flowed into each other, they did, forming one. The wind howled around the stone formations and whipped around the couples as dark clouds formed and floated across the full moon. Darkness enveloped the land." Erin wrapped her arms around herself. "Only the golden glow of the Books remained." Erin paused to glance at her for a couple beats. 'Twas a glorious day—night."

Mesmerized, she leaned forward, intent on every word. When Erin didn't continue right away, she whispered, "What happened then?"

Erin smiled. "It was silent. When the storm clouds parted, the moon shone blood-red with a muted ring of rainbow colors encircling it. The chanting ceased, and the books slowly separated, returning to their ancient leather-bound form."

She sucked in a breath. "And the curse was broken?"

"Yes, and the spells bound the gates of Hell tight. The portals were destroyed, and the fabric of time strengthened so there was no possibility of escape. For now." Erin's eyes cleared and a faint smile curved her lips.

"For now?" she squeaked.

"Yes, for now. The remainder of the legend has yet to come full circle. And is not my tale to tell. We cannot control the behavior of man, so there will always be a need to patrol magic kind. Tristian and Bruce do a great job with the help of other magic creatures. You see…we must all work together."

"I see." She wished she could have been there and witnessed the ceremony with her own eyes.

"I'm afraid you don't. Love is a magical gift that you must not ignore." Erin pinned her with her gaze.

"You know, in my short lifetime, I've had enough of people telling me how to live, what to do and…who to…"

"I'm not doing any of those things. Only here to warn you dark times may be on the horizon. The man who walks beside you is your mate and will be of great help to you when the time comes. Don't shut him out. He's already committed to you, and you know what that means for a gryphon."

"I can't endanger anyone should trouble come my way again. I'm not as I once was." She stared sadly at her defective leg.

"That's where you're wrong. Everyone in this life has a purpose. You can't just throw that away because you're afraid." Erin gently touched her shoulder. "Gavin has already given—" She paused a couple beats. "Gryphons take only one mate, and that is for eternity. You knew that, right?"

"Brandy shouted something like that at me during one of our arguments. Said her brother would never be whole thanks to me."

Erin shook her head sadly. "If something happens to that mate, the other will spend the rest of their life alone and never search for another. Some choose to follow their mate in death. The act of lovemaking seals that bond. It's a hell of a commitment for anyone other than a gryphon to understand—let alone agree."

She flinched choosing not to discuss the intimate details of her life with a person—a witch—she'd known only a short time. "Afraid. Me." She snorted. "You have no idea who I am, or what I've endured. I'm not afraid. I've earned the right to decide… As far as Gavin and me, it's private."

The witch raised her hands in a gesture of surrender. A polite smile turned up the corners of her mouth. "True. There are different kinds of fear. And I know you don't fear battle. It's matters of the heart that confound you. But your purpose has yet to run its full course. Believe me when I tell you the risk will be worth the reward."

She pursed her lips and crossed her arms over her chest in a sign of defiance.

"Visit Gale, she can help heal that limp. The problem be not physical. Dark magic inadvertently transferred from Baltizar when he used it against you and needs to be drawn out. She can help. You'll need to learn to control his dark magic and use it to your benefit. We doubt—" Erin glanced around "—that Baltizar knows the magic was transferred. Gale will be indispensable when the time comes."

"So the legend claims you were from a very powerful family of witches. Is Gale a relative then?" she asked.

Erin's smile widened as she wagged a finger at her. "You're not only talented but intelligent. It appears the stories about you are also true. Yes, Gale is a descendant and a powerful witch in her own right. Though she downplays it to avoid unwanted attention."

She shifted her gaze from Erin to the fading colors of dawn as the sun shone bright in the blue sky. "I hate to cut this conversation short, but Gavin will be here soon to pick up Storm and me. We are having dinner with his family." She put Storm on the ground and released a little of the rope.

"That's wonderful. Please heed what I've told you. If you ever need Tiarnan's or my help, you can find us on the cliffs at sunrise," Erin said.

Because her neck was getting sore being twisted at

such an angle, she shifted on the rock. When she turned back around to face Erin, she was gone. *Did I really see—have a conversation—or is my imagination working overtime?* Sitting still for a couple beats, she surveyed the area. No sign of anyone. She sighed.

"Looks like Tiarnan isn't the only one who disappears without warning," she grumbled shoving up from the rock. Brushing her hands together to remove the tiny rock particles, she tugged on the rope then called to Storm, who ignored her. She tugged on the rope harder then started down the path. The pup chewed on the leash and barked as she was forced to follow. At least this time, she didn't roll over, or become limp as a rag in protest forcing her to pick her up. She smiled. They were making progress.

When they rounded the bend in the trail, Gavin's truck was parked in front of her cottage. He was unloading several bags and setting them on the porch. As she approached, he smiled making her feel all warm inside. *Do I tell him? Will he think I've lost it? Better keep it to myself for the time being. What about the warning?* Her thoughts were spinning in all directions. She shoved the whole incident to the back of her mind to deal with later.

Gavin held up a bag and swung it back and forth in front of her.

"What have you brought us?" She made a quick swipe for the bag and missed.

He grinned and held it higher. "I called you earlier, but you didn't answer your phone."

She patted her right coat pocket, stuck her hand inside, nothing. "I guess I must have left my cell in the cottage." She pulled out a set of keys.

"Not a good practice. Please make sure to have your phone on you at all times," he said sharply then softened his tone. "But I figured you and Storm were out walking the beach. So I stopped by the market and bought a few things." He fished a paperback book out of the sack he was carrying. How to raise a well-behaved puppy was emblazoned across the front of the book.

She eyed the several bags lined up in front of the door including the one he was holding. "A few—things?" She took the book from him and thumbed through it. Storm promptly pounced on Gavin's boot and began to chew with gusto.

Gavin shook his boot in an attempt to dislodge the chewing machine. When his efforts failed, he took what looked like a rolled piece of leather and pushed Storm off his boot with a short "no" command. When she backed off, he gave her the chew toy. "Smart little thing."

"Anyone come into the pub looking for her?" A knot formed in her stomach at the possibility of someone claiming the pup.

"Nope. Ma and Da asked around this morning on their walk. No one had even seen that pup before."

"You went to the pub this morning?"

Gavin picked up the rest of the packages and waited for her to open the door. "No. Called them to see what time they wanted us over. Ma was all flustered. Something about Brandy's boss taking a turn for the worse and her vacation being postponed again."

She whirled around to face him. "Wow. Is he going to be all right?"

He tossed the bags on the couch and began taking

items out. "Guess so. Anyway, now she can't come back until the mid or end of December. The wedding's been moved to end of December, depending on when her boss returns and can resume his full responsibilities. I guess it complicates the wedding preparations." He shrugged. "Not my department." He held up two ceramic bowls with pink trim and a paw print on the inside. Spreading out a woven mat, he set the bowls on top of it.

She paused for a beat. "That's too bad." Picking up the bag of puppy food, she stored it in the cupboard and closed the door tightly. "But you know New Year's Eve would be a great time to have a wedding. Start the ceremony before midnight and time the vows to end right after midnight. Great way to start a new year—a new life together." Thoughtful for a moment, she suddenly snapped her fingers. "You know video chat would help Brandy and Mary work out the wedding details face to face—or face to screen." Snickering, she added, "I'll bring my computer along just in case."

"Good idea." Holding up a purple harness and matching leash, he called Storm to him. "Aye, not a bad idea. Might run that past Ma. She's all upset. Seems like it would be better now that she has longer to plan. But she was hoping that Brandy would be able to spend a while here before the wedding." He caught the wriggling ball of fur around the middle in the doorway to the bedroom, knelt, and put the harness on her.

Storm plopped down and pawed at the harness, rolled on the floor all four feet flailing in the air. When that didn't work, she got to her feet, shook, then raced off. Gavin laughed tossing a few toys around the floor. "I'm going to leave a couple in the bag to take with us to Ma's house."

"Oh…" Secretly she was relieved that his sister wouldn't be back anytime soon. The fact that Baltizar had sent her to kidnap or kill Brandy didn't endear her to Gavin's sister. It didn't help things when he made moves on her. Brandy was furious. Guilt edged into her relief, she didn't wish the wedding postponed…but…

"Hey, we gotta get going. I promised Ma we'd help with dinner since she's so upset about Brandy. Got one more thing out in the truck to bring in then you're set." He straightened and eyed the box at the foot of her bed. "Mended the box I see." He dumped the contents of a bag out on the kitchen counter. Took the two bottles of liquid and set them upright on the kitchen counter. "Dog shampoo."

She wrinkled her nose. "Yeah, couldn't have her getting out and into things while I slept last night. I was so tired I was afraid I wouldn't hear her." Pausing for a moment, she eyed the bottles. "Do we have time to give her a quick brushing and bath before we take her to your ma and da's? She stinks."

"You'll have to brush her out first, or she'll mat—bad." He pushed the door open and disappeared outside.

She stood and looked at the rag-a-muffin. "We can do better than this. She rubbed her hand over the pup, took off the harness, ran her fingers through Storm's coat. A light shimmered then she stood back and admired her work. "It would've hurt too bad to brush all those snarls out of your fur." She cooed. "This was much better. Let's get you in the bathroom." She grabbed one of the bottles, the pup, and started toward the bathroom.

Gavin carried in a huge wire crate with a pink

fluffy blanket inside "This will hold her for a few months." He shoved the cardboard box out of the way with his foot and placed the crate at the bottom of the bed. "Here all right?"

She nodded. "You've spent my first week's wages on this dog. What do I owe you?" She reached for her bag.

"Nothing. You were kind enough to take the puppy in. The least I can do is help get her settled." He glanced at his watch. "If we are going to clean her up, we better get to it. I see you took care of the mats."

Synn bristled. "It would have taken forever to brush them out, and it would have been so painful." She scratched the pup behind the ears. "So I used a little magic. It was for her benefit not mine."

He raised his hands up in a gesture of surrender. "I didn't say a word. Not judging."

Chapter Nine
Sunday Dinner and Wedding Plans Gone Amuck

Running later than he'd planned because after giving Storm a bath, Gavin couldn't tell who was wetter, Storm or Synn. She had to change before they left, and he took that opportunity to use a quick drying spell on his own clothes. How one little pup could drench two adults, he'd never know. Finally, he turned the truck into his parents' driveway and stopped out front.

He opened the back door and unlatched the small used crate he'd borrowed from a friend last night to save his truck's interior. Storm charged out. He held her back long enough to clip on her leash. She didn't even look like the same pup from last night, all fluffy and smelling great. He put her on a patch of ground away from the mud puddles left from last night's rain.

Synn reached over the back seat and snagged the bag of dog toys, then slid out of the front seat. Before her feet hit the ground, he was standing in front of her, caught her around the waist, and pulled her to him.

"I deserve a kiss for all the hard work getting your pup settled and bathed. Don't you think?"

"Do I have a choice?" she teased and wrapped her arms around his neck.

"Always have a choice." He brought his mouth down on hers in a searing kiss. During the pup's bath the inadvertent brush of her breasts over his back or side as he held the dog left him aroused. Even the bumpy ride to his parents' house hadn't diminished the feeling. Okay, the way her wet blouse clung to her curves and allowed that red bra she wore to show didn't help either. He had to get this relationship back on course, or he was going to lose his mind. *Didn't women have needs too?*

She molded to him as he kissed his way to the juncture of her neck, the tip of his tongue teased the hollow of her throat before he breathed a kiss there. She moaned when he returned to her mouth. Storm barked and bit down on her shoe. The sharp needle like puppy teeth cutting through her sock. She howled in surprise then anger. The spell was broken. Gavin cursed and looked down at the excited, happy pup wriggling all over and couldn't find his mad.

Synn rubbed the side of her foot inside her shoe. "You little beast," she said without heat. "I'll take her around back and let her loose in the back yard to run off the puppy energy. Thought the bath would wear her down. Guess not."

"Good guess. I'll meet you in the house." He tossed her a couple toys from the bag and walked to the house whistling a tune.

His da greeted him at the door. "Wondered if you were going to come in or bed her right in front of God and everyone."

Gavin paused in the doorway, heat rising to his cheeks. He turned to look around and grinned. "I don't see anyone, and God 'tis having a good laugh at my expense. I'm sure."

"So things back on track with you two?" his da

asked.

"Working on it. Still a ways to go, I fear. How's Ma?"

"She's in the kitchen cooking off her disappointment. She'll be fine now that you and Synn are here."

"That anxious to add a demon to the family?" Gavin teased.

Tim took off his hat and rubbed his head. "I don't know where we went wrong with you kids. Hannah married a warlock without even letting us know until it was all over. Brandy is engaged to a vampire, and you're chasing after a demon." He turned around shaking his head, but the quivering in his shoulders betrayed his laughter. "What's wrong with the gryphon lasses and lads?" he asked over his shoulder.

"Too tame." He threw back his head and roared with laughter. "Wasn't meant to be, Da. Our family needed a bit of diversity."

"You and your sisters sure saw to that."

"Hey, I'm not the only one to blame," he shot back.

"You're the one that's here." His dad grinned and slapped him on the back.

"Story of my life. I should have fled the country too," he grumbled.

"Oh, you love it here, and you know it. 'Tis the girls that got the wanderlust like Mary."

"You're telling me. Synn is out back with Storm. She needed to run off some excess energy."

"Storm or Synn?" Tim chuckled. "She can leave the pup out there if she wants. I repaired the hole in the fence this morning and checked the full length of the yard. It's tight."

"I'll go tell her." He walked through the house into the kitchen, kissed his ma's cheek, and reached for the door just as Synn pushed it open. He took two steps back and grinned at her. "You don't know how many times I waited for my sisters to do exactly what you did, only to scare the bejeebers out of them."

"Oh, sorry I didn't see you there. Hi Mary. Tim. What can I do to help?" She turned making sure the pup was still happy playing in the yard alone.

"She'll be fine until she notices you're missing. Then she'll set up a howl." He caught hold of her arm guiding her into the living area.

She gasped. Every flat surface was covered with pictures of wedding dresses, flower arrangements, wedding cakes, bridesmaids' dresses, tuxes, and several bride magazines opened to marked pages and strewn over the floor. On the couch was a huge binder opened to wedding invitations, menus, and a pad with scribbling on the page.

"What happened in here? A wedding planner blow up? Is Brandy here?" Synn asked, surveying the chaos.

"No… Oh dear, Brandy's wedding has to be postponed." His ma bustled in wiping her hand on the dishcloth tucked in her apron. "Isn't that a shame?"

"Doesn't that give you more time to plan the wedding?" Synn tilted her head up at Mary.

"Yes and no. The designs and things may not be available by then. I can't reserve or order dresses without Brandy's approval. She is swamped at work and doesn't return my calls promptly." His ma held her hands on either side of her head. "Don't know what to do."

"Ma, Synn had a great idea—well not about the

dress but the wedding." He nudged Synn with his elbow. "Tell Ma about your New Year's Eve idea."

Red patches bloomed on her cheeks and spread down her neck. "It was only a thought. I'm sure Brandy has a date in mind. I wouldn't want to interfere."

"Tell me. At this point the winter solstice is out, so we're open to anything." His ma ran her fingers through her hair, arranging her disheveled curls in a more orderly fashion.

Synn blew out a breath. "The New Year's Eve party you have planned for the pub could run into a reception for the wedding after midnight. If you could find people to work the party while the wedding is going on. It's a family business after all. So it might not work."

She sat quietly for a couple of beats, then a wide smile spread across her face. "That just might work. If Brandy and Stefan are agreeable. Thank you, dear. Now about the dress…"

"Can't you video chat with her? Show her the dresses. You know her sizes. Right?"

"Video chat? What is that?" She looked from Synn to Gavin and to his da who just entered the room.

"You can use your phone to see Brandy and show her the dresses in the stores and let her decide."

She stared at the phone on the coffee table. "How?"

Synn giggled. "Not that phone. A smart phone like this." She held out her phone for Mary to see. "Or we could use my laptop computer to chat. Do you or Brandy have a dress picked out?"

"Sort of. But styles come and go…" Her eyes brightened. "We could go look at the dress together and show Brandy."

"I don't think that'd be a good idea. I have to look after Storm. She couldn't stay in the crate all day while we were gone." She glanced at the floor. "Not to mention, I'm not one of Brandy's favorite people."

"She is going to have to get over that," he said in a determined tone.

His ma looked thoughtful for a couple beats.

"Ma, what are you thinking?" He narrowed his eyes, suspicion in his voice. He'd seen the look in his ma's eye before, and usually nothing good came from it.

"Aye Mary, what's on your mind?" His da glanced from red faced Synn to Gavin.

"Why couldn't you and Gavin take turns watching the l'il pup for a few hours? Synn and me could see the dress, phone chat—"

"Video chat, Ma," he corrected.

"Let Brandy see the dress and make sure the store can alter the dress when Brandy gets here, if need be. It would be such a big help," she wheedled, her eyes blinking up at Tim.

He made an exaggerated effort to roll his eyes and glanced at his da. *Yep, we're stuck.* "When did you have in mind to go?"

"As soon as I can cover Synn and my lunch shift. We'd be back by dinner. Katie won't mind the extra hours, since the kids will be in school."

Tim scrubbed his hand over his face and sent Gavin a covert glance.

Shit he's going to cave. He drew in a deep breath and let it out slowly.

"Not Monday or Friday. Maybe Thursday?"

His ma pounced on it. "Thursday it is." She peered at Synn who was staring wide-eyed switching her attention from him, his da, and back to his ma.

"I still don't think this is a good idea." She shook her head slowly.

"It'll be fine, lass." His ma patted her shoulder and took the phone from her. "How does this talk thing work? I'd like to tell Brandy our plans and see if she can be available. The five-hour time difference should work to our advantage. Don't you think?" She beamed at Synn.

Shoulders slumped she sighed. "I guess so."

"Let's try." She sidled over beside Synn, pushed the phone toward her.

The panic-stricken expression on Synn's face smoothed to resignation as she reached for the phone.

"Ma, can't this wait? What about dinner?" he asked.

"You and Da can handle it. We'll only be a few minutes."

A burbling, hissing sound was coming from the kitchen. Gavin sniffed. "What's that?"

"Probably the sauce for the salmon, it was a bit full," Mary commented. "You might want to check on the salmon too." She paused, finger to her chin. "I put it on a while ago."

He glanced at his da, and they both sprinted into the kitchen.

"'Tis a fine mess ya made of my Sunday." Tim glowered at him. "Know what's gonna happen. Brandy will be spiteful to Synn, your ma will ignore it for a while, then all hell will break loose. Someone will end up in tears, probably me Mary. Dinner will be ruined and… Our bloody day of rest blown to bloody hell."

"Da, don't be getting ahead of yourself. I'll handle Synn, Ma, and Brandy. You take care of dinner, and everything will be fine."

Tim crossed his arms over his chest. "Bollocks to that. Ruined I say."

"Just watch dinner. Ma will be back to take over soon." He walked out of the kitchen to hear Mary's voice raised in frustration.

"Brandy, do you want a dress or not? Synn is only trying to help, 'cause I asked her to. Not butting in anywhere." Mary brushed the back of her hand across her forehead. "You can always wait until you…" Mary had her hand on the phone frowning into the screen.

Synn locked eyes with Gavin, shoved the phone in his hand, and stormed out into the back yard, leaving the door wide open.

"Shit—Sis, take a breath. We're only trying to help. Synn is here to stay. Get used to it." *I hope.* He paused a beat for effect. "She can be a big help to Ma and you, if you'll…"

Brandy disconnected the call. *Right on cue.* He bit the side of his cheek to keep from grinning. *Predictable.* He turned to see his ma blinking back tears.

"See what you did," Mary cried. "She'll go off and elope, and it's all your fault. I won't get to see any of my babies married."

He cocked an eyebrow, patted his chest, then raised his hands in question. "What am I?"

She sniffled. "You don't count." She sucked in a breath looking chagrined. "Didn't mean—you're not a…"

Putting his arm around her shoulder, he hugged her tight. "Ma, listen. Brandy will think about it. Stefan will talk her down. Bet she'll call back before the evening's over. I know my sis."

"What if she doesn't?" She fisted one hand on her hip.

"I'll cook Sunday dinner for the rest of the month. Wash the dishes too."

"I heard that," Da called from the kitchen.

Ma wiped her cheeks. "I'll take that wager." She bustled into the kitchen and squealed. "Tim what have you done?"

Gavin beat feet out the back door. *Not winding up in the middle of that.* He found Synn sitting on the porch swing with Storm in her lap, conversing in low tones with the pup. "Mind if I join you?"

"It's your house."

"Brandy will come around. I'm so sure of it, that I bet Ma fixing Sunday dinner the rest of the month and cleaning up too. Since you shoved the phone in my hand and stormed out, it's your fault I wound up in that situation. Sooooo, you have to help in the off chance I'm wrong. Never happen—but giving you fair warning." He grinned broadly.

Her eyes rounded. "Me. I didn't do anything." Storm leaned across Synn, gave Gavin's face a wet sloppy lick, and jumped off her lap to pounce on a squeaky toy and drag it across the yard.

"Maybe you and me isn't such a good idea. What if I bring harm to you or your family. That's what Brandy thinks."

"Life doesn't hold guarantees. You grab hold, hang on for dear life, and hope all goes well. That's all any of us can do." He leaned over and kissed her lips. "You don't get rid of me that easy."

His ma pushed though the screen door of the house. "Gavin talk some sense into your da." She wiped her hands on the towel at her waist and threw it down on the bench next to Synn staring expectantly at Gavin.

"What's wrong now?" Gavin paused. "Or do I want to know?"

Chapter Ten

A Secret Unravels, but the Story is True—Dinner is Served

"What's wrong?" Synn asked watching Storm shake and toss her new toy then race the perimeter of the yard.

"Oh, nothing dear. I just wanted a few minutes alone with you." Mary's blue eyes twinkled with mischief. "Don't let Brandy upset you. She's always been high strung. A lass that speaks her mind without considering the consequences or other's feelings. I'm sure Gavin is right. She'll cool off and call back. I need your help with pulling all the wedding plans together since Brandy will be across the pond for most of the time. The video talk is great. We can get a decision on the spot."

"I'll do whatever I can to help, but I don't want to cause a problem."

"Oh, hon, the way my son looks at you—" Mary sighed. "I remember when Tim looked at me like that." Her eyes went dreamy for a beat, then cleared. She sat up straighter. "Brandy is going to have to get used to you being around. Once she knows you like we do, she'll be fine."

Synn shrugged. "I don't know about that. I did try to—well you know. She'll never trust me, and I can't blame her."

"That's all in the past. Things are different now. You're not the same person." Patting Synn's thigh supportively, Mary grinned and turned her attention to Storm. "Come here, Storm, you li'l monster." She called to the pup, who rolled on her back, chewing on the bottom picket of the fence. "She's going to be a handful."

"Oh, there's no going to be about it." She laughed. "But Storm is a lot of company." The mild breeze ruffled the pup's fur in the sunlight as the women watched in companionable silence for a few moments.

"Aye, I can see that." Mary started to push up from the bench. Synn put her hand on her arm.

"Can we…I mean I saw—"

"Spit it out. lass." Mary eased back onto the bench her forehead creased in concern. "What did you see?"

"Erin and Tiarnan early this morning walking the rocky ledge."

Mary gasped, her hand flew to her mouth then she blew out a breath. After a beat she asked, "Are you sure it was them? A lot of people walk that path in the early morn hours. The view is spectacular as it was today."

"Yes, I'm positive. They stood behind me when I stopped to sit on a rock to let Storm play and sniff around. Erin and Tiarnan talked to me. Well, Tiarnan only for a minute before he disappeared in thick mist. Erin—she told me what happened the night the curse was broken." *The rest I'm going to keep to myself—for now.*

Mary jumped up and paced in front of the bench. "Me own Brandy relayed the tale to us after it was over, but no one has seen them since. I mean until now—at least no one wagged their tongues about it if they did.

99

Believe me if they had, it would have been all over town. Did you tell Gavin?"

"Tell Gavin what?" Gavin and Tim sauntered across the lawn. Tim wrapped his arm around Mary's shoulder and kissed her on the cheek. "Everything 'tis handled. Dinner will be ready in a few minutes." He smiled knowingly. "Everything good here?"

She stared at Mary and gave a little shake of her head.

"Well it seems like I let the cat out of the bag." Mary laughed, red blotches bloomed on her cheeks. Her gaze touched on each person before she said proudly, "Our own Synn talked with Erin and Tiarnan this morn."

"What? Why didn't you tell me?" Gavin moved to face Synn, kneeling in front of her placing his hands over hers.

"I was thinking about it but wasn't sure if you'd think I was daft. Or having a breakdown. Which I'm not," she said firmly.

"What did they say?" Tim asked with interest.

Synn relayed most of the conversation she had with Erin, adding in the moments of conversation with Tiarnan. She left out the warnings of possible trouble as well as about Gavin and her. She wasn't ready to air her feelings in front of the whole world, or at least what constituted her world. When she glanced at Gavin, she saw doubt in his eyes.

"What—you don't believe me?"

"I didn't say that—'tis more to the story, I can feel it." He lifted Synn's chin and she looked away from him.

"Ahh…leave the—" Mary's comment was

interrupted by Synn's cell phone ringing.

Gavin puffed out his chest. "Told you so."

Checking the caller ID, Synn handed the phone to Gavin. "I'm not answering it."

He glanced at the screen and touched speaker. "Hi, sis."

"It's Stefan. Brandy wanted to make sure you answered rather than Synn."

"That's tough, since it's Synn's phone." His face lit up in a devilish grin. "You know, Stefan, my sis is going to have to come to grips with the situation."

"I'm well aware. That conversation is slated for later tonight. Right now, Brandy wants to talk wedding."

"Okay, let me give the phone back to Synn so we can arrange—" Gavin said.

"I've a better idea. Let's all go in the house, I'll fire up my laptop so we have a big screen and we can all—I mean—Mary and Brandy can set around the table and discuss the wedding." She backed away from her phone as he was trying to hand to her. "I'll need Brandy's video chat ID to get her connected."

"No, you had it right the first time, Synn," Mary said in a determined voice.

"Gavin, what's going on? Where's Ma?" Brandy's voice came over the phone.

"Sis, I need your video chat ID so she can connect the call to the computer screen rather than the phone." He paused for a moment glancing from his ma to Synn. "And if you continue to act like an arse, I'll kick yours the next time I see you. She's just trying to help Ma give you the dream wedding you discussed before leaving here." His words were met with silence on the other end. "Until life intervened."

"I'll text my ID to this phone so you won't get the numbers wrong, little brother." She emphasized each of the last two words.

Storm came bounding up to the group, barking and growling, alternately squeaking her toy, pushing it at her.

"When did you get a dog?" Brandy asked.

"It's Synn's puppy. Poor thing looked like a drowned rat when she found it outside the pub but she took it in. The pup has Ma wrapped around its paw as well as Synn." Gavin grinned.

"Right. I'll hang up and text you my number."

"Okay, but don't mess around. Dinner will be ready soon," Gavin said. His ma shoved an elbow in his side. He frowned at her. "Well, we are almost ready to eat."

She picked up Storm and carried her into the house. After making sure there was food and water in her crate, she coaxed the pup inside and closed the door. Storm objected for a minute, then crunching came from the crate, laps of water, and the pup curled up head on her paws.

Gavin brought her laptop in from the pickup and set it up on the dining room table. She entered the chat ID from her phone and connected to Brandy. When Brandy came into view, she backed away stepping behind the computer. Mary tugged on her sleeve forcing her to sit in the chair at the table. Within a few minutes, Mary and Brandy hashed out the ideas and set a time to reconnect and look at the wedding dress in Dublin. All the while she sat quietly next to Mary. Brandy only glowered at her twice.

It was nearing midnight in Montana, and Brandy was scheduled for an early morning hike, so everyone gathered around the laptop to say their goodbyes. Relieved, she disconnected the call.

"See that wasn't so bad." Mary snickered. "Told you'd she'd come around. Da, need some help in the kitchen?"

"Aye." Tim brought out a plate piled high with buttermilk fried chicken. "Thought you'd like a little taste of home for Sunday dinner." Tim narrowed his eyes at Mary. "Since the earlier entrée got burnt to a crisp."

Synn's forehead creased, and she tilted her head. "What do you mean?"

He waved his hand in dismissal. "Yanks have fried chicken, mashed potatoes, and gravy with rolls for Sunday dinner. Right?" Tim asked, placing the platter in the middle of the huge scarred wooden table that had seen many meals over the years.

"I guess so. We didn't have any family traditions. Or at least I don't remember any. I was young when—my parents died."

Mary came out of the kitchen with a large bowl of mashed potatoes and a round of soda bread wrapped in a towel. "Son, the gravy is simmering. Please pour it in the bowl sitting next to the stove and bring it out."

"Aye." Gavin sent her a sideways glance. "I'll be right back." He strode into the kitchen, returning a few seconds later with the gravy boat and ladle.

Once they were all seated around the table, Gavin reached for the plate of chicken. "What's the schedule look like for tomorrow? Can you spare us? I'd like to show Synn some of the sights, visit a few castles beginning with Blarney Castle." He picked up a breast and thigh, set them on his plate, then offered the plate to her.

She stuck her fork in a breast, pushed it onto her plate with a knife. "Pass the potatoes, please."

Tim handed the potatoes to her and reached for the gravy boat. "I guess we could work that out. Since tomorrow is the only dry day this week. Might make for a slow day what with people staying outside enjoying the nice weather."

"Aye. We'll be slammed the rest of the week. It'll work well for everyone." Gavin agreed scooping potatoes onto his plate from the bowl she held before she passed it on to Mary.

She dug into her chicken and popped a piece in her mouth, chewed, scooped up a fork of potatoes and gravy, and pointed it at Tim. "This is fantastic. Thank you." She slid the fork in her mouth. After she swallowed, she turned to Gavin. "Will we be gone all day?"

"Aye. If the weather holds."

"What about Storm?"

"We'll take her with us. Give her a good walk before we leave to tire her out. She'll sleep in the crate. We'll take breaks, grab a bite, and let her out during the day. The weather is cool enough. She'll be fine."

"He loves the old castles. When he was a kid, he was always poking around those ruins. It's a wonder he didn't fall and get hurt the way he climbed around," Mary said on a laugh taking the last bite of her roll. "I'll wrap up the leftovers, and you two can have a picnic tomorrow." Her gaze shifted to Tim. "Remember our picnics years ago?"

"Aye. Every blasted time we took off, the rain came out of nowhere, or one of your sisters followed and spied on us."

"Da put them up to it." Mary giggled. "He said you were only after one thing. Quite a skirt chaser—that one."

"Aye, 'tis true. But I fell under your spell." He patted her arse as she leaned over gathering the dishes. Mary swatted his hand away, her cheeks blushing.

After helping Mary clear away the dinner dishes, she let Storm out of her crate and escorted her to the back yard. Gavin excused himself and followed her.

As soon as they were out in the yard alone, Gavin slipped an arm around her waist and asked, "Now tell me what else Erin said to you." Letting his hand slide to her hip, he pulled her to his side steering her farther from the house and behind the grove of trees as the pup bounced and ran over the entire yard.

She glanced at his arm. "So are we doing this already? What happened to our agreement?" Stopping, she leaned back against a tree peering up at him.

"I'm done with it, and by the way you've been acting, I'd say you are too. A nice ride in the country side and exploring a few castles will be a fresh start."

She nodded and caressed the back of his neck. Standing on tiptoe, she brushed her lips over his.

"Not going to work. I want to know what else Erin told you." Gavin eased her hand from the back of his neck, entwining his fingers with hers, and pressing her against the tree trunk.

Shoulders slumped, she leaned into him and sighed. "Erin says dark times may be coming, and that I shouldn't push you away."

He paused for a beat as if digesting that information. "She did, did she? And Tiarnan?"

"He was only there for a few seconds. Erin shooed him away. Girl talk. You know."

Gavin raised a brow. "That's all?" Their joined hands slipped down her side, he caressed the side of her breast with the back of his hand. He nuzzled against her neck, teasing the tip of his tongue along the juncture of her shoulder, then lower inside the V of her sweater. His breathing increased.

He was too close his excitement pushed against her belly. She was tempted to tell all yet held back. "Yep, that's all." Leaning her head back, she allowed him access. It had been so long. She breathed in his outdoorsy scent. A soft moan escaped her lips, moisture gathered between her legs as his tongue licked the swells of her breasts. His hand moved from her hip to under her sweater, pushing her bra aside, his mouth closed over her breast. Her pulse raced.

"We better move this elsewhere, or I'm going to take you right here." Gavin growled. Her fingers let go of his, moved to stroke the baby fine hair at the nape of his neck. His thumb flipped open the button of her jeans, his fingers slipped inside as his knee pushed between her denim clad legs spreading her.

The pressure of his thigh against her tender parts and his fingers teasing around her center ignited a firestorm. She writhed against him and shuddered as the peak of ecstasy flowed through her. She buried her face in his chest to muffle her screams. When the pulsing subsided, she looked up. A smug smile curved his lips.

"Ready for more?" He thrust one finger inside, then another.

"Oh, Gavin." She breathed then the real world spun and careened on its axis, she gasped in sweet agony against him. Still his fingers gently tapped a tattoo on her sensitive bundle of nerves.

The outside light flicked on. Barking happily, Storm bolted for Synn, ramming into her leg, biting, and tugging at the bottom edge of her pant leg.

She tried to pull Gavin's hand from inside her jeans, he refused. One final thrust of his fingers had her sucking in a breath as desire bloomed again. "Stop it. What if..." At last he allowed her to remove his hand. He kissed her lips, his tongue teasing inside before he slipped his hand from under her sweater, pulled it into place and whispered seductively, "Your place or mine?"

Her body and mind still in a sexual haze, she managed a horse whisper, "What?"

"I'm far from finished with you." He grinned.

"You revved me up, so I would let you in my bed tonight?" The haze began clearing and twisting into a gut-wrenching anger. He'd taken advantage of her; worse, she'd let him.

"Oh, I did a lot more than that, lass."

Sparks sizzled at the end of her fingers. He covered them with his hands. "Temper... temper."

"Temper this." She raised her hand to slap him.

He caught her hand in his and waggled a finger in front of her face with his other. "No violence. Remember." He paused as if cooling his own temper. "I wanted to remind you what we had—have." Bending over, he picked up a toy, threw it toward the house. Storm let go of the bottom of Synn's jeans and bounded after the toy.

"Do I want to bed you? Hell yes, you're driving me crazy. I've taken more cold showers in the past months than in my entire life." He grabbed her hand and tugged her toward the house.

She jerked free. "There's plenty of women that would crawl into your bed at the snap of your fingers."

"Aye you're bang on. I just—" He paused, pinched the bridge of his nose with thumb and forefinger. "I don't want to fight. It's been a brutal day. Let's start over tomorrow when I pick you up to tour the countryside. We can go inside thank Ma and Da, and I'll take you home. Sound all right?"

"I guess, but I don't know about tomorrow."

"That's your choice. I'll stop by in the morning, if you don't want to go— I'll be on my way."

"Okay." She followed him into the house.

****

He stopped the truck in front of her cottage. "If you don't mind, I'd like to walk you to the door and check the inside before leaving you and Storm alone."

Her first thought was to decline politely, but it was out of spite. With Erin's warning, safety had to be first, though the whole discussion had been derailed by their lust. A wave of regret washed over her. He could have left her as she left him. But he hadn't. He'd sated her well.

What did it matter if his ulterior motive is to get laid? He's male after all. What is a matter with me? I could have driven him into the arms of another woman. Is that what I want? She bit her lip. *It wasn't.* For once she'd thought before opening her mouth.

He opened her truck door and held out his hand.

"Works for me." She clipped the leash on Storm,

took Gavin's offered hand, and climbed out of the truck. Walking up to the path, she dug in her pack for the keys, unlocked the door, and pushed it open allowing Gavin inside.

Storm wandered off the porch, squatted, and rushed back to the entrance.

Within a few minutes, he returned. "All clear."

"Thank you. What time do you want Storm and me to be ready?"

A slight smile curved the corners of his mouth. "Half past seven?"

"See you tomorrow." Synn closed and locked the door leaning her back against the wood until she heard his truck start up and drive off.

She made sure Storm had food and water in her crate, waited for the pup to reluctantly step in, and she closed the door. "Nite girl." She undressed, stepped into the shower, and turned it on letting warm water cascade over her for a few minutes. Then she lathered up, rinsed, toweled off, and pulled Gavin's t-shirt over her head before crawling into bed.

Darkness engulfed her. The voices in her head returned calling her a traitor suggesting retribution would be sweet and exacted soon. She fought against the words and covered her ears. As suddenly as the booming words came, it was silent. The dream shifted to a dank room, without windows, or light, and a darkness she could almost feel. Scraping sounds against a large wooden plank door grated on her nerves.

Magic failed her leaving her drained and unresponsive. She curled up in a fetal position. Baltizar's voice whispered again in her mind. "I still control you. They're all going to die a horrible death at my hands. You will get to watch. Just like when you failed to save your family."

His wicked laugh echoed though her mind and faded. A warm liquid flowed over her hands. She looked down. They were covered in blood. Bodies were strewn over what looked like the dirt floor of a cave. Screaming, she awoke soaked with sweat, head pounding, and blood trickled from her palms where her finger nails had sliced through the skin.

A loud bark came from the foot of her bed. She stumbled out of bed and rushed to Storm's crate, knelt, and yanked open the door. A warm, fur ball bounded into her lap, the dog covered her face with kisses. She sat on the floor, tears streaming down her face dripping on the soft fur she buried her face in.

Never allowed to cry, she allowed the flood gates open, and cried for her family, mistakes made, decisions forced upon her, and wished she'd died in the battle with Baltizar. She wouldn't be responsible for the deaths of her new friends, Gavin and his family, or Storm.

Chapter Eleven
Exploring the Irish Countryside Brings Shivers at the Castles

Gavin walked up the stairs to his house, shoved open the door, kicked off his boots, and shed the rest of his clothing. Stepping out onto the porch, his form shimmered and transformed to gryphon. With two beats of his wings, he was airborne and free. Gliding through the inky darkness with only a few stars trying to peek out from behind the clouds, he left his earthbound problems behind.

Soaring over the tree tops, he banked out over the ocean. After a while he landed on Hy-Brasil, one of the Phantom Islands claimed to be south west of Ireland. In the mortal world, these islands have appeared on maps and been considered to be real places, only to disappear from maps later when others were unable to verify their existence. This island was his secret place of reflection.

The islands have been seen or even visited by seafarers. Discovery of the islands is precipitated by a sudden dense fog descending upon their ship. When the fog clears a rocky shore appears only to later vanish without a trace. Still others claim catastrophic events like volcanic eruptions, earthquakes, or underwater landslides are to blame for the disappearance.

Steeped in mystery, legends born of curiosity and wonder claim the Phantom Islands are supposedly a mystical land inhabited by mythical creatures. He snorted through his beak, ruffled his feathers, and stretched his wings out. If the mortals only knew how close to the truth the legends were.

Pushing off with hind feet, he felt the wind beneath his wings. The magic from the island carried him into the night, over the sea, and back home in the blink of an eye. Touching down a few paces from his home, he transformed to a human and sauntered inside not ready to resume life as he knew it. Not yet.

He showered, pulled on sweats, and stretched out on his empty king-sized bed. After his long flight, a peaceful sleep came quickly until Synn's nightmare invaded his dream world. Gut wrenching terror tore through him until he was able to disengage himself from the nightmare. There'd be no phone call this time. For a moment he considered shifting, but he might need a vehicle after arriving at her home. He yanked off his sweats and pulled on jeans, a sweater, donned a coat, and grabbed his keys.

He found her sitting cross-legged on the bedroom floor. Storm curled in her lap. The usually active pup was lying still just peering up at her. When Gavin approached, Storm moved one ear forward and turned her head to look at him. "It'll be okay, girl." He knelt in front of Synn, brushed the hair away from her face. A vacant stare met his gaze into her eyes like she was in a trance. *This couldn't be good.*

He'd seen her nightmare. Something was trying to control her. He wouldn't let it happen. Releasing a breath, he took hold of her shoulders. She'd been like this once before. When she came out of it anyone within arm's reach could be in danger. Though her magic was tempered these days, it wouldn't be for long… Changing strategy, he repositioned himself behind her, caught her up in a bear hug, and pushed the pup out of her lap. Storm yelped and went grudgingly but refused to leave her side.

"Synn, it's me Gavin; you're safe." He gave her a little shake. Arms and legs began flailing. She let out a blood curdling scream and kept screaming until he thought the neighbors a few miles away would hear and call the police. He held her tightly, sat down on the floor, and pulled her into his lap. "Synn. Synn. You're all right. We're at the cottage." The screams turned to sobs. She leaned her head back and blinked.

Panic seized her. "Gavin, you've got to get out of here. He's coming for me and will kill everyone associated with me, including Storm." She reached for the pup cuddling her close to her chest. "I'm so sorry. I knew this would never work. I don't deserve a normal life."

"That's enough. It was a nightmare. That's all."

She turned her large aqua eyes on him and raised an eyebrow. "Really?"

He couldn't lie to her. "Okay…but you're not going to fight this alone. We won't let him win. You have magic to ward him off—use it."

She sadly shook her head. "Bruce limited my powers. I'm not strong enough." She tried to get up. He refused to let her go.

"You're strong enough to force him to try to use the dream world to get to you. During your waking hours, you're keeping him away. If Erin saw this coming, she must have told you more. What exactly did she say?"

She stared at the floor then slowly brought her gaze up to meet his. "She said I should talk to Gale. She's a relative of Erin's. Also the injury to my leg is not only physical, but when Baltizar threw that fireball of magic at me—he transferred some of his magic to me. But she doesn't think he is aware. Erin claims that Gale could heal me and help me learn to control the dark magic."

"Let's go see Gale." He paused a couple of beats running his fingers through his hair. "Why didn't you tell me this before?"

"You were—uh—we were otherwise occupied."

Gavin swore. "No more sexual games or teasing until we get a handle on this." Helping her to her feet, he paused to make sure she was steady, then he paced. Thinking was easier if he was on his feet.

"Agreed."

"Get…better get dressed. I'll fix a quick breakfast, and we'll be on our way. We'll stop by Gale's place before taking a drive. Don't want you staying here alone any more. Gather the things you need for a few days. You'll be staying at my home."

At her frosty gaze. He paused. "Or I'm moving in here. Your choice."

"We might be a bit cramped." She conceded and walked to the closet, pulled out jeans, a shirt and sweater, then carried them into the bathroom leaving the door ajar.

He fried bacon and eggs, put four slices of bread in the toaster, and buttered them when they popped. Put a slice of cheese on two pieces of toast, layered bacon and egg before placing the other pieces of toast on the sandwich. Storm circled his feet. He dropped a piece of egg on the floor before filling her food bowl and getting fresh water. Opening cupboard doors, he found a small basket to put the egg sandwiches in, added bottles of water, and poured a couple glasses of orange juice. *Not bad for breakfast on the run.*

Storm finished eating and slurped water. When she was through, he snapped the leash on her while waiting for Synn to get dressed and packed. He carried the pup's crate, dishes, food, and bag of toys out to the truck nearly tripping over the exuberant pup twice as she wound in and out between his feet. Opening the truck door, he strapped the crate in the back seat and was putting the pup inside when he heard her footsteps on the porch.

She carried a couple duffel bags out the door, paused, dropped bags on the porch, and locked the door. Picking up the duffels, she slung them over her shoulder and strode down the path toward him. "This is only temporary."

"Of course." Gavin held her door open and offered to help her climb in. She clambered into the truck without his help glancing at the basket setting in the middle of the front seat. She sniffed. "Is that for us?"

He picked up a glass of orange juice from the floorboard where he's set them and handed one to her. "Yep. Figured we'd better put food in our bellies before doing any exploring. Ma packed a picnic lunch for us last night. It's still at the house. But cold chicken didn't sound good for breakfast. I'll pick up lunch when I drop off your bags and Storm's stuff before we drive over to Gale's."

They ate in silence as Gavin started the truck and Storm whined in her crate.

A few minutes later, he pulled up in front of his

house, dropped off the bags and pup supplies, then returned with another basket. When they stopped in front of Pixie Magic, the closed sign hung on the window, and there was a note taped to the inside of the glass door.

She got out and walked up to the door. Peering in through the windows, she returned to the door and read the note loud enough for him to hear. "Closed for the day, will be back tomorrow." Synn trudged back to the truck. "She's taken the day off."

"So I heard. It's a gorgeous cool summer day. How about we continue on as planned. Staying around home and worrying about things won't change the situation. I left a cryptic message for Bruce while you were reading the note at Gale's place. I imagine he'll call as soon as he gets a chance."

She looked at the blue sky where a few puffy white clouds floated, then faded away. "We can't leave Storm in the truck all day."

"No. But we discussed taking a break and going back to the truck to let her out then return to continue our exploration of the castle. I'll leave all the windows cracked a bit creating airflow."

She brightened. "Okay, I've always wanted to explore the castles around here. So much history and legends."

"Yeah and we might see a ghost or two," he teased.

The color drained out of her face. "I don't think—"

"Only kidding. It's been years since I've seen a ghost. Besides they only come out for tourists." He nudged Synn in the ribs and grinned. "Except the Blarney Castle where we are headed today. A pretty lass such as yourself could bring out many a wayward ghost. Lots of battles have been fought here." He paused for effect. "Much blood of brave young men spilled."

"So you say. You silver tongued devil. How many times have you kissed the Blarney Stone?"

"I've no idea what you are talking about." He glanced over at his passenger.

"I believe legend of the Blarney Stone is that anyone who kisses it will receive the gift of fair speech and skillful flattery. I've seen you at your best in the pub storytelling, teasing the young women, and goading the men."

"Darlin', that's the life of a publican, and yes, I am well suited to it—runs in the family. Shaughnessys have made a living that way for generations. What do you expect? Brandy, now she's our Seanachi. Best storyteller in all of Ireland."

"Really," Synn said her voice cool. "I wouldn't know. All I've experienced from her is… Never mind."

"We'll have a story night when she returns. You'll see," Gavin said cheerfully. "Where would you like to start our tour? Drombeg Stone Circle better known as The Druid's Altar or Kealkil Stone Circle in West Cork. We'll end the tour at Blarney Castle."

Quiet for a moment, Synn shivered. "I'd rather pass on the Drombeg altogether. Don't wish to become someone's offering."

"Okay. Kealkil Stone Circle it is."

"Ummm… I don't want to tempt fate. The magic is restless. I don't need a bunch of ancient druids appearing and stirring up trouble. I'd rather go straight to Blarney Castle."

"Your wish is my command. But there are tales of

druids there too." He turned the truck onto the road toward Blarney Castle.

"Yes, but somehow the tales of the witch of Blarney Castle seem more benevolent." She shrugged and shifted in her seat watching the scenery pass by appearing to be deep in thought.

Turning onto the highway, he wondered how much of a toll this morning's events had taken on her. Would she go back in her shell, after making so much progress and new friends? She was good with the customers at the pub and seemed to enjoy the work.

He shoved the unpleasant memories to the back of his mind and snorted. "What tales of the Blarney witch have you been reading? If we'd left a little earlier, we may have been in time to see the dying embers of her fire in Witch's Kitchen."

She flipped around to face him. "She doesn't still exist there?"

"Depends who you talk to." A mischievous smile curved the corners of his lips. "Some say to this day she takes firewood from the estates for her kitchen. In return she must grant visitor's wishes made on the Wishing Steps."

Synn snickered. "Sure she does. One of your far-fetched tales, I'll wager."

"I wouldn't wager unless you are willing to lose. By the way, what might you be wagering?" He glanced out the corner of his eye at her for a beat, then his gaze returned to the road. The sign for Killinagh whizzed by on the left. "Would you like to stop in Castleview or Midleton on our way through? Too late for Killinagh."

"Not this trip. I'd rather take a look at the Blarney Village and spend most of the time at the castle."

After a couple beats he said, "Probably a good idea, there is a lot of grounds to cover as well as the castle. You gonna kiss the Blarney Stone?"

"Absolutely not," she huffed, straightening in the seat.

He chuckled. "Why not? Then you might be able to compete with my persuasive eloquence of speech."

She threw her head back and roared with laughter. "Think mighty highly of yourself."

"Just rephrasing what you accused me of earlier."

She slapped his shoulder. "Don't believe everything you hear. Boyo."

Feigning innocence, he tried to keep a straight face, but in the end, a broad smile curved his lips. "What was that for?"

"You know."

After about an hour, he turned the truck onto The Groves to The Square in Blarney. "Did you know that Blarney Village is actually one of the last estate villages that remain standing in Ireland? An eighteenth-century landlord built the village so the castle workers had somewhere to live."

"That was awfully nice of him."

"It was. Old witch probably put a spell on him," he teased while driving through the streets of Blarney Village. Pulling in front of an eatery, he cut the engine.

At her quizzical look and glance at the picnic basket he said, "We'll have the chicken Ma fixed for us after the tour. But we need sustenance for trekking over the castle and grounds. Want to do a bit of shopping while I run into the café and get a snack for us?"

"Not this time. I'll wait here for you. It seems the Blarney Witch was more inclined to cast a spell on the

Blarney Stone in thanks for a king who saved her life."

"So the story goes. You've been studying up on the Blarney Castle."

"I've wanted to visit this place since I arrived." She reached behind the seat and tickled Storm through the opening in her crate, then rolled the window down, and sniffed. Gavin sprinted into the café. A few minutes later, he came out with a wide smile and a bag. He climbed into the truck.

"The fresh bread aroma wafting from the café when you opened the door was mouthwatering."

"Oh, I know." He drew a round of brown bread out of the bag and handed her a slice. I had the waitress slice and butter it for us. Figured we'd eat it right here. Best when it's warm, right out of the oven."

She tore off a small piece of her slice and fed it to Storm.

After they ate their fill of bread and drank from the bottles of water, Gavin pointed out the window. "The castle is hidden behind those woodlands, only a few hundred yards from here."

Chapter Twelve
The Castle Blarney—Quite the Unexpected Experience

Gavin started the engine, turned on the road that led to the castle, and parked. "We're here. Where to first?"

"Let's just follow the trails and paths around the castle. After all that's where the true magic is. Then we can go inside. Is it true a river runs under the walls of the castle?"

"Aye, 'tis true." Opening her door, he offered her a hand.

She reached for his hand and clambered out of the truck. Opening the back door to the truck, she unlatched Storm's crate, checked food and water, then snapped on her leash and lowered her to the ground. The pup raced around for a bit, squatted, and did her business. Synn returned her to the crate. "We'll be back in a little while." She rubbed Storm's ears and closed the crate door.

Fingers twined, they started down the path to the castle. "The true magic of the grounds is only found after you've ventured out into the numerous walks around the estate."

"Lead the way." After wandering several of the paths around the castle, they took the one leading through the standing stones. Synn stopped in the middle and seemed disoriented. She let go of his hand.

"You all right?" He paused at her side, reached for her.

"Yes, I thought I heard something, must have been the wind." She stopped to touch one of the stones, then hurried up the path toward the poison garden. Skull and cross bone signs warned of the dangers of Cannabis, Opium Poppy, Wolfsbane, European Mandrake, and other traditional poisons. "Maybe I should use a bit of magic to harvest some of the plants for potion making." Synn rubbed her hands together just a little too gleefully.

"Not a good idea, even in jest," Gavin said in a solemn voice. He glanced back at the stones and then at Synn and began tugging her down the path away from the poison gardens.

Dragging her feet, she continued to look back at the gardens. "True, I'm sure Gale could get what I need." She snickered, a sound that sent shivers up his spine and not in a good way.

Several yards down the trail, he grabbed her shoulders and spun her around to face him. He stared into her eyes, giving her shoulders a little shake. "Synn…"

She blinked up at him. "What?"

"Are you okay?"

"Sure. I just got a bit confused coming out of the stones on which path to take." She glanced around. "We passed the poison garden already?" She studied his face. "What did I do?"

"Are you able to weave a spell of protection from spirits' influence?"

"Of course. Why?"

"Because you just suggested use of magic to harvest a few of those plants." He pointed his thumb over his shoulder toward the gardens.

Wide-eyed, she gasped. "I did?" She wrapped her arms around her body, murmured a few words, and drew a necklace of black stones infused with red from her pocket. At the center of the necklace hung an amulet of several shimmering green stones caged in silver. She slipped it over her head. "Sorry about that. I should be fine now."

"What did you put around your neck?"

"A necklace my mother gave me." A faraway look came into her eyes. She paused to finger the stones. "It's made of Fire Agate and Green Amethyst. The agate bounces negative energy back and builds an impermeable shield of protection. The amethyst clears disharmonious energy and assists inner vision."

Gavin gaped at her. "You were expecting—a problem?"

"Maybe."

"Then why the hell didn't you tell me?"

"You would've refused to bring me. I can't live my life in fear or in a bubble of other's protection. I have the means—at least I used to—have the ability to protect myself." She shivered. "I hope we hear from Bruce soon. For now I'm fine." She led the way through the Fairy Glade.

He gave her a dubious look. "One more episode and we are out of here."

"Fair enough." She sighed. "Better avoid the Druid's Circle and Sacrificial Altar." She looked up the well-worn path where several visitors milled around taking photographs. "Do you feel that?"

"I don't feel anything." He raised an eyebrow.

She took one step, paused, and took another toward the Witch's Stone in close proximity to the Druid's Circle.

"Whoa... Not going there." Wrapping an arm around her waist, he moved toward another path.

"But it's calling to me... Don't you hear it?"

"No," he said firmly, pulling her tighter against him moving forward with the crowd of people.

She stiffened and became rooted to the spot. "The Witch of Blarney has been with us since the dawn of time. Supposedly she's the one who told MacCarthy about the power of the Blarney Stone. Legend has it that she only escapes the Witch Stone after nightfall. So we're safe."

He gave her a little squeeze and smiled at the people around them. "It's not working," he whispered.

Quietly, she said, "Sure it is. I'm in control. Wanted to touch the stone to see what she had to say."

"Not a good idea. Now get moving."

"I suppose you're right," she said ruefully. "Spoilsport. This is such a beautiful place."

"Aye."

They wound their way toward the Witch's Kitchen. The opening was narrow. She touched the moss-covered rock wall and backed away.

"It's believed this was home to the very first Irish cave dwellers to cross the mists of time," Gavin said in a deep mysterious voice.

She giggled and gazed up at him for a beat before returning to stare at the narrow pathway. "Too close quarters for me. I'm not claustrophobic but I don't like the vibe. It's soooo cold in here. She touched her necklace and trembled. Taking the next turn, she headed toward the Rock Close and the Wishing Steps.

The sun disappeared behind the clouds, and a mist settled around the castle on their approach. "Can you climb the steps with your eyes closed?" Synn asked a devilish smile curving her lips. "You know it's said that if you can, your wish…"

"Aye. And I can do it jogging backward."

She blinked at him. "Really?"

He closed his eyes at the bottom of the stairs, whipped around to face her, then jogged up and back without a misstep. He opened his eyes and grinned. "We used to challenge each other as teens. I can't tell you how many times I landed on my arse before I mastered the task. Cracked my noggin a couple times too. By the way, I did it without thinking about my wish." He puffed out his chest, rubbed his finger nails against his jacket. "If you believe the legend—my wish should come true within a year." He chuckled.

Synn closed her eyes, placed her hand against the rock wall just above the railing, and slowly walked up the stairs. At the top she turned careful to keep her hands on the wall and descended the stairs. At the bottom she opened her eyes and smiled. "I did it…without thinking of my wish. It wasn't a problem, because I was thinking about how I could fall, crack my head wide open, and die."

"Drama queen." He snorted. "Where next?"

"Explore the castle. The view from the top is supposed to be spectacular."

"Aye, it is. That's where you can kiss the Blarney Stone too. You have to bend over backward, and it's a wee bit cramped in there. But it's worth the discomfort if you believe the legend. Besides, now there are hand rails to support you."

She smirked at him. "We'll see. First, let's eat lunch. I'm starved. Then we can let Storm out for a romp. I don't want any accidents."

"Great idea." Avoiding the Druids Cave, he took her hand and followed the path to the boardwalk. They strolled by the water garden and waterfalls on their way to the truck to retrieve lunch.

****

Inside the castle walls, Gavin wrinkled his nose at the damp, musty scent. "Smells like the castle keeper should take a page from the people who lived here in ancient times. A little orris root, rosemary, lavender, woodruff, or rose petals would be helpful."

Synn laughed. "Why don't you enlighten them?"

"With my luck, they'd suggest I do just that on a volunteer basis. Learned that lesson as a lad." He snickered.

"It must have been awful cold and damp in the castle for the inhabitants. There's no coverings on the windows, but bars."

"Each room usually had a fireplace for heat. The kitchen and great halls had more than one, besides the people back then dressed a lot different than we do today."

She shook her head. "Still, must have been a rough life."

"'Tis true. But they didn't know any different. This was their life."

She paused in the large open area entitled the family room, tilted her head up, and stared at all the levels of the castle. "Wow, there'd be no way to keep heat in here."

"Aye." He glanced up then followed her as she continued up the steps of the castle interior exploring every hallway and room on the way to the castle roof.

At the top, she briefly leaned on the black iron railing to look over the wall in several places around the roof. "Wow, the climb was worth it. The view is breathtaking." She glanced at the line waiting to kiss the Blarney Stone.

"Well, what are you waiting for? You know you want to kiss the stone," Gavin teased moving her to the end of the line with very little resistance.

"This is silly." Still she waited her turn and kissed the Blarney Stone. After she got up and straightened from her position at the stone, she stood on tiptoe and kissed his lips. "I guess we better get started back. Thank you so much for today. I've had a wonderful time."

"My pleasure. Next time we have a day off, we'll visit more castles and ruins."

"I'd like that."

They wound their way down the castle stairs, revisiting a couple of rooms Synn thought she'd missed. At the truck, she clipped the leash on Storm and walked around the area for a bit, then returned the pup to the crate over her loud objections. On the ride home, she rested her head against the seat watching the scenery pass by. She was quiet for a long time. He hoped it was from the physical day, not the nightmares and magical interference. They stopped once on the outskirts of town to let Storm out to do her business.

The road to her cottage took them by the pub. He didn't want to spoil a great day by stopping by

Shaughnessy's. But he had a nagging feeling that was exactly what he was supposed to do. Prior experience taught him nothing but trouble would come if he ignored his gut. "Mind if we stop by the pub on the way home. Storm can stay in the truck for a few minutes. I want to make sure—"

"Everything is all right?"

"Of course it's all right. I've taken time off before." Gavin bristled. "I had a life before—" He stopped mid-sentence. No way was he going to spoil this day.

She shifted in her seat to face him. "Before what? Me? Before your sister married an assassin? Or Brandy became engaged to a vampire? Before your world came crashing down amid demons, vampires, witches, and world ending shit?" She paused, closed her eyes, and leaned her head against the seat again. "I didn't mean that. I've been on edge since the dream—nightmare—premonition. Call it what you want. Today was a nice reprieve. But when we hit the edge of town—what'd you call 'em—" she tapped her temple. "My spidey senses went off." She shivered.

"I have to admit the dreams you have been so kind to share are disconcerting. If we were in danger, Bruce or Tristian would have contacted one of us. They aren't going to leave you hanging in the wind."

He turned on the street behind the pub. The parking lot was full to running over. Weaving through the cars without finding a space, he pulled back onto the road. After circling the block, he parked down the street and cut the engine. "Stay put for a sec." Gavin stepped out of the truck and surveyed the area. Nothing seemed out of place or unusual.

A slow creak indicated Synn had opened her door. "Stay girl. We'll be back." She eased the door closed.

He strode to her side and glared down at her but said nothing. *Not looking for a fight.* Slipping an arm around her waist, they strolled to front of the pub. He yanked open the heavy wooden door. Friendly voices, raucous laughter, and the yeasty scent of the pub spilled out. Tension eased in his muscles. He released the breath he hadn't realized he was holding. Synn walked through the door first and froze.

Chapter Thirteen
And so it Begins—Family History and Sword of Kilara

Seated at the bar were Hannah and Tristian. Synn sucked in a breath. This was bad, she could feel it. "Looks like your sister and her husband have come for a visit."

Gavin smiled wide and rushed through the crowd pulling her behind him. Hannah squealed as Gavin snatched her off the barstool. He swung her around in a circle, nearly colliding with several patrons waiting for their pints. Katie narrowed her eyes at him as she cautiously approached the bar and picked up a tray full of drinks.

"Boyo, you make me spill this and you're a dead man," she warned, making her way back through the crowd.

"Gavin, put me down," Hannah demanded.

"What are you doing here?" Gavin asked lowering her to her feet. He gave her a quick hug and kissed her cheek before letting her go.

She backed away to stay clear of Gavin and his sister. The ebb and flow of the crowd pushed her farther and farther away from the bar. Suddenly a hand snaked around her wrist and pulled her through the crowd.

"Don't be getting lost." Gavin chuckled. "Guess the weather didn't make the difference we thought."

"How long you staying?" He wanted to know.

Hanna shrugged. "Don't know." Tristian has business here. I came along to see if I could help Ma and Synn with the wedding plans. Where'd you two sneak off today? Da said Synn's been helping out here too."

"No sneaking around. Had the day off. We went sightseeing. Drove by a few ruins on our way to the Blarney Castle where we spent most of the day. The Wishing Steps, Witch's Kitchen, and Stone intrigued her."

"Oh, what fun."

"No...they gave me shivers and—" She gave herself a little shake. "I did enjoy touring the castle. The views are spectacular, especially from the top. The gardens and waterfall were mesmerizing."

"We were on our way home, noticed the crowd, and stopped in to see if Da needed help. Looks like the staff's got it well in hand. Synn's pup is in the truck, so we need to be on our way."

Tristian's bar stool swiveled around until he faced Gavin and Synn. "Good to see you too."

Gavin grinned and offered his hand. "Sorry, didn't mean to ignore you. So what are you doing here? Or do I need to ask."

"Probably not. However, I'd like a word with Synn." He glanced around the pub. "Somewhere quiet."

Gavin hesitated for a beat and glanced over at her.

She nodded, wiping her sweaty palms on her jeans.

"Sure. Down the hall, past the bathrooms take the first left. That's our office. She knows the way."

Tristian got to his feet and held up a hand. "I need to talk to her alone first. Give us a few minutes. Tristian leaned over to his wife, brushed his lips over hers. "I'll be back."

"Is your business with them, then?" Hannah narrowed her eyes.

"Unfortunately, yes. Been chatter they should be aware of—and." He blew out a breath. "A few things Bruce wants brought to Synn's attention."

"Anything I should be concerned with?" Her eyes clouded with worry.

"Given the volatility of the world these days, there's always reason for concern." His reassuring gaze swept over her and Gavin, then landed for a split second on Hannah. "Nothing I can't handle."

A title wave of fear washed over her. Rooted to the spot, her feet wouldn't move. She couldn't catch her breath. The Overlord's assassin wanted a word with her. Was this the end she'd wished for in the early hours of this morning? *I'm not ready.* She wondered at her change of mind and attitude. *What has changed?* She knew in her heart but couldn't come to grips with it.

Adrenaline flooded her system; the fight or flight response was alive and well. *What was he saying?* Her heart pounded so loud in her ears she couldn't make out the words.

A wave of nausea hit. Covering her mouth, she ran for the ladies' room, shoved open the door, rushed into the first stall, and bolted the door. When she turned, her stomach's contents spewed into the toilet.

After a few minutes there was a soft knock on the stall door. "Synn?" Bridget's voice was a welcome relief. "Are you all right?"

"Yes. I'll be out in a minute." She took a couple of

deep breaths. *What the hell is the matter with me?*

"You sure?"

"Yes." Waiting until the bathroom door squeaked open, she unbolted the door, walked to the sink, splashed water on her face, and rinsed her mouth out. "This day just gets better and better." Her words echoed in the empty room. She yanked open the door and glanced down the hall. Tristian and Gavin were waiting for her outside the office door.

"What happened?" Gavin asked. "You all right?"

"Don't think my stomach liked all the bumpy roads today."

Gavin looked skeptical but shrugged. "Okay, come get me when you two are finished with your secret meeting. There are a few things I'd like to discuss with Tristian too."

A wane smile turned up her lips while Tristian's expression remained unchanged.

Tristian held the door open and closed it behind her. Once inside the office, he motioned for her to have a seat. His gaze fixed on her. "First there is family history Bruce wants you to be made aware. It's why I asked to talk to you alone. I wasn't sure if you'd want anyone else privy to that information. The overlord would have come himself, but he's meeting with the council and time is of the essence."

As she eased into the chair, her roiling stomach settled a bit. *Should I bring up my shared nightmares? No, I'll wait and see what he has to say.*

Clearing his throat, Tristian sat in the black leather chair behind the scarred wooden desk, moved aside a pile of invoices, and began. "When Bruce provided protection for the information you had on Baltizar and the Book of Shadows, he didn't just take you at face value. It seems your ancestors were members of Andre's elite guard known as the Guardians Guild made up of magical creatures formed over a millennium ago."

She looked up from the worn gray carpeting and wrinkled her forehead in confusion. "Who's Andre?"

Tristian rested his arms on the desk and templed his fingers. "Andre is Bruce's father. He was the Demon Overlord before Bruce and is married to Matiah, an angel. The Guardians were tasked with protecting those creatures that were not of pure blood. This was before the covenants were put in place to discourage mixed races. But during that time the mixed were still viewed as outcasts. Fear of mixing the magic would create an invincible creature was the reason for the covenants."

"I'm sorry. I don't understand. Isn't the overlord's mate a witch? Those covenants aren't enforced anymore, are they?"

"Not in the Western Hemisphere that Bruce controls and many other locations are beginning to see the light." Tristian leaned back in the chair and rubbed his forehead. "The only way creatures evolve is through new blood."

She met his glaze. "What does this have to do with me? I'm of pure demon blood." She paused her eyes rounding. "This isn't over my seeing Gavin, is it?"

Tristian pinched the bridge of his nose with his thumb and index finger and muttered an oath under his breath. "No. It's not." He drew in a breath and let it out slowly. "You're not of pure demon blood. Your family is mixed with those of the ancient Fae Warriors. The majority of your mother's family was Fae with a couple demons mixed in. Your father was demon royalty. The mixing of those Fae and Demon blood lines created an extraordinarily powerful magic. Only one child of their union was born with their combined talents.

"But I have—had—a brother and sister." She wiped her hands on her jeans again.

"May I continue?" Exasperation seeped into Tristian's voice.

"Of course."

"This individual would one day be able to wield and control such magic. Unfortunately, word spread of the possibilities, and your parents were murdered before the extent of this child's power was determined."

She rolled her eyes but said nothing.

"Baltizar wanted control of the powerful magic and the one who wielded it as his mate. To his thinking his blood mixed with that of the child, when grown, would create an invincible magic being. His calculations were off. The child wouldn't come into its powers until fully matured."

"So the joke was on him. The blood line ended when he killed my parents and siblings." Her gaze fell to her lap where her fingers picked at the edge of her aqua sweater.

"No, he got part of the equation correct. You were the child with their combined talents. Baltizar didn't wait long enough for you to come into your powers. Thought he'd made a mistake. While you were extremely talented, it wasn't what he expected. By the time he realized his error, you'd requested protection from Bruce."

"Wait—" She paused dragging her bottom lip

through her teeth. Her mind was whirling with questions, possibilities, and trepidations.

Tristian held up at hand. "Let me finish. When an old acquaintance brought the matter to Andre's attention, he contacted Bruce and vouched for you. The overlord accepted your terms. Those of us in Bruce's inner circle thought he was crazy to trust one of Baltizar's minions. My boss didn't see fit to share this little gem of information regarding your heritage with us until recently. Now it's my job to bring you up to speed." The irritation in Tristian's voice belayed his frustration.

She nodded. "Is that why Bruce bound part of my powers when he gave me my freedom?"

"Yep. It was fortunate you wanted to stay in a land where myth and magic are real and most people don't bat an eye at the unexplained." He shoved up from the chair and paced the room for several minutes finally settling in the chair next to her. He rubbed the back of his neck.

With wide eyes, she watched him silently waiting for him to continue.

A cell phone buzzed in his pocket. Pulling it out, he checked the screen, then put the phone to his ear. "Boss. I'm talking with her now." He paused and listened for a couple beats. "No, I haven't gotten that far. Only to her family history. Sure." He reached out and handed the phone to her. "Bruce wants to talk to you."

With trembling fingers, she took the phone. "Hello." She willed her hands to still and the tremor in her voice to even out. *Get a grip. I keep this up, and I'll have to turn in my demon warrior card.*

"Synn, I'm sorry. This must be quite a shock. I wish I'd been able to be more forth coming when this all went down, but I had to make sure you were made of the stuff my father thought you were."

"It's been…unexpected, yes."

"There's more. Tristian is there to unbind your powers, to test, and hone your talents. The whispers we are hearing are while Baltizar remains in the seventh level of Hell, he's using what magic he has left, his minions, and their power in the mortal world to destroy those responsible for his fall from grace so to speak." Bruce snorted a laugh. "It's been my experience that displaced demons use the dream world as a contact point. So I'm warning you, the first level of defense needs to be honing your ability to shield yourself and mind while you are asleep, as well as, during your waking hours."

She blew out a breath. "He's already made contact. In fact he's infiltrated my dreams—nightmares—which are somehow broadcast into Gavin's mind or subconscious. Oh, hell Gavin shares those nightmares while he's still at his home and I'm in my cottage. How is Baltizar doing that?"

Tristian, his mouth set in a thin line, leaned back in the chair, and shook his head. The muscle in his jaw worked overtime.

"He's not involving Gavin. You are…" He paused long enough for the statement to sink in. "…by seeking help from the one person you have access to and trust completely."

"So what I am seeing—will it happen or…" Synn asked.

After a pause, Bruce answered, "We're not sure."

"I think we better bring Gavin in on this meeting." She peered at Tristian.

He nodded in agreement. Getting to his feet he walked to the door. "I'm going to go get Gavin and myself a drink. Do you want one?"

She nodded, still holding the phone to her ear.

"Whiskey or stout?" He turned the knob. The door squeaked open.

"Whiskey. The good stuff."

Tristian smiled. "You got it. I'll be back." He closed the door quietly.

She returned her attention to the phone and Bruce. "Now what?"

"This is where it gets complicated. Your powers and talents have matured without training. We aren't sure how they will manifest themselves. Tristian can train you to shield your mind."

"I've talked with Erin and Tiarnan," she blurted. "Well, more Erin than Tiarnan. Erin said if I needed their help, I had only to meet them at the cliffs at dawn."

Silence reigned for several beats. Unable to cope with the uncomfortable silence, she hurried on. "Erin also said that Gale who owns Pixie Magic, a store here in town, could be of help to me. Also Erin claims my limp is not permanent. Kinda a manifestation of the dark magic I stole from Baltizar." *Shit...why can't I stop babbling?*

"Hmmmm. Sounds like you have learned a thing or two on your own. Good job. Take Erin's suggestion and visit Gale. Let Tristian know how that works out. Better yet, take him with you, or least keep him in the loop should you or she need help. Gale is a witch then?"

"I believe so. Since she is a descendant of Erin, wouldn't that make her from a very powerful linage?"

"One would think. I've got to get back to the council meeting. Let me talk to Tristian."

"He went to get drinks and bring Gavin into our conversation. It's real busy at the pub tonight."

"Tell him I'll call later tonight. Be safe and don't take chances. Visit with Gale, soon."

"We stopped by Gale's today. But the sign on the door said she was closed. We'll go see her tomorrow."

"Good plan." He disconnected the call.

The door handle twisted. She stood. Tristian pushed through the door with a tray of steaming bowls. Gavin followed carrying a tray with a bottle of whiskey and three glasses.

She handed the phone to Tristian. "He had to go back to the council meeting. Said he'd call you tonight."

Gavin poured three fingers of whiskey in the glass and handed it to her. "You might want to eat something before you down that whiskey." He poured the same amount in the other two glasses and set them on the desk.

She inhaled deeply. "That stew smells great." She took a bowl and spoon from the tray and slipped a spoonful of stew into her mouth. "Mmmmm." Taking a piece of brown bread from the tray, she took a bite, dabbed it in the stew, and took another bite. After swallowing, she filled the others in on her conversation with Bruce.

Tristian groaned at the mention of the visit to Pixie Magic, took a swig of the whiskey, then reached across the desk for a bowl of stew and piece of bread. He sauntered behind the desk and sat in the chair. Gavin plopped into the chair next to her, listening intently. When she finished, Tristian took another drink of his whiskey and filled in the holes that she left. He held his glass out for a refill.

Gavin eyed the glass but said nothing, pouring another three fingers of whiskey into Tristian's glass. "Thought you didn't drink on the job. Preferred a clear head?"

Tristian gave him an eat shit and die look, took another sip of the whiskey. "Things change. Still have a clear head and you shouldn't question my abilities."

"Of course."

"Synn shouldn't stay by herself until she gets a handle on shielding her mind and subconscious while asleep. I'll be working with her on that." He shifted his gaze to Synn. "Also, Bruce has authorized me to restore your powers to full strength. Not that we expect a battle in the near future, but we have to be ready for anything."

Her eyes rounded. "Now? You're going to return my powers here?"

A devilish smirk played at the corner of his mouth. "Not exactly. First order of business, you need to pay a visit to Gale. See what she can do about your injuries. More than likely the repair by magic will release the dark magic unwittingly transferred to you by Baltizar. You'll have to learn to control his power as well. We'll do this in phases."

"I see." She squirmed in her seat.

"No, you don't, but you will," Tristian snapped. "Sorry...sleep deprivation makes me—difficult."

"You knew about this situation for a while?" Gavin

raised an eyebrow, his tone accusing.

"No, the rumblings from our informants got louder in recent days. Then we confirmed that Baltizar was up to something, but no specifics which is why I'm here."

"Hannah is aware?" Gavin asked.

He swirled the amber liquid in his glass and watched as the light glinted off the drink. "Not exactly. I couldn't jet off to Ireland without offering to take her with me. Luckily her work load was light enough she could accompany me. She may have to work a couple days a week, but she brought everything she'll need. Her computer is set up at your parents'. They're excited to have her here to help with the wedding. The rest is on a need to know basis, and right now, she doesn't need to know. However, that could change at any moment. I'll read her in if necessary."

"Are you planning to stay a while?" she asked picking at the edge of the upholstered chair.

"Afraid so. No telling how long Baltizar will take before acting on his plan. He can't leave the seventh level of Hell, but I imagine he's got demons in the mortal world willing to do his bidding." His gaze pinned her. "You are in no shape to take him on by yourself, even with a gryphon's help."

"I understand." She squirmed under his gaze. "I don't want to put anyone in danger."

"Good girl." Tristian smiled. "Given the new circumstances, I'd prefer you pay Gale a visit before I restore your powers. Deal with one situation at a time. How do you feel about that?" He finished the whiskey and pushed his glass away.

"Sounds like a plan. I have a full shift tomorrow, so won't be able to visit Gale until Thursday at the earliest. I could be at her place most of the day. So I'd rather do it on my day off. Does that work with your time frame?" She fingered her amulet as she spoke.

Tristian leaned over to get a better look at her necklace. "Do you have more to tell me?"

Gavin glanced at her. "You didn't tell him about what happened at the Standing Stones and Witch's Stone at the castle?"

"We hadn't gotten to that yet," she snapped.

"Someone want to start talking?" Tristian leaned forward both hands flat on the desk.

She brought him up to date with what happened at Blarney Castle. What she'd experienced and how she'd used a spell and her necklace to protect herself.

"Nice job." He nodded approvingly. "It's a good start, but…"

Chapter Fourteen
Business as Usual, Until Heat Sizzles

"But what?"

"What you experienced at the castle with a few benevolent spirits is nothing compared to…"

"Oh, I've already gone up against Baltizar. He doesn't scare me," she said with more bravado than she felt.

"He should." Tristian smirked glancing at her leg. "We all know how your last meeting ended." Pausing he nodded toward her. "Sorry, that was uncalled for. We don't want him to get to you under any circumstances. Especially after you embrace the power he inadvertently transferred to you and I've restored your own power."

"Are you going to Gale's with me?"

"Nope. Unless you encounter problems. You can handle it. But I want a report as soon as you leave her shop."

"I'm not one of your employee's to be ordered around like—"

Tristian cut her off. "If you want to stay alive, you'll listen, and do exactly as I say. I've no intention of putting myself or anyone else in unnecessary danger because you have a death wish."

"I don't."

"Good. I don't have to tell you there's a lot more at

stake here than the last time you battled with him. Surprise is what we want on our side. By the time we engage him, he'll have no idea what hit him."

"He can't get out. Can he?" She steeled her expression, but inside she was a ball of nerves.

"Not under his own power—at this time. Things change, we want to be prepared. We have a plan. What hours do you work?"

"Usually two in the afternoon until close. Unless someone calls off and I have to cover."

"All right. We'll meet at eleven during the week and work on your mind cloaking until it's second nature. Eventually, you'll be privy to—well never mind. We'll start Friday. If something changes, I'll let you know. I want you to afford me the same courtesy. If he continues to invade your dreams, I want to know immediately. His means of entry has been cut off for now. But he's smart and devious. We'll not make the mistake of underestimating him. He'll find another way. By that time, I hope to have you solid in your ability to keep your mind impenetrable whether you're awake, asleep, or unconscious."

The last part of his statement bothered her, but she didn't want to know what Tristian expected. Maybe she should, but for now she had all she could handle. "My amulet will strengthen my abilities."

"But if it gets ripped off—I don't want you compromised. It's best if you rely on the magic you wield to keep the shields up and protect yourself."

A soft knock sounded on the door. Hannah stuck her head in. "Ma and I are headed home. Da will be here a bit longer to lock up and count the till. Ma wanted to know when you planned to leave. If it'll be a while, we can take Storm home with us."

"Nope, we're finished here for now." He paused eyebrow raised. "Who's Storm?"

"My pup."

"Okay. Have a good night." He shoved up from the chair, walked to Hannah, and wrapped an arm around her waist. "Let's go. I'll escort you and Mary home."

Hannah smiled up at him clearly besot with her husband. She wondered if such happiness would ever come her way.

Tristian opened the door. They slipped out leaving the door ajar.

"Ready to go?"

"More than. Tim doesn't need your help?"

"Nope." He waited for her to clear the door, then closed, locked it, and pocketed the key.

"I bet poor Storm is tired of being cooped up all day."

"She can run in the back yard at my place. The fence is puppy proof. New surroundings will keep her busy while we move your stuff in."

She'd nearly forgotten she wouldn't be going to her cottage. Why did she feel like her independence was slipping backward instead of moving forward? Giving herself a little shake, she followed Gavin down the hall into the main pub. *It's not forever, only for the time being.*

After bidding goodnight to everyone, Gavin helped her into the truck. Dare she hope Gale could restore the strength in her leg? She smiled for a moment. Walking with a limp made her whole body hurt, making her job difficult by the end of the night.

The ride home was quiet except for Storm's

continual commentary in various whines and whimpers begging to be let out of the crate. She couldn't blame the little girl. It'd been a long day for everyone.

"We're here," Gavin sang out. "If you want to take Storm around back, the gate is on the left side. I'll stow your gear in the house and join you two out back." He took the pup out of the crate, held her while she clipped on the leash, then set the antsy ball of fur on the ground.

"Fair enough." She picked her way across the front lawn, opened the gate, and let Storm loose. She raced around the yard, barking, yipping, and sniffing, coming back to check in every couple of minutes. The length of time between returns became longer as the pup became familiar with Gavin's yard. She pulled a squeaky toy out of her bag and tossed it. Storm barked with delight and promptly pounced on the toy. The pup began squeaking it, oblivious to anything else.

How nice to have no cares in the world and have someone to take care of you. But not long ago you were homeless, not knowing where your next meal would come from. I changed all that. She called Storm over and was shocked when the pup actually bounded toward her. Picking her up, she hugged the warm, wiggling furball to her. "I'll always take care of you." She rubbed her cheek on the soft tawny fur and put the pup on the ground. Legs already going before her paws hit the ground, she thundered off to attack her toy again. Squeaking echoed all over the yard as Storm raced around.

"I see it didn't take long for the pup to make herself at home."

She jumped, letting out a low squeal and whirled around looking for the person belonging to the intruding voice. She relaxed at seeing Gavin standing here. "I didn't hear you come out."

"I didn't. After putting all your stuff in the house, I went back to the truck to make sure it was locked up and walked around here from the front. Didn't mean to frighten you. It's such a beautiful night." He grabbed a couple chairs from the patio and moved them to where she stood. "We can sit here and watch the pup wear herself out. Then we can all get a good night's sleep."

"I hope so. Won't your neighbors complain about the noise Storm is making?" She craned her neck and noticed there weren't any other houses around. A barn type structure stood off in the distance, washed in silver from the moonlight, but that was all. "Don't you think the half-moon looks like a canned half peach?"

"What?" Gavin peered at her, an incredulous expression spreading over his face.

She giggled. "Well?"

"Never thought about it." He tilted his head back to get a better look. "Aye, it kinda does." Reaching over he cupped her chin in his hand gazing into her eyes. "Tough day."

She nodded leaning into him. "There were good parts to the day also."

He bent closer to her, brushing his lips over hers almost as if asking for her approval. She wrapped her arms around his neck and deepened the kiss. Not wanting it to ever end. Feeling safe and secure was a luxury she'd rarely experienced since childhood.

Gavin slipped his arms around her and scooped her into his lap without breaking the kiss. His excitement was obvious as she settled into his lap. She didn't care. Turning she straddled him, pressing her breasts against his chest while her center felt the heat of his arousal through her jeans. Reaching between them, she undid the button of his jeans and pulled the zipper as far down as their position allowed.

His tongue traced the outside of her lips before slipping inside to tease in a sinuous dance with hers. His flavor spun into her as he kissed and licked down the side of her neck to the juncture of her shoulder. He breathed a kiss at the hollow of her throat before moving to the neckline of her sweater. He snaked his tongue as low as her shirt would permit, his breathing increased. "Stand for a second." He braced his hand on one side of the chair, raised himself up, yanked his jeans below his knees, and settled back on the chair.

"You have too many clothes on," he rasped, pulling her down on him, stretching the neck of her top so he could nuzzle and lick between her breasts. His hand burrowed under the shirt, flipped open the back of her bra, allowing her firm mounds to spill out. Lifting her top, he buried his face in her breasts. "Much better," he murmured, sucking first one nipple then the other, the vibration of his words sending jolts of lust though her.

She arched against his mouth. A soft moan escaped her lips. He tugged at the waistband of her jeans, unbuttoned them, pulled the zipper down, and slid his hand inside. "Too tight." He grasped her around the waist and lifted her up. "Take them off," he ordered.

She kicked her shoes off, pulled her knees to her chest, and pulled the pants off one leg. Before she could get the other off, he positioned her over him, moved her underwear aside, slid a long, thick finger inside, and curled it to her sweet spot. She muffled a scream, writhing against him, while waves of ecstasy crashed over her. When she stilled, he ripped her panties off. He groaned as he pushed inside her, burying himself to the hilt. She rested her feet on the ground, easing off him and slamming back down.

If he'd not enjoyed the pleasures of other women, he won't last long. And she knew in her heart that he hadn't. Her lips curved into a wicked smile. She lifted up and ground down on him. He groaned her name and grabbed her around the waist with both hands holding her down on him until his climax subsided. Putting a hand on both sides of her face, he brought her lips to his, kissing her hungrily before moving back to her breasts. He scraped each nipple with his teeth before soothing with his tongue and then sucking.

"You always were a breast man." She snickered.

"You got that right." He hummed against her nipple. "But I'm not through with you until I've tasted every inch of you." He licked his lips as his gaze slid downward.

Desire ignited inside her. She wasn't sure if he'd ever gone completely limp. But he was filling her again. She spread wider for him, reveling in the sensation. She'd miss the intimacy, his touch, and his masculine scent. If things were going to go south, she was going to ride him without any thought of consequences. If things didn't, she'd face the music when the time came.

Storm barked and growled somewhere in the back of the yard. Gavin turned his head to where the sound was coming from and cursed. She followed his gaze. "You little shit!" Sometime during their interlude, Storm had stolen her jeans. The pup had them in her mouth shaking her head from side to side, her paws placed on the material she was tugging and ripping the clothing.

"So much for play time." She attempted to get to her feet.

He held her thighs securely. "Oh, no you don't. I'll buy you a new pair of jeans."

Chapter Fifteen
Will the Magic Find a Way or Who will Pay the Price?

The next few days passed without incident. The pub was busy. Synn worked her shift and met Tristian daily for practice shielding her mind. Thursday didn't work with Gale's schedule, so their meeting was put off until the following week. Tristian relayed the potential dangers of Baltizar's dark magic being released during the healing process.

When she arrived at Pixie Magic, she paused to watch the multifaceted crystals hanging in the window sway in the breeze casting rainbows on the walls of the shop. At the opening of the door, a melodic chime sounded. Inside the pleasant aroma of sandalwood, pine, cloves, cinnamon, and a few scents she didn't recognize wafted through the air creating a calm atmosphere.

It was a quaint store with books shelved on light oak. Comfy chairs were scattered in the book nook. Glass cases lined in red velvet with mirror backing held assorted stones and crystals that shimmered in the light.

With a black, amber, and blood red stone shimmering in her hand, Gale turned and grinned. "Finally, our schedules allowed a meeting. What can I do you for? Lotions? Fragrances?" She tilted her head and raised an eyebrow. "A love potion? As if." She snickered. "I see the way Gavin looks at you."

She had spent most of the walk here trying to decide how to broach the subject with Gale. All plans went out the window when she blurted, "No. Erin sent me." *So much for using a tactful touch.*

"Erin who?" Gale asked, confusion clear on her face.

"Erin the witch who walks the cliffs with Tiarnan, King of the Faeries."

"Ohhhh, that Erin." Gale gently returned the stone to its place in the glass case and wiped her hands on the cloth she'd been cleaning the glass with. "So is it potions, then?"

She sighed. "Let me tell you a story." She began with meeting Erin and Tiarnan on the cliffs and ended detailing her encounter with Baltizar in which he chastised her for loosing track of Brandy and Stefan. Then he lobbed a powerful fireball at her which caused debilitating injuries. She included the fact that she turned to the Overlord of the Western Hemisphere, Bruce for protection, relaying all information she had on Baltizar, and his search for the three Books of Shadows.

Gale nodded. "I'm aware of a lot of the history with Bruce, Stefan, and Tristian. Erin relayed the information to me when the curse was broken. I detected a magic signature when we had our girl's day out. That was great fun, by the way. Glad you could join us. I knew you weren't a witch, but your ability to cloak your power and scramble your magic signature was creative. Let me see if I've got everything straight. You're a demon that got crosswise with a more powerful demon who nearly killed you. But in the

152

process, we suspect that some of his black—uh—dark magic transferred to you. Your injuries left you with a limp and constant pain that you'd like me to heal if possible."

"Yep, that's about it in a nutshell." Heat crept across her cheeks as she paused for a moment. "Oh, except, I'm not of pure demon blood, apparently my mother came from a family of powerful Fae warriors. It's the reason Baltizar killed my family and took me to serve him. I only recently learned that piece of information from the overlord." She looked at her feet for a beat then brought her gaze back up to Gale. "I wouldn't ask, except—well—it's possible Baltizar may become a problem. Bruce and Tristian would like me to be able—" Shifting from foot to foot, she paused again. *How much information is too much? Don't want to scare her or…our friendship is probably a moot point now anyway.*

Gale put her hand on her shoulder. "Wow, you've had a rough go of it. I believe I can help you out." She gave her a reassuring smile. "Couple things. If the dark magic was encapsulated in the muscles and bones at the time of the injury, it's possible that when I heal the bones and repair the muscles with magic, it will release the dark magic as you said. Are you able to control it? I sense your magic is not as strong as it once was." She shook her head. "This procedure could be dangerous for both of us."

"I'm not positive. If I can bind it to my magic, I can control it that way. If you'd rather, I can have Tristian accompany me next time. He wanted me to do this on my own, but if it's too dangerous… He knows I'm here and will come if needed."

"No, that would only complicate things by adding another type of power for the dark power to connect to. Not what we want. Well, let's get started. Walk toward me without trying to compensate for your limp. I need to see what muscles and bones are involved."

She stood and walked forward. Her limp more pronounced today due to being on her feet several days in a row at the pub. Gale motioned for her to turn, walk back, and stop.

"Okay, hop up on my table." Gale snapped her fingers. An exam table with flowers spread over the padded cover materialized in the back of the store. She walked to the window, flipped the sign to "Closed," and locked the door, then pulled the shades. "Need a little privacy." Gale murmured a few words and passed her hand over the door before walking to where she waited.

Gale held her hands over Synn's leg and hip. A glow of rainbow colors passed from the witch's hands to Synn's body. After a few minutes, a bead of sweat appeared on Gale's forehead and trickled down her temple.

"Oh, boy, this is going to hurt. I've no way to lessen the pain. You ready?"

"As I'll ever be." She gritted her teeth. When the excruciating pain zinged through her body, she let out a blood curdling scream. The pain was gone as quickly as it came leaving an odd sensation of power bouncing inside her body. It exited in small bursts of red and black sparks from fingertips and burnt holes though her shoes where her toes emitted the same strange sparks. She squinted her eyes shut concentrating on controlling the wayward magic.

"I can help you bind the new power to your Fae

magic. Would you like me to try?" Gale tilted her head to one side. "I don't think it wise to attach it to your demon magic, which doesn't seem as strong."

"Agreed," she said through clenched teeth. Opening one eye, she was surprised to find herself and Gale inside a translucent purple bubble. Thin jagged bolts of what appeared to be electricity zinged around the walls of the bubble but never penetrated the interior.

The sparks emitting from her fingertips and toes subsided. Gale held her hands up. "I believe you've got complete control." She backed away farther. "Oops, your eyes are still red."

"Probably because I'm so tired. Not getting much sleep lately," Synn answered

"Nope. Not bloodshot. They're glowing red. My guess, dark demon magic is still spiking. Concentrate, you gotta close it down lass. Can't walk around town glowing." Gale reached up and touched the bubble slowing the electricity flowing through the skin of the protective enclosure.

"I'm trying. I don't feel out of control." She blinked her eyes and mumbled a few words.

"Good. But… That's better, still a tinge of light rose specs in your aqua eyes, but not too noticeable."

A sudden burst of sparks flew across the bubble and bounced back. "Shit!" Gale ducked. "Fist your hands."

She reached out and slapped the remaining sparks. They turned to black ash and drifted to the ground. With her hands closed, she glanced at Gale in warning and slowly opened them spreading her fingers. To her relief, nothing happened. She sat up and slid off the table. Her still smoking shoes touched the ground and she sighed.

Gale sucked in a breath and grinned. "You're going to need a new pair of shoes. Okay, I'm going to dissolve the bubble. Any damage to my shop will be your financial responsibility." She snickered at her patient's aghast expression. "Only kidding. Hearing any voices? Any urges to do harm?"

"Nope, I feel normal. Scratch that, I've never been normal. Probably won't start now." A slight giggle escaped her lips. "A little nervous since I didn't feel that last burst coming. Otherwise…"

"Okay, here it goes." Gale touched the bubble. It drew in around them, then released her from its boundaries. Gale remained inside the protection. "How do you feel now?"

"A little strange, like my body is humming—vibrating, but I'm not." She held out her hands and did a couple slow squats.

"It'll stop. Or should soon. Effects of all the pent-up power you released inside the bubble." Gale waved her hand. The protective shield disappeared. "Smells like burning embers." She peered around, walked to the window, flipped the sign around, and opened the door letting in a cool breeze in. It was heavy with brine. She sniffed. "Summer storm blowing in." Uncovering several colorful pots, she waved her hand over each pot and the pleasant aroma that greeted Synn when she had opened the door returned.

"Sashay across the floor for me."

Synn straightened then walked down and back the length of the store. Her gait was a little unsteady the first time, but when she made the trek again, it was smoother.

"Oh come on. Let's see sway to those hips, lass. Make believe you're passing a group of good looking lads."

She tilted her head. "I don't normally try to attract attention. Not in my best interest."

"Okay, pretend you are walking by that handsome hunk of yours."

"He's not mine." But she felt her cheeks heat then the memory of their last time together came flooding back. Her whole face felt like it was on fire. She did her best come hither walk.

"That's what I'm talking about." Gale's head flew back, and she roared with laughter. "So the boyo is off the market."

"It's not that—I mean—We're only fr—"

Gale waved her hand in a dismissive gesture. "Yeah, yeah, yeah. And I'm a mortal. Your mouth is saying one thing, and your reactions are saying another. Mark my words. You can't keep it hidden forever. Why would you want to?"

Her shoulders drooped. "It's that obvious?"

"Only when you two are in the same room, or someone mentions his name." Gale wiped her eyes, still chuckling. "It's nothing to be ashamed of."

"You don't understand… Brandy hates me. Hannah is cautious around me. Mary and Tim are great. But I don't want to cause a problem."

"Oh, as far as Brandy is concerned, believe me, no one is good enough for her baby brother. If she'd only seen the skanks he dated while she was across the pond." Gale snickered and patted her arm. "Don't worry about it. She'll come around."

"Our recent history is—well let's say—tainted."

She settled into a chair near the bookshelves reviewing the titles. She'd like to look around. But she was too exhausted. Gale bounced from task to task like she did this kind of thing every day.

"Okay, one more test. Sit on the floor and cross your legs." Gale watched as she followed her instructions. "Not bad. Now skip the length of the store."

She did as instructed, then wiped a bead of sweat from her forehead.

"Looks good. You'll be sore for a bit. Later today, I want you to squat, jump up from that position, and land in a squat again on the balls of your feet not flat footed. Muscles are somewhat atrophied from not being used. Need to build them up slowly. It's best done with physical activity not magic."

Gale walked over to her. "Speaking of the handsome devil, I think it wise to have him come get you. I don't think you'll have a meltdown, but I'd rather have one of those powerful gryphons escorting you home. Whether or not Baltizar or his magic could influence your decisions is yet to be seen." At her crestfallen expression Gale added, "The ancient Fae magic should keep it in check."

She patted her pockets for the phone. It wasn't there. After Gavin had warned her not to leave the house without it, she was sure she'd had it when she arrived.

"I'll just ring him up." Gale picked up her phone, tapped the screen, and put the phone to her ear.

Pulse racing as panic set in, her gaze swept the shop. *I know I didn't leave it at home. Not after...* Her gaze settled on the glass counter—and her phone. She blew out a breath and closed her eyes. Baltizar's image popped into her mind. Her eyes flew open, and she jumped to her feet. Her gaze darted from corner to corner all around the shop.

"He'll be here shortly." Gale paused. "You okay?"

"Who?" At her wide-eyed stare, Gale spun around to see what had alarmed her.

Chapter Sixteen
Will the Dark Magic Control or be Controlled?

Gavin pushed the door open to Pixie Magic and sauntered in. "Hi, Gale." A tawny streak thundered through his legs and over the hardwood floor. Storm skidded to a stop at Gale's feet, sniffed, looked up, snorted, and raced toward the bookshelves and Synn.

Gale narrowed her eyes letting out a melodic laugh as the pup sped across the floor. "Quite a ball of energy you got there. Yours?"

"No…well, yes. It's Synn's puppy, Storm. She rescued it from sure death on the street outside the pub a few nights ago."

"Good thing Mary didn't set eyes on it first, or she'd have had a fight on her hands for the little scoundrel." Gale glanced once more at the ball of fur now bouncing at Synn's feet, then returned her attention to the paper work on the counter.

"Don't I know it. She dotes on the little nipper every chance she gets." He paused glancing at the paper work. "Business good?"

"Oh aye. Trying to get the inventory put away before the late afternoon rush." She checked off something on her clipboard, looked toward Synn, and frowned.

"Good to hear." Following Gale's gaze, he spied Synn standing still as a statue, even as the pup raced circles around her feet in the book nook. At the look of alarm on her face, he strode over to her. Leaning over, he kissed her check. "Anything wrong?"

"Nooo. Gale thought I should have an escort home. That's all." Synn gave herself a little shake, took a deep breath, and picked up Storm. She snuggled her face into the pup's fur.

He narrowed his eyes, assessing the situation. "And so you should." If there was something bothering her, it was obvious she didn't want to discuss it there.

Gale slapped her hand on the counter and cackled. "Rumors confirmed."

Startled by the thwack on the counter, Gavin jerked around to stare at Gale. "What the bloody hell? Rumors, what are you talking about?" His eyebrows knitted together in question.

She fisted her hands at her hips. "Come on, boyo. I'm not blind, and neither are the people of this town. I'm talking about speculation that you are officially off the market. Rob who owns the barber shop down the street is taking wagers. So far the ayes have it."

Surprised, he gathered himself and winked at her. "Only time will tell." Taking Synn's hand, he rested it in the crook of his arm and walked toward the door. "See you later."

Once they were outside the shop and out of ear shot of Gale, he stopped and turned Synn to face him. "What happened in there before I came in?"

She waved her hand dismissively. "Well, first she knitted the bones and muscles together with magic. The procedure was quite painful. As expected, the healing released the magic Baltizar shared. I had little trouble controlling the burst of dark magic at first. But we fused it with my Fae magic and it was easier…"

"You know that's not what I meant." He gave her shoulders a little shake.

Tendrils of red electrical sparks snaked out and zapped his hands. He yelped and let go. Storm looked up at them and whined. "There was that little thing where I closed my eyes to rest for moment after everything… Baltizar appeared in my mind. I jerked to my feet, but it must have been my mind playing tricks on me."

His eyes rounded, and he reached for her. "What? When?"

She backed out of reach then touched his arm. "Now don't go all protective. Let me finish. There were no whispers. No feeling of any kind. Except I scared myself. It was merely a thought I unconsciously conjured up."

He shoved his hands in his pockets, pulled them out, then paced in front of her. "How can you be sure?"

She shrugged. "Did you feel anything from me? A vibe? Like the dreams? No. That's how I can tell. The memory of our battle will always be a part of me. I think that's where his image came from."

Gavin's shoulders slumped a bit as he came to a halt in front of her. "Okay, I understand, but…"

"If problems arise, you'll be the first to know. And on that matter, I'm not sure I want the whole town knowing about our relationship. If there is one. What if things go bad—between us—with Baltizar? I'll be run out of town." She paused for a beat, scrubbed her hand over her face.

He shook his head. "It's not like that. The town will stand with you."

Sadness flicked over her face for a moment then was gone. "This is the only place I've ever had friends, had a girl's night out, and real people trust me. I don't want to give that up." She paused, reached out, and tipped his chin down so she could look into his eyes. "If we don't work, I don't want to lose what I've gained here. Understand?"

Throwing his hands up in an "I give up" gesture, he groaned. "There are no guarantees in life. We'll do the best we can. I promise if we don't work, I'll never taint anyone against you. But I'm sure things will eventually meld, and it will be forever." He leaned down and kissed the tip of the nose. *If not, I'll spend the rest of my life alone. Not an option.*

"See that's what I mean," she mumbled.

"Aww hell, I kiss my sisters like that. I could give you a real kiss that will curl your toes." A devilish grin spread across his face. "Like the other night."

Reluctantly, she ducked her head away from him and surveyed the surrounding area. "Don't you dare." Giving a mild jerk on the leash, she got Storm's attention and walked toward the truck.

When they arrived at the vehicle, he held the door open for her as she climbed inside. He took the leash from her and closed the door. Sauntering to the driver's side, he put the pup in the crate, closed the door, and hopped in the seat.

Running her fingers along the dashboard and over the upholstery, she smiled. "Had the truck detailed. Now you'll have Storm's fur all over it again."

"Nope. Had Gale cast a spell banishing dog fur." His lips twitched as her eyes went wide.

"You can't—magic can't be used—"

He snorted a laugh. "Only kidding."

She slapped at him then folded her hands over her chest for a beat. Turning back, she slung her arm over the seat to check on Storm, then shifted to watch out the window.

"Tristian is waiting for you. Otherwise, I'd whisk you off to more ruins and steal a kiss, maybe more." He rolled the window down and rested his arm on the frame. Fresh ocean breeze whipped through the vehicle. *Warmer than expected.* The horizon filled with clouds as the tires whined on the pavement. "Could be in for a storm later. Will be a busy night at the pub."

"I'm not scheduled to come in until late. Want me to push that up a couple hours?"

"See how you feel after working with Tristian. There's been a lot of magic swirling around and through you today, not to mention your upcoming training session."

"I can handle it."

"Didn't say you couldn't, but let's not push it. Oh, by the way, Ma and Hannah are planning a trip to Dublin next week to make a decision on Brandy's dress. They want you to come along. We'll revise the schedule. Either Da or myself may accompany you lasses. Whoever pulls the short straw."

"I don't have to go. Hannah and Mary—"

"I don't think you have a say in the matter. Ma said to fix the schedule. You're going. They want to video chat with Brandy."

"Hannah can handle that."

He shrugged. "You don't argue with Ma when she sets her mind to something. You're free to discuss the matter with her. Be prepared to lose. I've already revised the schedule. Oh, and Bridget had me schedule you both off on the same day in a couple weeks. She said something about a girl's night in and that you two wouldn't be fit to work the next day."

"Really?" Synn raised an eyebrow. "She didn't mention anything to me about it."

"Don't know. Just relaying the message. Be it far from me to meddle in the affairs of the female persuasion." Gravel crunched under the tires as he slowed and pulled up in front of his house. Tristian was sitting on the porch, feet propped on the railing, and head back against the chair. Long blades of grass waved in the breeze at the bottom corner of the stairs.

As the vehicle door squeaked open, Tristian got to his feet. "It's about time. How'd it go this morning? Any problems I should know about before we begin?"

Synn filled him in on the morning's events. "I haven't used magic since the healing. But I gotta tell you it feels so good to walk normally. The muscles are still a bit sore, but wow." For the next hour, Tristian invaded her mind, taught her evasive mind games, and in the end, gave her a nod of approval.

"Doing much better than when we started. Your ordeal today didn't put you off your game. Good job."

Watching the practice made him tired. He'd stayed at Tristian's request, presenting another distraction. But Synn never wavered. Pride swelled within him. "So are you done for the day?"

"I believe so. We'll skip a couple days. Hannah's schedule is clear, and we're going to spend time together." He waggled his eyebrows with a devilish grin. "She's going to show me the insider's guide to Ireland."

"I bet she is," he teased, tilting his head as Tristian strode down the path to his sports car, stopping once to turn and wave. *The man, scratch that, warlock, brother-in-law had sure changed since the last time he was here.* He glanced at his watch. "I gotta get ready for work. Are you going to come in early or rest up a bit?" Leaving her alone wasn't advisable right now.

Tristian's warnings still rang in his head. They didn't have any idea how Synn would react to the additional dark magic's influence once she let down her guard. Not that she had ever been all sunshine and rainbows. She had a dark side, no doubt about it. But his ability to sense people's true being, told him she wanted to be good, make acceptable decisions, and leave her past behind. Still the dreams they'd shared worried him.

****

Synn was tired, but the last thing she wanted was to sit alone and think. Take a nap, nope. In her frame of mind, she could conjure the unwanted demon. She didn't even want to think his name. Hard to tell what effect the new magic would have. Truth be told, she was a little worried about going to sleep. Letting her subconscious run wild, even with the lessons Tristian had taught her, it could be a crap shoot. "I'm fine. If you need me, I'll come in," she said absently, picking at the hem of her shirt. What would be perfect was to sleep under the watchful eye of Tristian. No way would she ask such a thing of the Overlord's right-hand man. She sighed. "Storm seems to be worn out so she should be fine for an extended shift. What did you two do this morning?"

He eyed her speculatively. "Took the path to the

166

cliffs then down to the beach—a couple times. She chased anything that moved and wore herself out. I suspect she was looking for you."

"No sign of Erin or Tiarnan?" She bit the side of her cheek to keep from smiling. Intuition told her he was a little jealous that she'd seen and conversed with the pair. Maybe they were keeping tabs on her too unsure of her true intentions. She didn't like that thought—at all.

An amused voice floated through her mind. *Synn don't over think your situation. I'm the only one monitoring you and only to help control the dark magic released into your body, if necessary. I don't think that will be the case.*

She answered him in kind. *What the hell are you doing in my head?*

Price you pay for the talents you possess or will possess.

She stamped her foot. *You can't just waltz into…*but Tristian was gone from her mind. She looked around sheepishly heat creeping into her cheeks. Though she was angry at the invasion, it was reassuring that she wasn't being left alone to cope with whatever was to come. For some reason, that irritated her also.

Gavin's eyebrows shot up nearly to his hairline. He tilted his head to one side, crossed his arms over his chest, and stared at her. "No. I wasn't looking for them. Only wanting to wear your little critter out so I could get a few things done without her under foot and getting into trouble the minute my back was turned."

"Oh—sorry. Thanks for taking care of her while I visited Gale. I appreciate it."

Yanking the shirt over his head, he balled it up,

took aim, and tossed it across the room into the laundry basket. "Going to take a quick shower. Wanna join me?" His eyebrows waggled, and the corners of his mouth turned up in a seductive grin.

She gave his offer serious consideration, tapping her finger to her lips. "No foolin' around?"

"No guarantees." He chuckled and swaggered into the bathroom.

Chapter Seventeen
All's Well Until the Magic Teaches a Lesson

When Gavin tugged at the pub door nothing happened. "The door must be swollen with all of this moisture." He tugged at the door again this time it made a sound like nails on a chalk board as it gave a little. One final yank and the door came open sending him a couple of steps backward. Synn moved out of the way just in time, then walked in ahead of him. Hannah's voice wafted through the pub. But she was nowhere to be seen. Tristian sat on a stool at the end of the bar deep in conversation with Tim.

"Da, you know the damn door is swollen again? Nearly dislocated my shoulder trying to get it open."

"Aye. Your ma and I had the same problem an hour ago when we arrived. I hired a handyman a few weeks ago to sand and seal it. Whatever he did didn't solve the problem. It made it worse."

Gavin examined the wood while she waited. "The edges of the door are still down to the bare wood. He didn't seal them and did a poor job sanding 'em. Got his name and number? I'll call him and get the job done right. We don't need to throw good money after bad when he should have completed the job right the first time."

"He can't do anything about it now. Too wet." After rifling through the records drawer, Tim ducked

169

under the pass through and handed Gavin the handyman's card.

"Our customers will have to use the back door. This one will never open again if we shut it." Gavin moved the door back and forth, pushed it to the door frame, but didn't force it closed. He huffed out a breath.

She searched the area for Mary, Hannah or—she hesitated as the warlock got up.

Tristian moved from the end bar stool to where Gavin stood examining the door frame. He glanced around at the empty pub, passed his hand over the wooden door. "Don't believe you'll have any more problems." Tristian gave the door a shove. It closed without even a groan. He swaggered back to his seat.

"Show off." Gavin grunted handing the card back to his da.

"I'm going to the back room. Too much testosterone in here for my likes." She sashayed across the room and pushed the swinging door to the kitchen open. Hannah and Mary were leaning over the counter looking at the laptop screen. When she heard Brandy's voice, she backpedaled toward the kitchen door.

"Synn, glad you're here. Ma and I were discussing when would be the best time to take a trip to Dublin. Sis found THE dress for her wedding. A bridal shop in Dublin has that particular one in stock, but we want to see it before forking out that kind of money. What days are you off this week?"

"I work all week. Besides, you know how to video chat. So you don't need me." She shoved the door open with her backside. Before she could scoot out the door, Hannah grabbed her arm, pulled her into the kitchen, and motioned to the computer monitor. "Brandy hold up the magazine picture again so Synn can see your dress."

Brandy mumbled something unintelligible and held up a page. A one shoulder, formfitting, cream gown, with Irish lace overlay came into view. The dress was split nearly to the thigh, sported an uneven hem, and tiny peach rosebuds embroidered on the bodice. At the bottom of the page was a picture inset of a scalloped sequin lace bolero the same color as the rosebuds.

"That's beautiful." She examined the dress on the screen, then Brandy took the page down. "It'll look great on you. I can see why you want to see it in person. That type of lace could be elegant and drape perfectly or stiff and look terrible." Her hand flew to her mouth, she grimaced.

Surprise in her voice, Brandy agreed. "My thoughts exactly. Ma, Hannah when can you make the trip to Dublin?"

Mary narrowed her eyes at the computer screen effectively cowing her daughter.

"And Synn," Brandy conceded. "Didn't mean to leave her—out. I, um, figured she'd have to hold down the fort while you and Hannah were gone."

"We have more than enough employees to cover while we have a day off. If we leave early enough, we'll be back for the evening shift." Mary cut her gaze to her and smiled.

"On that note, I gotta get back to work. Let me know which day you decide. Weekends work best for me. Thursday is my day for paperwork, so I could be available then unless something unforeseen comes up."

"Weekends don't work for us," Mary said. "Thursday it is."

Bridget burst into the kitchen. "Is that Brandy I hear?"

"Aye." Brandy smiled from the computer screen. "Bridg, how are you doing? Married Quinn yet?"

Bridget threw the towel she was carrying at the laptop screen. "Nope. But if people don't quit asking me, we're going to elope and never tell a soul." Bridget stuck her tongue out at Brandy.

Hannah's face turned bright red.

"Oh no, you didn't tell her, did you? I mean—"

Mary, patted Bridget's arm." No, hon. We're discussing Brandy's wedding. She has weddings on the brain. Eloping is a touchy subject around here. Since that's exactly what Hannah did, and didn't tell anyone for nearly a year. Thus the red face. As it should be." She winked at Hannah. "But it's all good now."

"Tell me what?" Brandy repeated above the din around the computer.

Mary kissed her fingers and touched them to the screen. "Talk to you later." She closed the laptop and sent a warning glance in Bridget's direction.

She watched the interaction with interest. "Is there something I should know?" She sent a pointed look in Bridget's direction.

Bridget blew out a breath and plopped down on a chair. "I've been talking with Mary about renting the pub for a Sunday soon."

"Why?"

"To throw a Cèilidh after Quinn and me tie the knot. Nothing fancy, a party so Ma won't get her knickers in a knot. But I haven't told Quinn yet 'cause he'll blab it all over the County Cork."

Heavy footsteps sounded as Quinn pushed through

the kitchen door a puzzled look on his face. "Tell Quinn what?"

Bridget buried her face in her hands.

Synn turned her back to him to keep him from seeing the grin on her face. Mary calmly said, "We're going to put you to work behind the bar if things get too busy tonight."

"Oh no you don't. If I'm back there you won't allow me even one pint until the night's over." He shook his head vehemently as he backed out the kitchen door. "Hey Gavin, you should keep a better eye on your womenfolk." His voice faded away as they burst in to gales of laughter.

Wiping her eyes, Bridget said, "You sure knew what to say to send him running."

"And he'll never wonder back to that conversation again. So your secret is safe for now. But better make plans sooner than later."

"I will." Bridget picked up her towel, tossed it in with the dirty clothes, and grabbed a fresh one. Tying her apron on, she nodded toward the door. "Come on Synn. Customers are trickling in already. Oh, don't breathe a word of what we were talking about." Hannah watched the kitchen door swing shut. "Ma, did Quinn ever tell Brig?"

"Not to my knowledge."

"She's going to marry him without knowing?"

"He can't let that happen. Either he'll have to tell her or maybe already has, but I'll not be asking her." Mary pointed her finger in Hannah's face. "And neither will you."

"Yes, Ma." Hannah raised her hand in surrender. "But you know the rules, he can't…"

Synn's gaze shifted from one person to the other then her brow creased in puzzlement. "Do I want to know?"

"No," they said in unison.

Tristian swung in through the kitchen door. "Hannah, you ready to go? I'm looking forward to an evening alone in front of the fireplace with my woman."

"Yep. Ma fixed us a care package for dinner. We're all set." Hannah wrapped her arm around Tristian's waist as he bent down to kiss her.

"Go on the two of you. Get outta here." Mary grumbled. "Kitchen's never been this busy even on New Year's Eve."

"I heard that." Hannah paused at the back door. "You wanted your family around you. Careful what you wish for." She snickered and waggled her finger at her ma.

Tristian grinned but said nothing as they exited and closed the door.

"I better get out there before Bridget skins me alive." She grabbed her apron and order pad. Tying her apron around her waist, she scooted out the door.

Mary hurried after her and grabbed her apron strings. "Check with Bridget on your schedule. Next week we're off to Dublin. Don't want to wait any longer." At Mary's yank, Synn's apron came untied and fell to the ground. Her order pad, cell phone, and pencil skittered across the hardwood floor.

Mary's hand flew to her mouth in an effort to hide a chuckle. "Sorry about that."

"Not very convincing." She gathered up pad, pencil, checked her cell, all seemed to be fine. With a final tug, she tested her apron strings, then shot a glance at Mary. "May I go?"

"Of course. Remember to."

She tilted her head and rolled her eyes. "Ask Bridget about my schedule." She flounced out into the pub, slapped the bar where Gavin was standing, and grinned. "Don't be standing around, boyo," she teased.

Gavin jumped the bar landing in front of her on the balls of his feet. "Mighty cocky, aren't ya?"

"Maybe, but I know the family and—" She licked her lips with the tip of her tongue to tease him. It seemed like forever since she'd used her womanly wiles. It felt good as the men standing in a group to the side of the bar turned their attention to her. "They're my friends." She finished and winked at him.

Gavin leaned back, elbows braced against the bar, and grinned watching her with male appreciation as she negotiated the crowd. Feeling his gaze on her, she turned and put her fingers to her lips, kissed them, and blew him a saucy kiss. The action caused a ripple of wolf whistles from the crowd.

"Gavin, get back behind the bar. There be customers to serve," Tim scolded, but one corner of his mouth turned up in a half grin.

Vaulting back across the bar without touching it, he turned to face the customers. "What'll you have?"

A strange face in the crowd answered the question. "I'll have some of that cute little lass you were toying with." The burly redheaded man reached out a hand and snagged her around the waist. He slobbered on her cheek attempting a kiss as she carried a tray of drinks through the crowd. She bobbled the tray a little as she swung an arm free in an arc, breaking his hold and sending him howling to the floor. She leaned over him, pasting a puzzled expression on her face. "What happened? Raining outside, huh? Really should wipe your feet before walking on the hardwood floor." She reached for the man to help him up, but he scurried across the floor like a frightened crab. He hoisted himself up at a nearby table and pointed a finger at her.

"Did you see that," he said getting in the face of one of the men at the table. "She tried to fry me. She did."

A stocky, bearded man got up from table where the red-haired man remained. The stocky man took him by the arm and shoved him away from the table. "You've too much to drink. Move on. You don't treat our waitresses like that in Shaughnessy's. This is a family establishment."

"It's a pub. Jackass."

"I asked nice. Next time…" The stocky, bearded man gave the stranger another little shove.

The stranger turned and swung a right hook at him. The stocky man ducked and rose up under the red-haired stranger and hoisted him over his shoulder. "Be right back. Gotta take the trash out."

Gavin exchanged glances with his da, then he threw up the pass through and sprinted after the two men who'd now made it outside.

Shrugging, she delivered her tray of drinks and returned to the bar. "He wasn't a regular. I've never seen him in here. Did you?" she whispered to Bridget who was standing at the bar gawking at the scene that had played out.

Bridget shook her head. "Nope. First time I've seen him. Didn't belong to the group of tourists in here earlier either. Sounded like a Scot. Glasgow bur, did you notice?"

"Not really. I was too busy attempting to keep the drinks from spilling."

"And a good job you did." Bridget gave her a pat on the back and moved out in the crowd with her tray of pints.

Tim put a hand on her arm. "We don't need trouble makers in here. Don't worry about it. But…" He raised an eyebrow.

"Got it. Don't mess up the customers. I barely touched him." She shifted away from the bar. "Not much of a man." She sniffed as her forehead creased in thought. She'd let her temper guide her actions—again. Something Tristian warned her about that could have deadly consequences in battle. *I know that*. She drew in a breath and searched her mind for his presence. He wasn't there.

Blowing out a breath, she grinned, relieved. Another lecture from him was not on her agenda. He could be so damned condescending. It raised her ire which she was sure was his intent. She'd beaten his mind games a couple of times and could keep him out of her thoughts—mostly.

She should have had her shielding abilities up. She didn't. Had that been a test? Had he done that on purpose and would remind her of that failure next time they met. *Every time I must remember to check the magic signature or a disguising spell before… He could have*— Stamping her foot she whirled around and ran into the broad chest of Gavin. His eyes narrowed, he motioned to the office.

Tim waved a hand to Gavin, indicating he needed

177

to be behind the bar. Gavin nodded then held up an index finger and escorted her to the office.

"What just happened?" Gavin asked after closing the door.

"He slipped on the floor?" Synn suggested.

Gavin narrowed his eyes at her. "No magic?"

Synn blew out a breath. "Only a little and it was well controlled. Did you notice? No one else did." She was unable to keep the pride out of her voice.

"This time. All we need is a magic wielder in here, witch, demon, faery, you get the picture. Should they feel your power, read your magic signature and report back to…"

Shoulders slumped as she frowned. "I made sure there was no one with magic abilities in here, cloaked or not. Tristian drilled that into me until it's second nature."

"Aye, but it was your temper acting not your head."

"Got it. Won't happen again." *Sheesh, he's as bad as Tristian.* She walked toward the door. "If you're finished, I need to be out on the floor."

Following her to the door, he reached out and snagged her arm. "Your magic smells a lot different than before. Should we be concerned?"

Her temper flared, but she tamped it down glaring at his hand. He made no effort to remove it. "No. Tristian said that's to be expected. Next week, he's going to return the rest of my powers."

"Provided he determines you can handle it. After tonight, I'm not sure." He released her arm.

"I had complete control of my magic, even if my temper—and you know it." She reached for the door handle, turned the knob, and threw open the door. It banged once against the wall before Gavin caught it.

"Aye. Still…"

"I'm fine. Trust me. I got this." She sashayed down the hallway, stopped, turned toward him, winked, and hurried into the main pub. The rest of the evening passed quickly. When the last customer trudged out the door, she sidled up to Bridget. "Have you got next week's schedule set up?

"Almost. Looks like Wednesday and Thursday will be your days off. Quinn's band is booked for both Friday and Saturday. Cori will join them on Saturday. It'll be a full house." Bridget grinned.

"You love watching all those women flirt with Quinn. When the night is over, you waltz up to him, stake your claim, and leave a trail of hopeful hearts broken." She snickered and finished wiping off the bar.

"Not my fault they don't know better." Bridget gathered the empty glasses on to a tray and carried them to the bar.

"How are they supposed to know? Don't have a ring on him." She went behind the bar and rinsed out the cloth in the sink. Picking up a spray bottle of disinfectant, she walked to the tables.

"Don't need one. He's always had eyes for only me. Local gals know it."

She shook her head. "You are sure of yourself and your man."

"If I wasn't, I'd never consider tying myself to him." Bridget carried the final tray of dirty glasses to the bar where Gavin put them in the washer behind the bar.

"How about we have a girl's night out—really in—

Sunday night. I hear the men are gathering for a poker game at Gavin's house. You don't want to be there. We're not scheduled to work until Monday evening."

"Sounds great." She rolled her eyes. "We'll need it after the weekend."

"You bet. I'll bring the wine. Gale will bring the movies. She's got every chick flick known to woman. Colleen can bring the munchies. Katie will join us if she can. It'll depend whether or not Sean is going to the card game."

"What do you want me to bring?"

"Yourself and tales of that hunk you are shacking up with." Bridget snickered then broke out in gales of laughter.

"How did you know?"

"It's a small town, hon. Talk about a trail of broken hearts." Bridget waved her hand at the floor and covered her mouth subduing her laughter.

"It's only because of a plumbing problem at the cottage. Hannah and Tristian are staying with Mary and Tim. They have a house full. As soon as the cottage is fixed, Storm and I'll return home."

"The only problem with the cottage is you're there and he's not. You're in denial, lass."

Chapter Eighteen
Trip to Dublin Brings Surprising Results

Thursday morning, Synn gave Gavin a light kiss on the cheek before exiting. He stood in the doorway with Storm as she sprinted down the path to the awaiting car. She turned and waved as the driver's door opened. No sooner had the door to the house closed she heard Storm whining then saw her in the window letting out a mournful howl.

She pulled her coat tightly around her and sprinted toward the car. The green foliage turning yellow on the edges whirled in the north wind making a rustling sound. "I'll be back soon." She called to the pup. By the time she reached Mary's awaiting car, she discovered Tristan holding the back door open for her. She skidded to a halt. "What are you doing here?"

"Good morning to you too." Tristian's lips twitched as he raised a brow. "Are you getting in or staying?" There was a hint of amusement in his voice.

She slid into the back seat next to Mary. "I thought we were going alone."

"Last minute, Tristian had business in Dublin. He offered to drive us to the city freeing up Da to take care of a few things at the pub and Gavin to watch Storm." Hannah turned in the front seat to face her and Mary. The trip to Dublin was uneventful. Tristian pulled up in front of the bridal shop with ten minutes to spare before their appointment. "Ladies, give me a call when you are ready to leave."

"Okay. We're going to have lunch around the corner. You're free to join us," Hannah offered.

"I'll try, but no guarantees. Not sure how long my meeting will take." Tristian leaned over, put his arm around his wife's shoulders drawing her to him, and gave her a long affectionate kiss. "Miss me."

"Always." Hannah slid across the seat and got out as Mary exited the backseat.

She climbed out of the car and hesitated a moment letting the sun warm her face. She stepped around a couple of puddles on the sidewalk, glanced up and down the street, then hesitated.

"Don't even think about it." Mary reached for her arm. "Brandy is depending on us to help her confirm her wedding gown selection. That's exactly what we're going to do." Mary pulled the glass door to the shop open and chimes tinkled somewhere in the back. A variety of fragrances whooshed out.

Inside the store she sniffed. Bayberry, peppermint, vanilla, and lavender scents she singled out. *A relaxing combination, a good thing for nervous brides and their mothers.* Her lips twitched. Why all the fuss over a union of a couple that may or may not last. *A waste of time and effort in my opinion.*

"Are you coming or going to stand there all day?" Hannah chided her and waved to the woman behind the counter.

"Coming."

The woman at the counter, smiled. "Shaughnessy party?"

Mary nodded.

The woman held up her finger. "I'll be right back." She bustled to the back room. Quick as a wink, she was back with a white garment bag, unzipped it, and held the beautiful gown out for all to see. A white pearl essence shimmered around the dress then faded away. She stared for a moment. Glancing at the other women, she could tell they hadn't seen it. *What was going on here?*

Mary touched the fabric, a smile spread across her face. "Me daughter called you?"

"Aye, she did. Right after I disconnected from talking to you. She had a few unusual requests, but I was able to accommodate them."

Mary raised her eyebrow. "Like what?"

"I'm sorry, not at liberty to say. However, I can tell you, she asked that Synn—" The shopkeeper paused. "Am I pronouncing that correctly?"

"Yes, that's correct," she acknowledged. Tilting her head, she sensed an undefined magic element coming from the dress. She reached out, touched a tiny embroidered rose bud, and a feeling of calm washed over her. *Huh, there's more here than meets the eye.*

"You're to decide between these three bridesmaid dresses." She paused again. "Oh, forgive me. Where are my manners? I'm Molly O'Toole. This is my shop." She held her hand out to each woman. "My clerk failed to show up for work this morning. I've fittings, meetings… Oh, but you don't want to hear—"

The petite woman with silver strands through her dark hair hung the wedding gown on the rack, then disappeared behind a swinging door. Soon she returned with three pristine garment bags. When Molly unzipped the bags, a light blue pearl essence wafted out, floated on the air then disappeared.

Synn glanced around. "Did you see that?" A momentary look of surprise crossed Molly's face. She quickly schooled her expression to normal.

A perplexed expression crossed Mary and Hannah's face. "See what dear?" Mary asked.

"The blue glimmer—you didn't see it." She rubbed her eyes. There was magic rolling off Molly now too.

Both women shook their heads. "Are you feeling all right? You look a bit pale," Mary observed.

"I'll get you a glass of water." Molly rushed through a curtained doorway and returned with a glass of water. "Here you are." She smiled and handed her the glass.

"Thank you. I'm fine." She took the glass and drank deeply trying to figure out what just happened. "Seeing things. Must be sleep deprivation—I guess." She grinned and concentrated on the three beautiful dresses Molly had displayed on the rack.

She reached out and touched the first emerald green dress. It was soft like silk but with a touch of something stretchy. She rubbed the fabric gently between her thumb and forefinger. Fashioned with one shoulder, the dress was meant to cling to the curves of a woman that wore it.

The next one, baby blue, had a semi-fitted bodice with rosebud embroidery that matched the bridal gown, lace sleeves, and flowed from the waist to the floor in a slight flare.

The last one was in her opinion obnoxious. The bodice was also fitted, lace peeked out along the strapless top, and the skirt flared from the waist reminisces of the ballgowns during the Elizabethan period.

Yuck. By the look on Hannah and Mary's faces, they shared her opinion. Though she didn't know Brandy well, this wasn't the type of dress she would even consider. *Was this a test? Or an affront to me? Of course not.* She shook her head. "I'm not sure what this dress was created for, but it wasn't for Brandy's bridal party." Heat rose in her cheeks when she realized she'd said her thoughts out loud. Her hand flew to her mouth. She mumbled, "I'm sorry."

Mary burst out laughing. "Leave it to our Synn to tell it like it is." She leaned over and whispered, "Me thoughts exactly."

Hannah joined in the laughter. "That dress is just plain ugly."

She blew out a breath and slid a glance to Mary and Hannah in turn. "Unless it's for the mother of the bride." She gulped then giggled at Mary's expression of horror.

The look disappeared in a second replaced by raucous laughter. "Wow, teasing me Synn. That's a new one." Mary couldn't have appeared more pleased.

With a shrug, she stared at the dress again. "It was the only explanation I could come up with."

"And a good one it was," Hannah said still laughing and touched her on the back. "Let's connect the video conference and see what the heck Brandy was thinking."

Stiffening, she glanced at the other two dresses. "I haven't decided which dress."

"Yes, you have." Hannah wiped her eyes. "I saw the look of pure desire when you touched the green dress. I like it too. So it's decided."

"I like the blue one." Mary peered at Molly. "Do you have my size?"

"Of course. Brandy thought you'd like it." Molly walked to the counter, jotted down something on a pad of paper.

"Mary, if you don't mind my asking, how did you find this shop?" She touched the green dress again and fingered the bride's dress as Molly whisked them away. A slight feeling of calm flowed over her.

"Oh, I believe it's owned by a relative of Angie's best friend. You know Angie—Tristian's sister, Bruce's wife."

"Would that be Willow?" She'd heard Angie talk about her. Met Willow once at the Wycked Hair.

"Yes...yes...that's the one. Molly created Angie and Willow's wedding gowns for their double wedding. Angie said Molly's creations are magic. Brandy was so excited to discover that Molly could make the dress she saw in the magazine. Why?"

"Just wondering. Brandy was lucky." *That explains a lot. Willow's family are faeries. Bet there is faerie dust in the material.* She touched the green dress once more. "It's settled then. Better call her."

Hannah took out her cell phone and touched in Brandy's number. A few seconds later, Brandy's face appeared on the screen. "Hey, girl. We're at the bridal shop. Your dress is perfect. The lace is soft."

Brandy's face split into a wide smile. "I'm so glad. Angie said Molly was the best. What about the bridesmaid dresses?"

Hannah shifted the phone so Brandy could see the green dress on the rack, then without warning handed the phone to her.

"Uh… If it's all right, we decided on the emerald green dress." She held the phone out toward Hannah.

"Perfect. I thought you and Hannah would love that dress. What about fittings?"

Molly returned with pad and pen in hand. "Oh, honey, I guarantee my dresses will fit. Don't worry about it until you get here."

"It could be as late as January," Brandy said. "I hope not, but…"

"No problem. The dresses will be ready. Be sure and let me know the wedding date as soon as you can." Molly smiled.

"What about veil and shoes?" Mary asked.

"Oh, I've already settled on those with Molly." Brandy turned her head on screen as someone walked into the office. "I gotta go. Thanks, everyone. We'll talk soon."

"Bye." Mary blew her daughter a kiss.

"Don't worry. We'll see to everything," Hannah promised and disconnected the call.

She blew out a breath. "That wasn't so bad."

"See, I told you. Brandy will come around." Mary bustled to the counter. "What about fittings?"

"We'll do it right now. Pick a dressing room. I'll bring the dresses in."

Her dress fit perfectly, no alternations needed. The others weren't so lucky. After an hour of trying on dress sizes and fittings, her stomach rumbled.

Mary hurried out of a dressing room with her gown in hand. "I'm all set and starved. Hannah, honey, call Tristian and see if he can meet us for a quick lunch. This has taken longer than I thought."

Hannah emerged with her dress already in a bag.

"Will do—"

The chimes sounded, and a smiling Tristian pushed through the door of the store. "Did I hear my name?"

Chapter Nineteen
Walking the Pup Brings a Surprise Meeting

This morning Storm had been a bugger when Synn left. The pup had looked up at him with those baleful eyes and whined. If that wasn't enough, she'd jumped on the bench in front of the window seat and set up a mournful howl. After a few minutes, he couldn't stand it anymore and clipped the leash on her harness. "Come girl, let's go for a walk."

It's not what he had planned. But that confound noise had to stop, and he didn't feel much like hanging around the house anyway. Synn's bouts of recent insomnia resulted in his house being cleaner than it had ever been. He couldn't find a damn thing. Rather than lay in the bed tossing and turning, she got up and quietly cleaned. Now he understood why her cottage was always neat and tidy. Sleeping in separate rooms probably had its advantages, but he still heard her every movement. Her scent was everywhere. It drove him crazy. Thoughts of the other night filled his mind which didn't help. When this was all over, she would be in his bed and in his life permanently, if he had anything to say about it. Until then...

After walking along the beach where Storm chased the waves along the shore and barked at the gulls, he turned and followed the path that led to the cliffs. Storm's tail wagged nonstop as her nose rarely left the ground.

At the top of the cliffs overlooking the ocean, he inhaled deeply. Floral fragrances of summer were gone. Crisp breeze and falling leaves whirled along the path indicated fall was in the air.

There was no doubt in his mind this was where he was supposed to be. After his sisters left for America, he often wondered if he should have followed them. But he didn't get the wanderlust from his ma as the girls had. No, he was content living in the home that generations of Shaughnessys had grown up in. Working at the pub, seeing the familiar faces every day, spinning tales for the pub patrons, and knowing his place in the world centered his life. All that changed when Synn barged in to his world. Things would never be the same.

The increasing cold north wind tousled his hair. He pulled the collar of his coat higher on his neck and tugged on the leash. "Storm, time to go." The pup scampered back to his feet. Switching direction to head down the trail, he'd taken only a couple of steps when a muscular man materialized in his path.

"Top o' the morning to you, lad." The man sang out in a cheerful voice.

He rubbed his eyes and looked again. Yep, the man was still standing in the way. Storm gave a friendly bark and pounced at the man. The leash pulled her up short.

Sucking in a breath, he swallowed hard. "Who might you be?"

"Tiarnan, King of Faeries."

"Sure you are." He narrowed his eyes and took a good look at the man. *Sure enuf, he fit the description.* "So what do you want with me?"

"Just checking in. Haven't seen your lass for several days. Everything all right?"

"You tell me." He paused and shook his head. "Sorry, I'm not in the best of moods. Things are as good as can be. I guess. Synn is on edge and having trouble sleeping."

He nodded. "To be expected. Her lessons with the warlock?"

"Going well. At least so I've been told."

"Tiarnan, are you over here?" A melodic voice carried on the breeze before a beautiful woman appeared. "Oh, you have company." She looked him over. "Gavin, how are you?"

"Good." He paused a couple beats. *This had to be Erin, Tiarnan's lady love. Be careful what you wish for.* "Erin, isn't it?"

"Aye, it is."

"Don't mind me. I was just leaving."

"No need. Did you tell him?" Erin looked expectantly at Tiarnan.

Tiarnan wrinkled his brow. "No, the warlock hasn't returned her power yet."

"Oh."

"Mind telling me what you are talking about?" He reached down and pulled the puppy to him with the leash.

"You'll see soon enough."

When he looked up, the couple was gone. "What the hell was that all about?" He directed his question to Storm. She didn't see fit to answer him. Only gave a quick wag of her tail in acknowledgment and tugged on the leash, anxious to be on her way.

Half way down the trail his cell phone rang. He

yanked it out of his pocket and stared at the screen. "Quinn, what's up?"

"Gee a bit testy? Want to meet at the pub for lunch?"

"Sure. Give me an hour. I'm walking Storm up by the cliffs. Gotta get home and cleaned up."

"See you there."

He put the phone back in his pocket and increased his speed toward the house. Storm raced behind him. Once at the house, he fed her and coaxed her into the crate while he showered and dressed. One last check and she was sound asleep in her enclosure. He closed the door, clicked the lock, and sprinted to his truck.

At the pub, he pushed through the door to find the usual lunch crowd. Waving to a few regulars, he made his way to the back. In the kitchen he got out meat, a fresh baked loaf of bread and sliced it. He spread mustard and mayo on the bread, stacked cheese and meat, then took two plates down and put the sandwiches on them. On the way through the kitchen door, he nearly plowed into his da.

"What are you doing here? Aren't you supposed to be watching the pup?"

He nodded. "We had a long, interesting walk this morning, and she's snoozing in her crate. Quinn is meeting me here for lunch. Thought I'd make our sandwiches rather than add to the work load." He held up the plates and nodded to Quinn standing in the pub.

Tim put a hand on his arm. "What about your walk?"

"I'll tell you about it later." A booth in the corner opened up, and he hurried over to stake a claim. Quinn sauntered up to the bar and waited. A few minutes later he slid into the both with two pints of stout.

"Starting early today, aren't you?" He tilted his head in question.

"Yeah, been a day already. Bridget got up on the wrong side of the bed. The gig tonight called and wanted it moved up three hours. Bridg started cleaning, and I left." Quinn took a long swig of his beer and set the mug on the table. The liquid inside sloshed from side to side threatening to overflow.

He slid one plate over in front of Quinn. "What is it about lasses that when they are upset or frustrated—they clean. Synn does the same thing. I can't find a thing in my own house." He bit his lip at the expression on Quinn's face. *Shit he didn't know.*

"You two living together now?" Quinn's eyebrow rose forming a question mark. "Wow… Why am I always the last to know?" He took a big bite out of the sandwich and waved it at Gavin. "Good stuff."

"It's not what you think. Her cottage has plumbing problems, and something is nesting in her chimney. Until those problems are corrected, I've two house guests. Synn and Storm." He ran his fingers through his hair and rubbed the back of his neck. This gave him time to make sure to keep his stories straight. He looked at his watch, picked up the mug, considered it, then took a swig.

"Landlord taking a while?" Quinn finished his beer and looked at the mug longingly.

"Da owns the cottage." He took a big bite of the sandwich and chewed slowly.

Rolling the empty glass between his hands, he looked up. "Oh, yeah, I forgot. Guess you need to do the repairs. Need help?"

"Naw, I'll get around to it. Besides sounds like you have your hands full." He took another bite.

Quinn gave him a lopsided grin. "Got that right. But I can make time for a friend. Week after next?"

"If I can find the problem and get the supplies that could work." He paused for a beat. "I'll let you know."

"So is Sunday night's poker game off?" Quinn stood mug in hand.

"Nope. Synn and the girls are going to your house for a girl's night. Watching movies, complaining about us, and heaven knows what else. Hope you don't mind a pup in your house, because Synn plans on taking Storm. Will that be a problem?"

Quinn paused for a moment. "Well, I don't want it chewing up my stuff."

"I can see if she'll leave her with me. But doubtful."

Holding up his empty mug, Quinn pointed to Gavin's mug. "Want another?"

"No, I gotta work tonight, and Da is strict about his not drinking policy."

"That's why I don't help out around here. I'll be right back." Quinn strode across the floor and plopped his mug on the bar. The bartender switched out the empty for a full. When he headed back toward the table, Bridget swung through the door and shot him the evil eye. She stopped in front of him, hands fisted on her hips.

Oh boy, doesn't look good for Quinn. He grimaced and looked away. That way he could honestly say he wasn't paying attention.

A few minutes later, Quinn returned to the table, drank about half of his beer, and slammed the mug on the table. Beer sloshed over the rim and onto the table. Quinn plopped in the seat.

"Hey, don't be breaking our mugs. We'll take it out of your earnings tomorrow night," he said half joking, half not and gathered up a few napkins sopping up the mess. At his friend's stormy expression, he was forced to ask. "What's wrong?"

"Women! Can't live with 'em or without 'em." Quinn rolled his beer between his hands, then grabbed the handle and guzzled the rest. In a deliberate motion, he set the mug on the table carefully.

He watched his friend's gaze travel from his empty glass, to the bar, then follow Bridget. "Hey, let's get out of here. From what you said, you got a gig in an hour. I've got to get back and let Storm out. Synn'll have my head if the pup has an accident in her crate." He wrinkled his nose. "Besides, I don't want to clean that up."

Quinn grunted and stood, mug in hand. He took a step toward the bar.

"You don't want to do that." He placed a hand on Quinn's arm. "Sunday, you can have all you want. We'll plan on you staying over."

His friend sneered and jerked his arm free.

"Your band is in high demand now. You start showing up drunk or impaired and…"

"I can hold my drink," Quinn shot back.

"Didn't say you couldn't. It's unprofessional to show up smelling like a brewery. We'd dismiss you on the spot. Not to mention trouble with Bridg. Not worth it. Go home and cool off. Get ready for your gig." He gave Quinn a hard look.

"Better get a cup of coffee in you." He patted his

friend's shoulder, turned on his heel, and headed for the door. On his way past Bridget, he touched her arm. "Don't know what's going on, but best give him some space." With a wave, he caught Katie's attention, pointed to Quinn, and mimed pouring coffee. She grabbed a cup and the coffee pot. He gave her a thumbs up.

The heavy wooden door groaned as he yanked it open and breathed in the fresh air. The breeze had a slight chill to it, but the sun was still warm as he made his way home. After letting Storm out, he leashed her, and they walked to the beach. He was careful to keep Storm out of the surf.

Trudging up the path toward home pulling a reluctant Storm behind him, he heard a car door close and voices. He quickened his pace as he came up over the rise and saw Synn standing beside the vehicle talking to Mary and Tristian. She waved to them as the warlock got back in the car and drove away.

Silhouetted against the sun with her dark tresses blowing in the breeze, she still took his breath away. Just like the first time he set eyes on her. The moment frozen in time shattered when Storm figured out Synn was back and began barking. The pup tugged on the leash trying to get to her. Synn turned toward the sound, a wide smile spread across her face, as she rushed toward them.

A knot formed in his stomach remembering the lukewarm goodbye this morning. The lass was a puzzle. She ran hot and cold. It was a disadvantage for him never knowing how she'd greet him. Still he was anxious to tell her about his visit with the warrior king of the faeries and his wife. Should he tell her what they said and the strange way they left the discussion?

"Storm, I missed you." She bent down and hugged the wiggling pup to her. "Were you a good girl?" Synn shifted those beautiful aqua eyes to him. "And how was your day?"

"Storm was good. My day— It was different."

"Do tell." She rose up on tiptoe and wrapped her arms around his neck. "I missed you too." She brushed her lips over his and sighed, resting her head against his chest.

He grasped her around the waist and held her tightly against him as he poured his feelings into the kiss. The soft warmth of her curves against him sent shivers of desire through him wiping all thought from his mind except bedding her. *Not a chance in Hell that's going to happen.* Easing away, he whispered, "Tell me about your day. Brandy's wedding plans all set?"

Synn threw her head back and laughed. "Not by a long shot but the wedding gown, shoes, veil, and bridesmaid dresses are bought. The flowers decided and the invitations ordered. Molly's wedding shop is kinda a one stop shop. She's a relative of Willow's—you know Angie's best friend."

"I don't know, but I've heard about her. Faerie blood, isn't she? Married a satyr, right?"

Synn's eyes rounded. "Faerie yes. But I didn't know who she married. Bet her family was in shock."

He shrugged one shoulder. "Don't know. But I had an interesting day. Talked with Tiarnan and Erin. Storm ran right up to them. Not a peep out of her."

"Wow. What did they say?"

"That's the thing. They had more questions than

conversation. Mostly about you. Then made a cryptic comment and poof disappeared." He shook his head.

"About me? What about me?"

He relayed the conversation word for word ending with the weird statement "You'll see soon enough."

"What do you suppose he meant?" Synn chewed on her bottom lip. "More trouble?"

"Didn't feel like that, but then I'm not an expert on Faerie kings. I guess the sooner you finish with Tristian and he restores your powers, the sooner we'll find out."

"Don't like surprises…really don't," she muttered.

"Guess we better get inside and get ready for work. Oh, as a warning, something happened at the pub this afternoon when I had lunch with Quinn. He and Brig got crosswise. She came in and he was having a pint with lunch." He hesitated a beat rubbing his chin. "Okay a couple of pints and she— I don't know."

"Did they get it worked out?"

"Beats me. I left before they got it settled out. I don't like to get in the middle of things like that. So consider yourself warned."

Chapter Twenty
Girls Night in and all Hell Breaks Loose, Magic
Wielders to the Rescue

The next couple of days whizzed by in a blur.
Quinn and his band played Friday night. Cori joined
them Saturday and the pub was at near capacity. She
and Gavin had fell into bed each night exhausted and
woke up in time to take Storm for a decent walk, then
pack her up and take her with them. The pup spent her
days in the storeroom at the pub so they could give her
the breaks she needed.

Synn rolled over and yawned wide, glad they
didn't have to work today. She was looking forward to
the girl's night in at Bridget's after an early dinner at
Mary and Tim's. Stretched across the bed, she listened
to the far off waves pounding on the shoreline and
wondered if all this could really last. The town had
embraced her. She had friends. Mary and Tim treated
her like family. She'd never been happier in her life and
intended to savor it for as long as she could. But she
wouldn't fool herself into believing there was a happy
ever after for her.

Darkness loomed and she could feel it getting
stronger each day. The nightmares were gone. Thanks
to Tristian and being able to block her mind while
sleeping. She crept out of bed and pushed the curtain
aside letting the warm sunshine wash over her. When

she slipped out of the bedroom, Storm was still asleep in her crate.

Gavin's eyes were closed as she tiptoed into his room down the hall from hers. She paused to watch him sleep. *How did I get so lucky?* Touching a fingertip to her lips then to his full lips, she smiled as the corners of his mouth turned up in a grin.

"Awake already?" he said in a sleepy whisper, reaching out to her.

Storm whined and let out several short barks.

"I'll let her out." She rushed into her room, pulled on jeans, a sweatshirt, and after tugging on socks shoved her feet into sneakers.

"If you wait a couple minutes, I'll go with you."

"Not sure Storm can wait. We'll be out front." She reached for the leash and unlocked Storm's crate. "Come on, girl." The puppy rushed out of the crate, all wiggles and licks. She clipped the leash on Storm's harness, crossed to the front door, and hurried outside.

A few minutes later, Gavin joined them pulling on a light jacket over his green shirt. He took the phone out of his jeans pocket, glanced at the screen, and stuffed it into his jacket. "How about a walk before breakfast?"

"Okay, but not a long one. I'm starved. Don't want to faint from hunger." She laughed. "You making a bacon, egg, and cheese omelet?" Storm raced around in circles at their feet, until the leash was wound around their ankles making walking impossible. "Storm halt." She reached down, grabbed the harness, and unclipped the long lead. When she stepped out of the coils of leash, Gavin did the same but caught a foot and nearly toppled over. Bumping into her, he knocked them both off balance. Laughing, she clipped the leash back on

Storm.

He chuckled scrubbing a hand over his face. "Too early. I need my coffee."

The pup led the way up the steep path to the rocky cliffs. At the top, a light breeze took wisps of short hair and blew them across her face. He reached out and tucked the wayward strands behind her ears. "Why so quiet?"

"A lot on my mind, I guess." She shrugged.

"Care to share?" He caressed his fingers over her cheek.

"Not yet. What do you need to get ready for your poker party tonight?" She reached up, caught his hand, and twined her fingers though his. Her stomach gurgled. "Better start back."

"Nothing special. The guys bring snacks and drinks. I've got the cards, poker chips, and will set them out on the table before we go to Ma and Da's. That's about it. Sure you don't want to leave Storm with me?"

"No. She'll be fine. Could you drop us off with the pup's crate at Bridget's after dinner?"

"That'll work. You call me when you're ready to come back. I don't think the crate will fit in any of your friends' cars."

"You're right about that."

He grinned. "Don't want Storm running loose in the house? Unsupervised?"

"No. She is doing so well. I don't want her to regress because she didn't have her crate."

"Good answer." He smiled down at her.

When they got back to the house, she left Storm outside in the backyard while they fixed breakfast, ate, and cleaned up the kitchen. Gavin set up for the poker game. She padded over to the window mesmerized by the seabirds swooping and calling to each other.

After he filled Storm's food bowl in the crate, he called out. "Do you need more than this?" He pointed to the bowl.

She turned her attention from the window to him. "That should be fine. We'll only be gone a few hours."

Gavin sent her a cheeky grin. "Unless you have too good a time." He snickered.

"We'll see." She called Storm into the house and waited. The pup circled toward the door, barked, and raced back into the middle of the yard. Eventually, she had to go outside and get her.

He slid the crate into the backseat of the truck, then went back to get the lemon meringue pies she'd prepared for the party and dinner. Finally, she appeared carrying Storm and scolding her.

"Having second thoughts?"

"No, she has to learn to come when called. Her recall sucks," she retorted.

"She's young. She'll learn." He took the pup from her and put Storm in the crate.

"Thanks for bringing out the pies. I hope your parents and the girls like them."

"I'm sure they will." He started the engine and guided the truck down the street. At his parents' house, the truck rolled to a stop. Ma and Da were waiting in the doorway.

"Where's my little angel?" His ma crooned making a beeline straight for Storm. His da rolled his eyes.

"We're having lasagna the Irish way." Tim said a twinkle in his eye as they passed by him into the house.

She glanced from Tim to Gavin. "What's lasagna

the Irish way?"

"Oh, you'll see, lass," Tim said with a chuckle.

"It means that Tim has been experimenting in the kitchen again, and we are the innocent victims," Tristian said his voice gruff.

Hannah elbowed him in the ribs. "The last thing you'd be is an innocent anything."

A twitch of Tristian's lips gave way to a hearty laugh. "His experiments are usually quite tasty." He slung an arm around Hannah and walked to the couch.

She took Storm out to the backyard and let her go. The pup did her business and rushed back on the porch. "Too many people to pester for you to stay outside?"

Mary bustled out and picked Storm up. "Don't you be mean to this little darlin'." She carried her into the house and put her down on the hardwood floor in the middle of a large pile of toys. "Our neighbor, Gemma brought over a few toys for Storm to play with."

"A few?" Gavin grinned.

"Dinner is ready," Tim called from the doorway of the kitchen.

As it turned out lasagna the Irish way tasted a lot like regular lasagna with a hint of thyme. She wasn't so sure about the garlic brown bread, but the green salad and fresh veggies were wonderful. Her pie was a hit. She hoped her friends felt the same way.

After dinner was cleaned up, everyone retired to the living room with coffee or hot tea. "Are you going over to Bridget's?" She looked over at Mary and Hannah.

"Oh, I wouldn't miss it for the world. She throws a great girl's night in," Hannah said.

"No. I'm looking forward to a quiet night sitting in

front of the fire. I have an exciting book, *A Witch's Journey*, that I've been trying to finish reading. Since Da and Tristian will be joining the lads." Mary glanced longingly at the book splayed open on the end table.

She followed Mary's gaze to the book. "What do you like to read?"

"Oh...a little of everything, romance, adventure, and mysteries. Thrillers give me nightmares." Mary shrugged one shoulder, and her cheeks pinked.

"Hannah, you want to ride with us?" Gavin asked, waving at the zonked-out pup at the front door. "I'm going to take Storm and Synn over and pick them up when the party is over."

Hannah quirked a brow as Mary handed her a bag. "Why?"

"Hannah, dear, make sure you hold that sack upright." Mary put her hand under the sack that Hannah was holding sideways.

"Because he doesn't trust me to drive his truck and we have to put the seats down in my car to get the crate in. It's a pain." She made a sour face.

"Oh." Hannah shot a quick glance at Tristian. "That'd be great." She held the bag up and put her hand under it replacing her ma's.

He nodded casting a glance in her direction. "I'll be over at Gavin's if you need something."

"Hey, Trist, you can ride over with me to drop the girls off," Gavin offered.

"Thanks, but I'd rather have my own vehicle."

"Okay."

"Let's go. Thanks for dinner, Da. It was delicious."

"Thanks so much," she added giving Mary a hug. "Sure you don't want to come to Bridget's?

"Aye. Don't get much of a chance to have the house to myself. I'm going to take it. Besides that book's been calling to me for days."

She put Storm in the crate and latched the door. When she hopped into the truck, she scooted over making room for Hannah. Gavin picked up the pie from the backseat, handed it to Hannah, and closed the door. He tossed his house keys to Tristian. "I'll be right over after I drop the girls off."

Tristian reached up and snatched the keys out of the air, then gave the thumbs up sign. "Tim, you want to ride with me?"

"Aye, let me grab a coat."

****

She and Hannah knocked on the door and waited. Bridget threw open the door. "Began to wonder if you two were coming."

"Awww… Bridg, we're not that late. Had dinner at Ma's you know how they are. Da had a new recipe that turned out really good. Bet you'll find it on the menu at Shaughnessy's in the next while."

"What was it?"

"Irish lasagna. There's samples in the bag." Hannah held up the pie and a paper sack. "Where do you want these?"

"Mmmm—sounds yummy. Put the pie on the table." Bridget took the bag and walked to the table where nuts, chips, dips, and other munchies were lined up. "Where's that little fur ball?" She turned and peered around Hannah.

She bopped in with Storm on lead. "She's right here. We took her for a long walk before we left this morning. The pup played herself out at Mary and Tim's place." She glanced over her shoulder at Gavin.

He followed the girls inside carrying the crate. "Excuse me, Bridg, where do you want the crate? Then I'll be on my way. Don't want to crash the girl's party."

Bridget waved her hand in the direction of the wall. "Over in the corner, where she can see Synn." Leaning over the table, she sniffed. "The pie looks and smells delish. Let me get plates." She opened the bag and took two containers out. "We'll need to warm these up later. I'll put them in the fridge."

Gavin set the crate down and opened the gate. He caught her around the waist and kissed her lips. "See you later. Have fun."

Colleen clicked her tongue. "Friends my arse."

She felt her cheeks heat, then bent over to unhook Storm so she could visit each of the women. She ignored Colleen's comment.

"The wine is on the table. The two glasses next to the bottle are yours. The rest of us have ours." She glanced at Gale, Colleen, and Katie. They held their glasses up and grinned. The red wine in the bottle was nearly gone.

Hannah poured wine in one glass. But when she went to pour the red liquid in the other, only a dribble came out. She swung the decanter around. "Hey, Bridg, we are going to need another bottle."

"I've plenty." Bridget came out of the kitchen with plates in one hand and two wine bottles, held by the neck, in the other hand.

"Girl, you're going drop one of those." Hannah lunged for a bottle.

She took the plates from her as she stumbled over Storm. "Sorry. I'll put her in the crate."

"You'll do no such thing. She's just fine." Gale grabbed the pup from under Bridget's feet. The other girls nodded in agreement.

"Okay, but if you get tired of her or she gets naughty, put her in her crate. She's got food and water inside."

"What movie do you want to start with?" Bridget asked holding several Blu-ray discs.

"How about the one set in the 50s at a resort. Dancing something." Hannah blurted out.

Bridget waved a movie box around. "Got it right here. All agreed?"

"Sure—if we can watch that one Mike something about male strippers next?" Gale shot back.

The girls moaned. She wasn't sure which one shouted. "Those guys are hot." But she had to agree after checking out the cover Bridget held.

"Fair enough, that's next." Bridget tossed the first one to Katie who put it in the player. Bridget dimmed the lights and set the big bowl of popcorn in the center of the coffee table between the group.

After a couple of hours and another bottle of wine, the popcorn bowl was empty, and Bridget tuned up the lights. "Ready for the male strippers?"

"Oh yeah, bring 'em on," Katie shouted.

Feeling a little light-headed, she glanced at Bridget. "How about I warm up the Irish lasagna?" She stood and headed for the kitchen but paused at the sound of Bridget's voice.

"Ohh, good idea. Let me get the movie in, and I'll be right there." Bridget popped open the movie case.

Inside the kitchen, she searched for the light switch. Unable to locate it, she made her way to the fridge and opened the door. Light flooded the dark kitchen. She took a dish of lasagna from the first shelf. Still not seeing the switch, she called out, "Hey Bridget, where's the light switch?"

"Be right there as soon as I get the Blu-ray dislodged. It's stuck in the player," her friend's frustrated voice answered.

"I'll show her," Gale called out.

She turned with the refrigerator door wide open and managed to set the dish on the counter. Suddenly, the door closed with a thwack. An eerie blue mist fringed in red rose from the floor. She screamed recognizing the shape as Baltizar his robes emitting a blue glow.

The fuzzy effects of the alcohol gone in an instant, she shielded her mind and took a step back. With a ball of energy snapping and popping in her palm, she reached out. Her hand cut through the image. *It's a hologram.* Her fist snapped shut, extinguishing the energy as an unseen force slammed her against the wall.

"You stole..." Baltizar's image grinned. He raised his hands, palms out. His uneven, yellowed teeth bared in the moonlight streaming through the window. The red edges of the image began to blur. "I want it back..."

She gulped in air. *He's not real. He's not real.* "I've nothing of yours," she retorted in a terse whisper getting to her feet. The ball of energy returned to her palm.

The light flicked on. The demon's image disappeared without a trace. Gale stood in the doorway, arms raised, and gaze scalpel sharp. "What's wrong?" Thunderous footsteps raced across the floor. The rest of the girls peered from behind Gale. Storm whined in the other room.

Her mind frantically searched for an answer that would satisfy the group without scaring the bejeebers out of them. *Keep the magic secret.* Wind howled around the house. Shadows danced on the kitchen walls from the trees outside silhouetted by the full moon. "The moving shadows surprised me when the fridge light came on." Her voice shook, and she took several deep breaths. "Sorry."

The others laughed it off and returned to the living room where Bridget cursed her Blu-ray player. Gale stood rooted to the spot. In a low voice she said, "That explanation may appease them, but I smell the magic, and feel the darkness. What happened? You all right?"

"I don't know—I mean—yes. A little shaken—but fine." Her voice gained strength as she spoke. *If I'd had my full magic, would I have unleashed it in my panic?*

"We'd better summon Tristian. And Gavin." Gale reached into her pocket.

"Don't spoil the fun for the others. It…he…was only a hologram."

"Aye, a hologram that slammed you against the wall. How is that even possible?" Gale shook her head. "Especially after expending the power it took for him to appear here from the seventh level of Hell?"

"I don't know," she shot back without thinking.

"Even more concerning is how'd he know to appear here?" Gale threw her hands up and let them fall to her side. "Fun would be spoiled if one or all of us ended up dead." Gale stared pointedly toward the next room.

"He's gone," she said flatly.

"For how long? What did he want?" Gale

demanded as she fisted her hands on her hips.

"Not sure. He accused me of stealing. But he didn't say what. Only that he wanted it back." She knew it was a futile attempt to keep Gale in the dark. *He wanted his magic back.*

"Bollocks to that. He discovered you have his magic, and he wants it back." Gale went silent, her eyes blank for several seconds.

"Gale…Gale, are you all right?" She put a gentle hand on her friend.

When the witch focused again she said, "Tristian and Gavin are on their way."

Gale moved to the counter, waved her hand over the lasagna, and steam rose from the dish. She snapped her fingers and a bell sounded. "Food's ready." Gale pointed to the cupboard to the right of where she stood. "Plates?"

"Wait, how am I going to explain the guy's appearance?" She got dishes out of the cupboard Gale indicated and walked to the door way.

"Let them handle it." Gale whirled around, waved her hand, index finger pointing to the cantankerous Blu-ray player. The disk popped out and sailed through the air landing on the carpet at Colleen's feet.

Colleen giggled and picked up the disc. She nearly dropped it, then turned it over peering intently at the object. "Not even a scratch on it. Lucky."

Bridget stood slack jawed staring at the machine with a flat-tip screwdriver in her hand. A second later she waved the tool around. "That'll teach it." Bridget slid another disc carefully in the player and touched a button. The drawer closed, and she blew out a breath. "All set. Come on over, fill your plate, and we'll watch the next movie."

Her gaze switched from Gale to Bridget and lingered on the front door. She could feel Tristian's presence, but...

"Thanks." Bridget and the others grabbed the plates out of her hands as they came through the doorway. Bridget stopped, opened the silverware drawer, and pulled forks and a large serving spoon out. Her friend commenced to scooping up portions of the lasagna and depositing the delicious smelling food on the plates.

Her stomach growled loudly. Bridget handed her a plate heaped with steaming noodles, meat, cheese, and sauce.

A loud knock sounded on the door. "Who the hell could that be at this time of night?" Bridget dropped the spoon back in the dish. Tomato sauce splattered on the counter.

"I'll get it," she said in unison with Gale.

Bridget followed the girls to the door, peered through the peep hole. "Well, I'll be damned." She opened the door a crack. "What are you doing here?"

"Good evening—or sorry morning to you too. May I speak with Hannah?" He held a bulky light green parka folded over his arm.

"Yes, of course. Come in." She opened the door wide, motioning him inside with her hand. "Can I get you something to eat or drink?"

"No. Hannah left her parka in my car. Figured she'd need it since it appears a storm is blowing in."

Hannah turned around to stare at the back of her chair and shifted her gaze to Tristian. A puzzled expression spread across her face.

She covered her mouth to hide a snicker. Hannah knew that coat was on the back of her chair earlier. A truck's engine rumbled out front. A door slammed. In an attempt to peer out the door, she cut in between Tristian and Bridget. He caught her arm. "It's Gavin. He drove me over."

Oh, I don't think so. You were here several minutes before he drove up. She answered telepathically.

Protecting my interests. His smooth deep voice wafted through her mind. *After being summoned by Gale, I put a protection spell in place. All of you should be safe the rest of the night. We'll discuss this when we return to pick you two up.*

A female voice interrupted inside Synn's mind. *"What the hell is going on?"* She put her hands to her head. There were too many people inside her mind. *Knock it off, all of you. I can't even think.*

Tristian smirked as Gavin rushed in, concern creased his face. He reached out and touched her hand. She nodded.

"In or out boys, I'm not heating the outside." Bridget wrapped her arms around herself and pushed on the door. The two couples clogging the doorway moved inside.

Tristian handed Hannah her coat. "Didn't mean to crash your party. Dropping this off and we'll be on our way." He nudged Gavin toward the door.

"All right, girls, male strippers up next." Bridget snickered all the way to the Blu-ray player.

Tristian's jaw dropped as he stared from Bridget to Hannah. Gavin's eyes went wide, and his gaze flew to hers.

"What!" they said simultaneously.

She coughed and covered her mouth to hide a giggle at the expressions on the men's faces. "It's only a movie." She kissed Gavin on the cheek and flounced away to secure her seat in front of the television.

Tristian regained his composure first. "See, you leave a gaggle of women to their own devices and this is what you get. Booze, debauchery and…" He smirked. "Come on Gavin. We got a poker game to get back to." Whirling around to face the women, a mischievous smile turned up the corners of his lips. "We could make it strip poker if you girls would like to play."

Gavin chuckled, turned the knob, and held the door open shoving Tristian through it as a bright blue pillow flew at them. The pillow hit the backside of the door, slid to the ground as the door closed with a bang.

"Those two men are—HOT." Colleen said looking from her to Hannah. "Maybe we should join the guys."

Hands on her hips, Bridget narrowed her eyes at Colleen. "I'm cutting you off, no more wine. We'd be the ones showing our assets, believe me." Bridget pushed the play button and dimmed the lights.

Chapter Twenty-One
Magic Hangs in the Balance as Decisions are Made

"I'm not comfortable leaving them alone unprotected," Gavin paused. Looking over his shoulder as he hesitantly climbed into the truck.

Tristian frowned. "I cast a protection spell over the house. Baltizar won't be able to even project an image within a hundred-foot radius. Still how he moved Synn across the room being only a hologram is troubling. He shouldn't be able to do anything except project an image." Tristian swung into the truck and closed the door.

"Obviously you're missing something. I don't like Synn not being able to wield all the magic that should be at her disposal."

"Don't kid yourself she's far from defenseless. Giving her magic back before she is ready is more dangerous than leaving her without it." Tristian rubbed his chin with thumb and forefinger. He was quiet for several minutes as the truck bumped along the road to Gavin's house.

He pulled the truck in front of his home, cut the engine, and turned to Tristian. "How did he find her?"

"I'm sure he's got spies embedded here watching. He may be tracking her by magic. Though, she knows to cloak her magic, if she has to use it." Tristian shoved the door open a little harder than necessary.

He raised a brow as he rounded the hood of the truck joining Tristian. They trudged up the path to the house. Welcoming lights in the front windows shone through the inky black darkness. "I'm going to wrap up the game and let everyone head home. Concentrating is going to be tough trying to watch the girls and still win." He pushed the door open to find the others sitting around with beers in their hands and the cards neatly stacked on the table. "Wanna beer, soda, or bottle of water, Trist?" He crossed the floor to the kitchen. All the snack bowls were empty and stacked in the sink.

"Soda will do," Tristian said.

Bottles and cans clanked as he took a couple sodas out of the refrigerator. He handed one to his brother-in-law.

"Quinn's lost all he can afford. The rest of us are afraid if we continue to win, we won't be invited back," Tim said with a cocky smile. The others nodded in agreement. "We cashed everyone out."

"In your dreams ol' man," Gavin said eying the pile of cash at his place.

Quinn stood and stretched his arms above his head. "Do I need to crash here tonight, or can I go home?"

He and Tristian grinned at each other. "Give it about another hour. One of us will drive you home. The girls are watching that XXL movie. If you're dead on your feet, crash in the guest room to the right of the hallway."

Quinn's eyebrows shot to his hair line. "A stripper movie? I thought only guys did that?"

"Apparently not." Tristian shook his head. "The women around here are a bad influence on my wife."

Gavin slapped Quinn on the back. "You'll reap the

benefits of their escapades tonight if you can keep her awake." He chuckled deep in his throat.

Tim stood took another swig of his beer and held it up to the light. "I'll be heading on home. Thanks for the invite. Morning shift is going to come mighty early." He shrugged into a light jacket and reached for the knob.

"I'll take you home and come back," Tristian offered.

"That's a good lad," Tim said sleepily.

"I'm going to head home soon as I finish this beer." Quinn held his bottle up. "See if I can sneak into bed without catching Bridget's attention."

"I don't think you're driving anywhere." He snatched the keys from Quinn's hand.

"The hell I'm not." Quinn made a grab for the keys, lost his balance, and face planted on the floor. He helped Quinn to his feet and pushed him into a chair. "Like I said, you're not driving anywhere." He paused for a moment considering the logistics of getting all the vehicles to their proper locations. "Tristian, I can pick up the girls and drop Hannah off."

"Naw, safety in numbers. Be right back." Tristian opened the door and followed Tim out.

****

An hour later, he locked up the house and opened the truck door. "Hey Trist, why don't you leave your car here and drive Quinn home in his car, then I'll follow you. We can pick up the girls in my truck. I'll bring you and Hannah back here. You can take your sports car home." He tossed Quinn's keys to Tristian.

"I can do that. Come on, Quinn." Tristian turned around and glanced at Quinn. "Hey, what happened to

216

your eye?"

"Tripped and hit it on the floor…or something," Quinn said sheepishly.

Tristian guffawed. "And you thought you were driving home?"

Quinn mumbled something unintelligible and followed Tristian to the vehicle.

When they arrived, Gale was climbing in her car. Hannah and Synn were standing beside the vehicle talking while Katie got in the passenger's side. Colleen clambered into the back. Bridget was standing in the doorway as Quinn made his way up the path with Tristian's assistance.

"Did you lasses have a good time?" Gavin asked getting out and opening the truck door.

Tristian swaggered up to the truck. "Quinn's going to be sleeping on the couch tonight by the expression and tone of Bridget's voice."

Hannah snickered crawling into the backseat. "Bridget enjoyed the wine tonight too. She'll have a heck of a hangover tomorrow."

"That'll probably be good for Quinn." Tristian stepped into the truck and closed the door. "Or not."

"To answer your question. We had a great time even after the incident." Synn jumped into the front seat holding a wiggling Storm under one arm.

Tossing the crate in the back, he closed the door, vaulted over the hood to the driver's side, and slid in the seat.

"Tell us exactly what happened," Tristian said.

Synn recounted the event from going into the dark kitchen to when Gale turned the light on. "Strange, even Storm didn't sense him. She's usually my first warning even when my nightmares started."

"He appeared without warning?"

"Yep, didn't feel or see anything out of the ordinary. I'd had a couple of glasses of wine but didn't really feel impaired."

"It only takes one to impair your judgment," Tristian said sharply. "It'd be wise to abstain until this matter is concluded."

"Didn't think about that. Sorry." Synn stared at her hands stroking the pup.

Hannah bristled and shifted in her seat. "She's entitled to have a little fun once in a while."

"Not with Baltizar looking for revenge and my wife in close proximity." Tristian growled. "Fun can have deadly consequences." He shot a dark look at Synn. "Not on my watch, when any misstep could be fatal," Tristian snapped. "Especially when Balti…"

"All right, I get it. It won't happen again." She squirmed under his gaze and sunk into the seat in a sulky silence. Her arms wrapped around Storm as she stroked the pup's fur slowly staring out the windshield.

Gavin opened his mouth to protest. But the thunderous expression on Tristian's face made him close it again without speaking. The ride home was quiet, too quiet. Not a sound from the creatures that roam the night.

"Good enough." Tristian slid his arm across the backseat and wrapped his hand around Hannah's shoulder. She kept her back to him.

His headlights swept the area as the truck coasted to a stop in front of his house. The porch light cast a pool of light over the front yard and the windows were dark. When Gavin stopped, Synn and Hannah rocketed out of the truck. He and Tristian exited and glanced at each other.

"See you tomorrow—scratch that, make that later today?"

"Sounds good. Just so you know, need to give Bruce a heads up before I return Synn's powers. But I'm leaning toward doing that tomorrow."

He raised an eyebrow and paused for a beat, glancing at Synn as she made her way to the house, Storm tugging on the leash in front of her. "Probably a good idea."

Hannah waited at the sports car as Tristian sauntered up behind her and opened the door. She slid into the seat and closed the door with a pop. Tristian grinned back at Gavin. "She'll be fine."

Inside the house, Gavin grabbed Synn by the shoulder and spun her around, kissing her soundly on the lips. "So, tell me about the rest of your night—the fun part."

"Gotta let Storm out first. Not in the mood to clean up puddles." She unclipped the leash and followed the pup who raced to the back door. The door opened with a groan, and the pup thundered out. Synn waited for Storm to do her business, then insisted that she come back inside. "Too many weird things going on for her to stay out unsupervised."

"Couldn't agree more." He leaned his chest against her back, his arm resting above her head on the door frame. "How about we leave her with Ma on Tuesday, and I'll take you away from all this for the day?"

Her aqua eyes sparkled as she twisted her neck to glance up at him. "Oh, we couldn't impose." She sighed. "It would be fun. What have you got in mind?"

The corners of his mouth kicked up in a deliberate devilish grin. "It's a secret. I guarantee you'll enjoy it."

A fist on her hip, she whirled around in his arms as one eyebrow winged up. "I will, will I?" She smiled wide. "Could use a little R & R around here. After the recent turn of events... I feel so bad I ruined your poker game and the girls' night out." Pursing her lips, she shook her head and stared at the ground. A single tear rolled down her cheek. "He's never going to leave me alone."

He'd hadn't seen her cry much. When she did it was disconcerting, but a sure sign the tough façade she'd built around her was cracking. "You couldn't be more wrong. And you didn't ruin the poker game. It was time to shut it down anyway. Quinn couldn't afford to lose any more—he had a bad night... A worse one once Bridget got a hold of him I'd wager." When he reached out to touch her cheek, she backed away. *Two steps forward, one step back—story of my life.*

She straightened, and her chin jutted out. A fierce expression spread across her face, and her eyes darkened. "I'm not going to let that son-of-a-bitch take the new life I've carved out for myself here." She paused. "For us."

His heart sang at her words.

She paced across the room as her voice got louder. "If it's a fight he wants... A fight to the death he'll get...his death." Skidding to a stop in the middle of the room, feet planted firmly a shoulder width apart. She fisted her hands at her sides. "How can I protect my friends? I couldn't bear it if they were hurt because of me. I need my powers back." The air surrounding her crackled with defiance. Even Storm stood at attention surveying the area as if looking for whatever had upset Synn.

"That's me girl." He reached out for her. This time she leaned into him wrapping her arms around his neck and burying her face in his chest. His warrior was back. It was always darkest before the dawn, and the proverbial horizon was on fire. "Your friends will stand with you, whether you like it or not. That's what friends do."

"It's my battle." She braced her hands, palms down against his chest, and shoved. But he held her tight.

Finally, he loosened his grip and glanced down at her. "Oh, think again. The odds of winning go up exponentially with Tristian, Bruce, Angie, and the rest of us by your side. Baltizar is no match for us. He's going to go down, once and for all this time."

"I can't let—"

He interrupted her shrugging one shoulder. "You've no choice."

The rush of adrenalin had run its course. Fatigue etched lines across her beautiful face. Stifling a yawn, she brightened suddenly. "Sure Mary won't mind keeping Storm on Tuesday?"

"I'm sure." In the worst way he wanted to tell her Tristian's plans to return her magic. But if Bruce nixed it, then she would be terribly disappointed. Besides the last place he wanted to be was crosswise with the warlock. However, given Synn's rightly placed anger, determination, and confidence, he was sure Tristian would return her magic.

The fall breeze that wafted through the still open door had a bite to it, reminding him that Samhain would soon be here. What better time to launch an attack on

Baltizar in the days leading up to the night the veil between the dead and the living was the thinnest. He sauntered over to the door and closed it.

She yawned again. "I'm going to talk to Tristian first thing tomorrow. Convince him I can handle the additional magic."

"You do that. But first I think a few hours of sleep would make you more persuasive." He kissed the top of her head and released her even though it went against all of his being. What he wanted was her in his bed. Where she was safe and secure with his arms wrapped around her soft, sensual body. *Okay, that wasn't the only reason I want her in my bed. Who am I kidding?*

Synn trudged down the hall with Storm trotting behind her. She pushed open the door to the guest room and paused. She turned blew him a kiss and closed the door quietly.

He hoped there'd be no nightmares. The hold Baltizar had over her was troubling not to mention the abilities he was able to wield from the seventh level of Hell. What could Baltizar do should he break free? An icy cold chill shot up his spine. *It didn't matter he was going down one way or another.*

Chapter Twenty-Two
The Time has Come for the Return of Magic and the Powers that Bind

The sun was high in the sky when Synn's eyes blinked open. *What was that God-awful noise?* Someone was clanking pans. The delicious smell of bacon and coffee assaulted her senses. She kicked the covers off, sat up, and stared at the clock. *How could it be one o'clock in the afternoon? I gotta be at work in three hours.* She howled as her warm feet touched the cold hardwood floor. Storm thundered up the hall and pushed her way into the room, all wiggles and snarfuling at her feet and legs.

Laughing, she bent down and rubbed behind the pup's ears. "Good morning to you too." Sliding her feet into her cozy slippers, she padded to the closet and pulled out a black pair of jeans, red sweater, and black boots with fringe at the top. Quickly she dressed and bounded to the kitchen. Yipping and barking, Storm cut in front of her nearly causing her to trip and go sprawling on the floor. *Wouldn't Gavin have a good laugh? Too bad, didn't happen.*

She rounded the corner into the kitchen. Gavin stood next to the stove stirring a pan of scrambled eggs. He scooped out the steaming food onto the plates next to a couple pieces of bacon. "Why didn't you wake me?" Her mouth watered at the enticing aromas.

"You needed your sleep to be your best when you meet with Tristian at three this afternoon. He'll be waiting at the pub for you."

"You set up an appointment for me with him?" Her voice had an edge of irritation to it.

"Nope. He called this morning. Set up the meeting. Mary told him you were scheduled for work by four. Said it wouldn't take long." He shrugged.

"Crap." She eased into the chair by the window and watched as the breeze swayed the trees. Conflicted, she considered her options. On one hand she wanted her power back. On the other, she worried she may not be ready. *I'll just have to trust that Tristian knows best.* She shivered. *That in itself was a scary thought.*

"Isn't that what you wanted?" Taking a pitcher of orange juice from the fridge, he poured the liquid in the two large tumblers on the table. "Toast should be up soon." He picked up a steaming mug of coffee, wrapped his hands around it, and stroked the handle with his thumbs as he slipped into a chair beside her. "Changed your mind?"

"No," she snapped.

"Touchy this morning. Huh?" He took a sip of the coffee. The toast popped, and he pushed up from the chair, buttered the toast, and brought the slices over to the table.

"Nooo. Wonder what he wants?" She forked up a bit of eggs, popped it in her mouth then reached for a strip of bacon.

This time he sat down across the table from her, set his coffee mug down, and picked up a glass of orange juice. He eyed her over the rim for a moment. "Better to get it over with than brood over it all day."

"I don't brood. But you're probably right." She finished her meal and took the plate to the sink, paused, walked to Storm's bowl scraped a couple pieces of egg into her bowl, then rinsed her plate, and put it in the dishwasher. "Are you scheduled at four too?"

"Yep. I'm going to go on in as soon as the kitchen is cleaned up. I'd like to know what he wants too."

"He wants to talk to me—not you." She rinsed the pan, flicked the remaining droplets of water in Gavin's direction, and put the pan in the dishwasher.

Gavin took the dish towel from his waist and snapped her arse with it. She swung around to swat at him, but he'd ducked out of range.

Wiggling his index finger at her he grinned wide. "Too slow, lassie."

****

When they arrived at the pub, Tristian was already there seated at the bar, rolling a pint mug between his hands while conversing with Tim. The wind caught the heavy wooden door and banged it shut behind them. Tristian turned and nodded, motioning them to the stools beside him. Hannah was nowhere to be seen. A few early customers milled around finally settling at the bar or sliding into a booth. Monday's were traditionally slow at the pub.

"A little early to be drinking," Gavin teased.

"It's root beer." He took a large gulp. "Want something to drink?"

"Nope. Just finished breakfast." She perched on the bar stool to his right. "You wanted to see me?"

"Yes." He wiped the condensation from his mug with a napkin and glanced at Tim. "Might we use your office for a few minutes?"

225

"Sure. No flying objects. You break something… you replace it." Tim's lips turned up in a lop-sided grin. "Only messing with you."

Tristian raised an eyebrow, eased off his stool, and jerked his chin toward the office.

She climbed off the seat and followed him turning to toss a triumphant glance in Gavin's direction before flouncing after Tristian.

Tristian paused, letting her go ahead of him, and looked over his shoulder. "Gavin, you're free to join us."

A slow smile spread across Gavin's face. "Be right there."

Tim shook his head and turned back to the stout he was building. He finished it up and slid the pint across the bar to an awaiting customer. Foam from the beer sloshed over and ran down the side of the mug. Tim grabbed a towel and mopped up the mess. Gavin snickered, before getting off the stool and sauntering down the hall.

Tristian took a seat behind the old wooden desk motioning to the two chairs in front of him. "I'll get right to the point. Bruce is concerned at Baltizar's ability to track you. For him to be able to physically move you across the room while projecting a hologram—not an ability we've seen. Hell, a hologram form should only be able to appear and at times talk. He—it should not have any physical attributes."

She plopped down on the chair, all frivolous thoughts and banter with Gavin forgotten. "What do you mean?"

He leaned back in the chair. It ground out a squeak. "I mean Baltizar is drawing magic from this world while he's in the underworld. A dangerous situation."

Gavin stood behind her resting his hands on her shoulders. "So what are we going to do about him?"

"Bruce and I discussed it at great length last night." Tristian paused shifting his gaze from her to Gavin and back again. "We've decided to return your powers."

She pumped a fist in the air, then let her arm drop to her side. *He's not going to like that.* Magic coursed through her body like lightning striking a tree, splitting it apart, and setting it on fire. She reveled in the feeling but feared being unable to control it once her magic is restored completely.

Eyes narrowed, Tristian held her gaze. "Not something to be taken lightly or celebrated. It's serious business. You must temper your emotions lest the power get away from you and harm innocents."

"It's just us," she argued.

"But you had no control. It was a reflex action. Not a metered or a calculated response. The combination of your full magic merged with that obtained from Baltizar is an unknown."

"It won't happen again." It seemed like she was saying that a lot these days. Tristian was right. She'd needed more control. "Can he control me though his magic? Can I control him?"

"I don't know. It appears he is using it as a conduit to track you. If he could control you, I think he would have tried by now."

"Good to know. What about me? Could I use his magic against him?" Her lips twitched at the thought.

"Another unknown. Bruce and Angie will be here by week's end. We will challenge you at every turn until your responses are automatic. Then we will gauge the strength of your magic and ability to control it with ease. Hopefully, we'll discover if you are tethered to Baltizar through his magic in any way. Gale, Erin, Hannah, and Tiarnan will be involved testing you when you least expect it."

"Oh goody. Work is off limits. Right?"

"No… Well…at first…in keeping our existence from the mortals. But what better place to test your abilities than when your attention is divided?"

"But what if I fail—here in the pub." She got to her feet, raised her hands, and spun around. "And the magic is observed by customers who know me—mortals?" She blanched then stared directly at Tristian. "You'll have to dispatch me."

Tristian chuckled. "My reputation must be worse than I thought." He rubbed his jaw thoughtfully. "Wouldn't let that happen. While we'll all be testing you, we'll have your back too. Failure is not an option."

"Yeah, right. Remember who you are talking to." She paced in front of the desk. Still her confidence didn't wane. The magic wanted to snap and sizzle at her finger tips, but she held it back with little effort.

"You have changed so much from the demon that I—we—knew over a year ago. You've gotten in touch with your Fae magic. It's strengthened and settled you. I can see it in our training sessions. You're hardly recognizable. I see no reason to expect anything different now that all your magic has been returned. But Baltizar's magic—we'll have to wait and see its effects. Once you're ready. We'll plan our attack and carry it out when the time is right."

"How much time do I have?"

Tristian frowned. "Not much. Training starts

tonight after your shift." An evil grin twisted his lips. "Maybe during your shift." He leaned over, rested his elbows on the desk, and tented his fingers.

"You can't."

"Oh, believe me I can and I will." He rose and strode toward the door.

"Wait a minute." Gavin held up his hand. "Tomorrow, I'm taking Synn away from all this for a few hours. Can we let her at least have that without tests and training?"

Tristian was silent for a couple beats. "No guarantee. Remember her life as well as yours may one day soon hang in the balance."

"Understood. But I'm not telling you where we are going."

"Fair enough. If we can find you two—game on." He yanked the door open and walked out into the hallway. "Until tonight." A flick of his wrist and he was gone.

Gavin wrapped an arm around her waist pulling her close. "You got this."

"I know. But at what cost to everyone I care about?" She squared her shoulders and strode out the door and down the hall.

At the end of the hallway where it opened into the pub, Bridget stood tapping her foot. "We have a full pub, and you pull a disappearing act?"

"No. Tim knew where I was. Had a meeting." She glanced around. Not a stool or table was empty. "Where'd they all come from? On a Monday no less?"

"I'm sure I've no idea." Bridget tossed her an apron, pad, and pencil. "Break time's over."

She caught the apron, tied it around her waist, and

stuck the rest in the pockets. Felt good to get back to something familiar. *I can handle this. I have to handle this.* Never had she wanted anything so badly as to settle in this little town in Ireland, have friends, family, and fit in without fear stalking her.

Anxiety zinged through her most of the night. A tray of mugs crashed to floor and shattered, she jumped and whirled around magic snapped from her fingertips. She fisted her hands to hide the reaction. Her heart pounded in her chest. A shoving match erupted. She cringed. Gavin told them to take it outside, and they did. Waiting, watching for something to happen made her one big ball of nerves.

Two hours into her shift, she changed her attitude. If Tristian meant to get under her skin by his innuendos in the office, she'd let him, and it couldn't continue. She straightened, squared her shoulders, and marched up to the bar gave Gavin her drink order and waited.

Gavin shoved a tray with a glass of wine and four pints toward her. "Off you go." He winked at her and moved down the bar taking orders and making change.

If this was a weekend night, she expected the crowds, but for a Monday, it was insane. Customers were crawling out of the woodwork. It was standing room only. She shoved through the crowd, taking orders, delivering drinks, making small talk, and trading barbs with the regular clientele. By the end of the night, her feet hurt, and her voice was hoarse from trying to converse over the boisterous voices who'd had too much to drink. A quiet fell over the pub as the last customer walked out the door, and Gavin clicked the lock.

He leaned with his back against the door. "Whew,

what a night. I wouldn't have believed it, if I hadn't seen it with me own eyes."

Tim counted down the till and put the funds in the floor safe. "Good job. Now the lot of you get out of here."

"Da, remember to make the deposit in the morning, I won't be in. We have the night off tomorrow." He shot her a grin. "We have plans during the day, and Ma is watching Storm."

Tim swept his hat off his head and ran his fingers through his hair. "So I've been told." The back door banged open. Steady footsteps sounded as someone made their way through the kitchen and pushed the swinging door open. All eyes met Tristian's gaze as he paused inside the room.

"What?" He glanced at the group staring at him and crooked a finger at her. "We have a date." His lips twitched, and a rare mischievous grin turned the corners of his mouth. "Don't tell my wife." He chuckled.

"Don't tell me what?" Hannah danced through the doors a couple beats behind him.

"We apparently have a date," she teased. "Can't it wait. It's been a hell of a night, and I'm beat."

"Nope. Time waits for no one, and we're burning starlight." He held one of the swinging doors open. As he passed by Hannah, he stopped and gave her a searing kiss. "See ya later."

She caught him around the neck and returned the steamy kiss, then turned attention to her da. "Ma sent me to remind you that you two have an early day tomorrow.

Tim nodded. "Aye."

She sighed and tipped her head back to look

skyward. "Let's get this over with."

With an eyebrow raised, Tristian leveled his gaze at her. "One would have thought a display of more excitement would be in order at having the remainder of your powers restored."

"Oh wow. After the initial—you meant to plant the seed of possibility in— Never mind. I'm ready."

"I did indeed. Took a while for you to settle down, but after you did…good job. Looking for trouble is not being prepared for trouble." He motioned her impatiently through the door. "I'll have her back before dawn."

"Better be before that, she needs a few hours' sleep to enjoy the day I have planned," Gavin growled.

"The day you have planned may be a bit different than anticipated," Tristian shot back on his way out the door.

****

It was the wee hours of the morning when she trudged up the stairs into the house. She took her boots off outside the door so as not to wake Gavin. It had been a grueling three hours. Her returned powers blended seamlessly within her. All was well until Tristian disappeared and reappeared behind her deliberately scaring the bejeebers out of her. All hell broke loose.

Her fingers flared sending sparks as far as the rocky coast line. Wind whipped around her enclosing her in a small tornado. To top it all off, thunder and lightning seemed to come from nowhere crashing all around her and huge rain drops dotted the landscape. Tristian stood frozen in place for what seemed like hours. In reality, it was only a few minutes. Finally, he'd shouted. "Take control. You've got to control all the magic. Rein it in—NOW."

Try as she might, the magic had a mind of its own. In the end, Tristian froze the scene, reached through the wind barrier, cracked it releasing her. Lightning bolts were stuck from midair to the ground, big rain drops were suspended all around them some in mid splash on the ground. The scene was surreal but beautiful at the same time. Tristian's irritated voice had cut though her observations. He didn't appreciate the moment. A tired grin turned up one corner of her lips at the memory.

It had been a massive failure. Eventually she'd been able to rein in her magic, control it, and clean up the mess. Subsequent exercises were more successful. She shook her head as she undressed. Never had she commanded so much powerful magic. Exhausted, she crawled into bed as a satisfied sigh escaped her lips. *I did it. In the end, I met Tristian's expectations. A feat in itself.* Snuggled deep under the covers, she drifted off to sleep. She tossed and turned through several nightmarish scenarios, waking often, until… surrounded by evil she couldn't identify, she screamed herself awake to find a gleaming silver sword floating over her. Storm howled in her crate, and Gavin burst through the door to the room.

"What in the hell?" He skidded to a halt at the foot of her bed.

In all the chaos, she was calm. Her sheets damp from sweat that beaded on her forehead. The sword glinted in the ray of sunlight streaming through the curtains. The jewels encrusted on the handle sparkled as the weapon slowly lowered toward her, handle first. When she reached out, Gavin made a strange sound in his throat. She touched it and wrapped her fingers around it. It was warm. A sudden sense of well-being flooded through her, then the sword disappeared.

"Well, that's quite a rush first thing in the morning. What the hell was that?"

"I've no idea." She sat up in bed and rubbed her eyes with the back of her hand. "Came with some of the ancient magic I inherited? Didn't feel like demon magic. Maybe we should contact Tristian."

"No. No way. Today we're going to have fun and forget all about magic, power, and dire consequences. Besides, Ma's waiting for Storm."

The pup whined then barked. She jumped up, shrugged into a robe, and released Storm from her kennel. The pup raced to the front door and scratched on the door frame. Opening the front door, she thrust the leash in a surprised Gavin's hand as the pup thundered out the door.

"I'll be ready in a minute. The alarm didn't go off. Or I slept straight through it. Then woke up to—well you saw it." Sprinting through the house, she tossed her robe on the bed, took a quick shower, and pulled on the jeans and a red sweatshirt she'd laid out last night. Quickly she pulled on socks then she slipped her feet into running shoes and grabbed Storm's bowls. Mary had a bag of dog food at her place, along with several packages of puppy treats and extra toys.

She yanked the door open to Gavin standing with his hand out as if he was about to open the door. "Ready." She blew out a breath and pushed the sword appearance to the back of her mind. There was only so much she could handle. Gavin was right. She needed to get away from it all.

"Storm's in the truck. I'll get her crate, and we're off. Ma can feed her at the house."

"Sure this isn't too much trouble for your ma?"

A grin like a Cheshire cat turned up the corners of his mouth. "The trouble will be yours, when she returns a spoiled pup that won't listen to a word you say."

"In one day. I doubt it," she said smugly.

He tossed the crate in the back of the truck and chuckled. "Don't say I didn't warn you." The truck bumped up the road. The rain last night had cut ravines in the dirt road. "So how'd it go last night?"

"Better than I anticipated. My control is good as long as I concentrate. I need to get to a point that reaction comes naturally, as it did before. The power, well, I can feel it surging through me if I pay attention to it." She snickered. "There were a couple of incidents. Singed boots, earth and that tree out back of the pub, well, it's a bit taller now. By accident, I conjured a thunderstorm. I couldn't control it. Tristian had to cast a freeze spell, so I had time to get control. I'm afraid it'll be a while before the night creatures venture anywhere near the pub." She paused. "Seriously though with all the power, I worry that my disguising ability may not be strong enough to hide my magic signature any more. Can you feel it?"

Giving her a sideways glance, he nodded. "Aye, it vibrates around you. Not type or strength of magic, but a kind of humming—an almost warning. You know what I mean?"

"That's about what Tristian said and indicated it was unacceptable. I should be able to walk through a group of magical beings without them being aware of what I am or the power I wield. By tonight, I have to be able to arrive for our lessons without Tristian being aware. Does that make sense?"

"It does, but that's a tall order." Gavin rubbed his chin between his thumb and forefinger. "But our plans today will work to your advantage." The truck slowed. Gavin turned the wheel toward the driveway and proceeded to where Mary stood outside waiting for them a picnic basket in hand.

"I thought you said early," she blustered, handing the basket to Gavin through the open window.

"Had to let Synn get some rest. Tristian kept her out so late last night, or I should say early this morning."

Mary crossed to the passenger side of the truck. "So how'd it all go?" Mary tilted her head.

"Not bad. Got a ways to go, but I'll get there." She stepped out of the truck and handed the leash to Mary with an apology. "Storm's not been fed yet or exercised. She may be a handful."

"Good to know. She'll be fine. Won't you, li'l darlin'?" Mary cooed, opening the back door to the truck. She clipped the leash on the wriggling pup which was making it tough to pick her up. When Mary set her on the ground, Storm streaked up the path until the leash stopped her short. The pup pawed at the ground, tugged at the leash, barked, and howled. "Wish I had all the energy." Mary waved at Synn dismissively. "Off with you two. Have a great time."

They got back into the truck. Gavin followed the road back to his house and got out of the truck. "Ready?"

She stared at him in disbelief. "What are we doing here?"

He opened the truck door and held his hand out. "We leave from here."

Chapter Twenty-Three

A Learning Experience in a Magical Place with Unexpected Results

She stepped out of the truck and into Gavin's arms. He lowered her to the ground and kissed her nose. Reaching into the truck, he took a small leather bag from the back of the truck. To her surprise, he stripped right there, stuffed his clothes in the bag, and tossed it to her.

"Where we're going requires gryphon transportation."

She stood transfixed. Her lips formed an O as she blinked up at him. "But won't we be seen?"

"Not with the disguising spell I plan to use." He grinned at her as yellowish feathers with a slight orange cast poked through his hair and framed his face. "As soon as I've shifted, climb aboard, put your arms around my neck, and hold tight. The edges of his form blurred, began to shimmer as a golden light spread across him. A tawny gryphon with large emerald eyes stood before her poised on his powerful hind legs, fur and feathers glistening in the sun. He leaned down nudging her with his beak.

She'd seen him transform a few times before, from a distance, but up close—she sucked in a breath—he was magnificent. Hesitantly, she reached out and touched the feathers on his neck caressing them. He nudged her again, and this time nearly knocked her over. She grabbed onto his neck to steady herself. He curved his body into hers, and she swung onto his back. Wings spread, he sprinted a few yards and with a couple beats of his powerful wings they were airborne.

The ground faded away. Tree tops spread out below. A flock of seabirds gave them a wide berth. She glanced down and saw nothing. They blended into the surroundings, air currents curved around their invisible bulk gliding though the bright blue sky. A couple times it appeared her hair escaped the disguising spell, as did a foot and her hand—for only a split second. Or maybe it was her imagination. She shrugged. Who could tell what was real or imagined as tired as she was.

The forest below gave way to white capped waves on the ocean. She tightened her hold around him. The flight was disconcerting, but she felt so free. The breeze swept her hair from her face, and her shirt flapped behind her. Awe of his ability crashed around her as he banked left and spiraled downward toward a tiny island. They landed in a lush meadow. Tall grass swayed in the backwash of air caused by their arrival.

Easing off his back, she set his bag on the ground and turned in a circle taking in her surroundings. She froze. Rustling in a bush only a few yards from where they stood caught her attention. A shimmering white unicorn bounded toward them but veered to the left at the last moment and disappeared.

She scrubbed her hand over her face and rubbed her eyes. When she opened them again, a water sprite appeared in the creek ahead of them for a moment, then her form returned to the babbling stream with a splash. Crooked trees surrounding the meadow seemed to get closer each time she looked away and then back.

The rock ledge's shape between the meadow and ocean was rounded when they first landed. Now, it had sharp outcroppings and appeared to be changing again. Creatures flitted in an out of the trees and slithered through the grass so quickly, she couldn't be sure what she was seeing.

Cool arms reached around her, and she squealed. Balling up a fist, she swung. When she opened her hand, sparks danced on her palm and froze. She was so entranced at the surroundings that she'd failed to notice Gavin's transformation. He shifted from behind to beside her and covered her hand with his extinguishing the sparks. "Remember, think before you react."

"Where the hell are we? Did you see the unicorn? It wasn't real, was it? Those are only myths. Right?" She wrinkled her forehead as her eyes rounded taking in the shimmering magic before her.

"We are on one of the Phantom Islands."

"But those don't really exist." She paused and stared at him. "Do they?"

Gavin raised an eyebrow and grinned. "Depends who you talk to. Aye…they are steeped in mystery. Many legends claim the Phantom Islands are a mystical land inhabited by mythical creatures. Which in my experience—" he spread his arms wide "—is exactly what we have here."

"Wh—You mean what I'm seeing is not an illusion of your creation, but real?" She abruptly sat on a large rock formation that appeared beside her.

A chuckle rumbled up from his throat. "You give me too much credit for magical talents." He paused. "I brought you here because you needed to get away, get your bearings, and consider all that's happened in the past few days."

"Can Tristian find us here?" She glanced coyly at him from under her black eyelashes. Taking his hand in hers, they walked down a path toward the ocean.

"Not sure. I've used this island for years when I needed to get away and think. Never been interrupted by anyone but the inhabitants of the island. And it's always here." He winked at her. "However, given Tristian's vast knowledge and experience in the magical realms, I'm guessing he is aware of this place. Though he may not consider we know about it as long as you can keep your magic under wraps."

"So my little inadvertent display a few minutes ago when you frightened me, he'd track."

"Probably. You're leaking magic regularly since your powers returned. I had a heck of a time keeping your magic disguised during my flight. Another reason we're here. Practice disguising your power and magic without interference from anyone. Hopefully."

"I don't leak magic. Never have. It could get you killed in my profession." She huffed out a breath.

"Things have changed. You've changed. You're not a warrior controlled by another—being. The Fae magic awakened inside you changes how your other powers react. Now you're not under duress all the time. That being said, the situation you are in now requires you learn to control it all and in a short time. Or the consequences could be devastating to all of us." He leaned over to the ground reaching out with his hand, caught a tendril dark mist trailing from her foot, and tossed it to her.

"Shit." She absorbed the mist in the palm of her

hand. "Was that me?"

He nodded. "My thoughts. Baltizar's magic is trying to escape the Fae influence coursing through your body. You don't notice it because it's not really yours. You need to own and control it if you've any hope of defeating Baltizar once and for all."

The wind whipped around them. Clouds obscured the sun, and the magical creatures disappeared. She landed unceremoniously on her ass when the rock she'd been sitting on disappeared into the earth.

A black cloaked figure glided toward her. The hood obscured his face. He raised an arm and pointed at her. The sleeve slid over his hand, and light glittered inside. Without warning, the figure zinged a bolt of white-hot magic toward her.

She gulped in air quickly raising a hand and absorbed it. *Wow...look at that.* Her heart raced, panic hit her, but without hesitation she took several steps back. Tugging Gavin with her, she raised her arms murmuring an incantation toward the rock that had disappeared moments earlier. The jagged stone erupted from the earth, between her and the figure, rising higher and higher until it formed a solid wall concealing both her and Gavin. It spread wider across the beach at the edge of the meadow. She sucked in a breath and to her surprise blew flames as she exhaled. "Holy shit, that's a new one."

Gavin's eyebrows winged up as he sidestepped her. "Interesting."

When she raised one arm higher, the sword appeared in her hand. Her eyes widened, and her mouth dropped open. The clouds split, and the sun glinted off the silver blade. A stone encased in the hilt of the weapon pulsed white pearlescent to a deep blue, then flickered red as she closed her fingers around the handle. Feeling one with the sword, the power was exhilarating. She fought for control.

In a split second, she had clarity of the situation and influence over the weapon. Holding the sword high over her head, she swung it in an arc in front of her.

A barrier protecting her and Gavin rose between them and the rock. "Identify yourself," she demanded sliding to the side of the rock where she had a view of the intruder. Prodding the figure's magic signature with her power she gasped.

The figure pushed back his hood and shifted to face her arms held out in front of him palms up. "Tristian, enforcer to the Overlord of the Western Hemisphere." He disguised a snicker with a cough. "I see you wield a new weapon." Disappearing, his voice boomed from the forested glade in front of them where he reappeared. "Nice. You've been practicing."

"No—you did that all night. It's become second nature."

"So I did." He stared pointedly at her foot. "But didn't bring forth your new addition."

Rather than follow his glaze, she concentrated her magic at her core and disappeared. Reappearing behind him. "What the hell are you doing? You nearly scared ten years off my life." When she relaxed her arm, the sword in her hand shimmered and faded. Narrowing her eyes at him she began, "I could have—"

"But you didn't. You showed control and forethought. Didn't even follow my gaze when I tried to throw you off your game. Good Job. Remember to keep your detection ability active at all times. Not sure you could have penetrated my disguising spell, but…"

"You didn't sense my arrival. With your powers, you should have."

"I did. Just before I peered around the rock. I sensed your magic. Faint, but there." She straightened her shoulders puffing out her chest a bit. "What do you know about this sword?"

"Over all, you passed this test with flying colors. I'll leave you to enjoy the rest of your day." Not even a breath of air out of place and he was gone.

"But wait." She stomped her foot.

"He's not going to tell you anymore than you're able to ascertain on your own." Gavin grinned wide. "Wow, my girlfriend is a kick-ass warrior with a blade to match."

"Synn always was." A lilting voice floated behind them.

Gavin grumbled and fisted his hands at his side. "This place is busier than the pub on Saturday night."

She whirled around to find Erin seated on a rock smiling. Tiarnan stood behind Erin, hands on her shoulders. His face was unreadable. "How do you like our little slice of heaven?"

Gavin bristled. "I've never seen you on my get-away visits. I've used it for years."

"So you have, laddie. But your moods were so dark the times you were here, we chose to leave you to your brooding." His eyes twinkled as his lips twitched.

"I don't brood. I didn't sense…"

Tiarnan waved his hand dismissively. "No matter. We've come to talk with Synn."

"Excuse me." Gavin backed away a thunderous expression on his face.

"Why what did you do?" Erin teased. "We'll only be here for a few minutes. Didn't mean to interrupt your little holiday. But the appearance of the Sword of Kilara required our intervention and explanation."

"The sword has a name?" Her eyes grew wide.

"Yes indeed. It belonged to your mother's bloodline. The weapon is infused with Fae magic to protect those who wield it."

"Why didn't it protect my mother when she really needed it?" She straightened, squared her shoulders, and stared defiantly at Erin.

"We don't know. The sword was lost centuries before the murder of your family." Erin sighed. "I'm so sorry. We were shocked to feel its presence in the universe last night. Figured you'd be the one that called it."

"I didn't call anyone—thing. I woke up from a terrible dream. Not like I haven't had those before. Even yanked Gavin into a few without meaning to. As you know. But there it was floating above my bed, over my body, shimmering, and pulsing… I don't know. I couldn't help but reach out and touch it. Then poof…it's gone. Only to reappear a few minutes ago."

"When you were threatened," Tiarnan suggested. "As it has always been."

"If the sword is truly yours, the gauntlets can't be far behind." Erin tapped her index finger to her lips. "I can't remember the last documented time those appeared. In ancient times they appeared together. Sword as defense and gauntlets to absorb evil magic and send it back upon the wearers command. Quite useful, though I've never had the opportunity to use either item. Wrong blood line, I guess." She sighed and brushed a bit of sand from her skirt.

"Aye, you were trapped by your own family problems." The corner of Tiarnan's mouth kicked up in a lopsided grin, and he wrapped his arm around Erin. "'Tis all good now. As yours will be one day soon." His gaze shifted from his beloved to her. "Enuff said, we're off—enjoy the rest of your day." In the blink of an eye, Erin and the King of the Faeries were gone. A bit of sand swirled where'd they'd stood before settling at the base of the rock.

Gavin scooped her up and sprinted across the glade, leaving footprints in the grass. An outline of a cottage emerged in the forested landscape as he slowed to a quick walk. "This is what I wanted to show you." Dew drops glistened on the broad leaves of the plants growing on the forest floor. Huge pink blooms with lavender centers swayed in the breeze.

He touched the far corner of the outline, and the full image of the cottage came into view. Flowering vines wound up the walls, and a variety of exotic blooming plants covered the building's roof. Walking through what appeared to be a solid door, he lowered her to her feet.

"Alone at last." Gavin sighed, gathered her into his arms, and lowered his head until their lips met.

Without hesitation, she melted into him. The touch of his lips was a delicious sensation. Her mind reveled in the velvet warmth of his kiss. Her lips parted as she nibbled on his bottom lip, soothing it with her tongue until his slid inside to tangle with hers.

Slipping his hands under her sweater, he unfastened her bra to caress her breasts. His thumb teased her nipples until they were hard. He eased away and pulled her sweater over her head. Planting a tantalizing kiss in the hollow of her throat before kissing his way to her breasts, he took first one nipple then the other into his warm mouth.

As if she were light as a feather, he swept her into his arms, carried her to the bed, and eased her onto it. He joined her, sliding his hand inside the waistband of her jeans. Before she could object, his hand found her moist center. His magical fingers explored, danced, and teased until she let out a low moan and shifted to allow him better access. He pushed her jeans to her knees and continued his ministrations.

On the edge of ecstasy, she reached for him and tugged his shirt over his head. She flicked the button on his jeans open, pulled the zipper half way down, slipping her fingers inside before he stopped her.

"I'm not through. Wait your turn." He captured her wrists in one hand and held them above her head wrapping the bed sheet around them. On his knees between her legs, he shoved her jeans to the floor with his foot. He trailed his tongue around her belly button, tracing the little dip then licked farther down. The ecstasy was pure and explosive. She screamed her release, writhing beneath him as his mouth found its target.

Rising up with a satisfied smile curving his lips, he whispered, "Liked that, did you?" He picked up a lock of her hair and caressed it gently. The fingers on his other hand continued to tease a bit more as she whimpered and shivers of pleasure followed his touch.

Without warning, she arched her back flipping him over. "My turn." She snickered and waved her hand. His clothes landed in a heap on the floor. "Oh…that's much better," she purred. Her gaze lingered over every inch of his luscious body. She straddled him and her fingers caressed his broad chest tracing the sinewy muscles down to the V of soft hair pointing between his legs. There she tangled her fingers in it until she touched him, teased him, and positioned him at her entrance.

"If you don't stop right now, you're going to regret it. It's been too long." He growled. Grasping her around the waist, he arched. She welcomed him into her body, and he buried himself to the hilt. Her breath came in long surrendering moans as the heat of his body rippled down the entire length of hers. She rose up only to have him pull her back down. Exploding in a downpour of fiery sensations, she rode him until the waves of ecstasy throbbed though him. His last thrust sent her over the edge again. Her body shivered, then melted against his, and her world was filled with him. He'd shattered the hard shell that she'd built so carefully around herself. *Now what?*

Chapter Twenty-Four
Preparing for Battle—the Wedding will go On

The trip home from the Island did nothing to quell his desires for Synn. She rode astride his massive gryphon body, the warmth of her sinking into him. He barely maintained control as he landed, lowered her to the ground, and shifted back to human. Even if he couldn't act on his desires, it was satisfying to know he had the same effect on her. Never had a woman touched him like she did. He had no intention of ever letting her go.

Reaching out, he tugged on her long braid as she started to walk off toward her bedroom to change and get ready for work. "Need some help?"

"I think you've helped enough. I barely have the strength to walk let alone work a full shift tonight." She paused for a couple beats. "Thanks to you."

"I aim to please, lass." He couldn't hide his smug expression. Gathering her into his arms, he bent to kiss her.

She placed a couple of fingers to his lips. "That you do." She smiled and wiggled out of his hold. Blew him a kiss before she slipped into her bedroom, closed the door and the lock clicked.

Her intention came across loud and clear. He blew out a breath and trudged to his room to change into work clothes.

****

A few dried leaves rustled as they blew across the street. He held the door to the pub open for her. Laughter, a delicious aroma of Mulligan Stew, and fresh baked bread spilled out into the cold evening air as he peered inside. Tourist season was upon them. There wasn't an empty seat in the pub.

The several hours they'd spent on the island was enlightening as well as a well-deserved break for both of them. By the looks of things, they were going to need it. He waded through the crowd, smiling and calling out to the regulars. Synn followed in his wake then escaped under the pass through and into the kitchen.

"Whew, what a crowd for a week night." From the peg on the wall, she grabbed her change apron, tied it around her waist, and checked the pocket for her pad and pen. The door swung open, and Gavin emerged.

"Aye. It's going to be a wild one tonight. A lot of new faces. The tourists have arrived." He kissed her on the cheek, grabbed clean towels, and piled freshly washed glasses and mugs on a tray. When he started toward the door, he heard footsteps and backed out of the way.

Bridget swung in through the kitchen door skidding to a stop a mere foot from him. "It's about time. Been like this since we opened. You ready?"

"Yep." She squared her shoulders and followed Bridget out into the pub.

Hoisting a tray of glassware, he pushed through the door and slid the glasses into place beneath the bar.

Customers were lined three deep at the counter. Tim and the new guy were working the far end. He scooted to the other end of the bar, taking orders and pulling pints. After a few hours, the crowd thinned. A group of tourists seated at a table in the far corner started a shoving match among themselves. It escalated, and a couple chairs toppled over in front of her. Her tray of drinks crashed to the floor as she tripped over a chair.

Gavin vaulted over the bar and sprinted to the ruckus. He grabbed one man by the collar and the other by the back of the shirt. The material tore revealing bulging muscles and ancient tattoos over most of the younger man's upper torso.

Quinn waded into the fray and encouraged the younger man to go outside and clear his head. When Quinn returned, Gavin had cleared the area. Broken glass and beer spread across the polished wooden floor. Synn brought a mop and a bucket. Katie carefully bent down and picked up the large shards of glass.

A rush of cold air blew through, and the young man returned to the pub. His face twisted, he took a swing at Quinn over the top Katie. Synn blocked the man's arm and shoved him backward with the mop handle. He reached out, grabbed her shoulder as another man cinched his arm around her waist. Gavin reached for her. A glint of silver winked on her wrist and quickly climbed up her arm.

She glanced down as silver encased her other forearm. A look of surprise then recognition spread over her face. Wrenching her shoulder out of the man's grasp, she kicked backward and connected with his groin. He went down like a sack of potatoes. Arms behind her back, she ran toward the ladies' room.

Tristian appeared at Gavin's back and took control

of the flailing young man pinning him to the wall. A hush fell over the crowd, and all movement ceased.

"What the hell is going on?" He stared at Tristian.

"Spell froze all the non-magical beings so I could get a handle on what's going on. This place reeks of magic, but I don't see the culprits that could be wielding…"

Gavin jerked his head in the direction she had disappeared. "It's Synn."

"Oh, no, she's not the only one. This one here—" He slammed the man's head against the wall knocking him out. "Belongs to Baltizar. The others…" He turned to find all the individuals that started the brawl had disappeared. "I suspect this was a test. We failed."

"But Synn, she's…"

"She was the target of this attack." At his sides, Tristian's hands clenched and unclenched. His face flushed with fury. Raising a booted foot, he placed it across the unconscious man's throat. "Not one of you noticed the magic?"

Gale picked her way through the paralyzed crowd pausing in front of Tristian. "I did. But I just got here. It was so well disguised. I'm not surprised no one else noticed." She glanced toward the ladies' room. "Then the Kilara gauntlets made their appearance and the magic was overwhelming which allowed the culprits to escape undetected. It wasn't Synn's fault. Her reactions were perfect to protect the mortals in this establishment."

Bridget stuck her head out of the ladies' room, and her mouth gaped open. "Oh, my God, what in bloody hell?" She ducked back inside and closed the door.

"Looks like we've got some explaining to do,"

Gale said calmly. "Let's hope she's the only one."

"How did she avoid—" Tristian scrubbed his hand over his face.

"If I had to guess, I'd say Synn inadvertently blocked the magic. Bridget must have followed her into the ladies' room where she probably witnessed the powerful Fae magic from the gauntlets." Gale tapped her index finger to her lips.

The ladies' room door creaked open. Synn stepped out tugging Bridget behind her. The faint traces of magic emanating from her direction ceased. Silver gauntlets gleamed under the lights in the pub. The stone in the center of each glowed red fading to blue then to opalescent white and back to red. "How the hell do I get these things off." She held up her arms and walked toward the group.

The corners of Gale's mouth twitched. "Relax. As soon as they sense no danger, they'll disappear. No appearance by your sword?"

"Oh hell—no." Synn glanced around apparently satisfied the sword hadn't made it into the fray. She closed her eyes and took several deep breaths. Gavin moved to her side wrapping an arm around her. The silver wrist guards faded.

"Tristian, I think you'd better remove the spell before we have more to explain than to Bridget—this is a public establishment." He glanced at his da rooted in place, eyes wide and mug in hand. The foam ran down the side of the glass and dripped on the bar. Tim shook his head, reached for a cloth, and wiped at the mess.

The warlock shrugged. "If mortals walk in the door, the spell will snare them. That's why I can't understand what the deal is with Bridget. She should be frozen. But you're right." With a quick wave of his arm, the spell was broken and activity resumed.

Her eyes wide, Bridget remained planted next to Synn.

Quinn stared at his girl. "You all right?"

She nodded slowly, her gaze shifting quickly from each of the persons in the magical group.

"Bridget, let's take a walk." Gale took her friend's arm and started toward the back door that led to the deserted porch.

"Hey, wait up. I'm coming too." Quinn strode toward them.

Synn took two steps to follow, and Tristian snared her arm. "We need to talk."

"Hey, I sure as bloody hell can't handle what's left of this rowdy crowd by myself," Katie howled. "Get your arses back here."

Her voice broke the uneasy mood floating over the group. Synn smiled while the others chuckled. "Point taken." She glanced at Gale and Bridget then locked eyes with Tristian, his expression stormy. "This matter will have to wait."

Tristian gave her a curt nod. "I don't like it."

Shrugging one shoulder, she flounced to the tables and resumed taking orders, then made her way to the bar.

Having returned to serving customers, he touched her arm as she approached the bar and rattled off a list of drinks. "You doing all right?" He searched her eyes before setting a tray on the bar, grabbing a couple mugs, and begin to fill her orders.

"I have to be." She picked up the loaded tray and sauntered into the crowd.

****

The next morning Synn sat at the kitchen table hands wrapped around a cup of steaming coffee turning it around and around. Storm raced in circles near the table and between Gavin's feet as he scrambled eggs and fried bacon. A pitcher of orange juice sat in the center of the table, and two small glasses waited next to the plates. "Synn, pop down a couple pieces of bread in the toaster." He glanced at the whirling dervish at his feet. "I can't move without stepping on your pup this morning."

"Sure." She grinned and got up doing as requested. "Any word from Tristian this morning?"

"Nope. I was surprised that he left the pub without talking to us—you last night."

Shrugging one shoulder, she took a sip of the coffee and set the mug on the table. "Hannah came in shortly after the commotion and said something to him. They left together."

She bounced a ball of crackling light from hand to hand, drawing it into different shapes, and colors. Storm settled at her feet intently watching the ball.

Though ill advised, he'd noticed playing with magic was a way of soothing her nerves or working out a problem. Part of the time, he didn't think she realized she was doing it. Of late, she'd made a habit of keeping her magic signature disguised as Tristian insisted in her training. "Expecting problems?"

"No. Not looking forward to working with Tristian today. I should have—" The toast popped. She jumped up leaving the ball of magic hanging in the air. Quickly, she buttered the slices and placed the stack on a plate.

The unspoken intent of her unfinished statement

255

hung between them. He jerked his chin toward the dog. "You better extinguish that ball before Storm pounces on you in an attempt to get to it and gets hurt. Breakfast is ready." Picking up the skillet off the stove, he slid eggs onto the plates, scooped the last bit of egg into a bowl over the pup's kibble. He left it on the counter to cool, put the pan in the sink, and eased into the chair beside her.

She stabbed a piece of egg as if it was the enemy and raised it halfway to her mouth when a knock sounded on the door. "It's Tristian." Slipping the bite in her mouth, she washed it down with a sip of coffee and picked up a piece of toast.

He snatched the piece from her, taking a bite and padded over to the door, letting the warlock in. "Good morning."

"Morning."

She took a bite of bacon and chewed as Tristian strode into the room. "To what do we owe the pleasure bright and early this morning?"

"Bruce and Angie arrived earlier. He wants us all to meet at the ruins of a castle on the coast within the hour."

She swallowed and raised an eyebrow. "Who all is included in this little impromptu meeting?"

"Magic folk involved in last night's fiasco including Bridget and Quinn." He took out a piece of paper from his coat pocket. "Here's a map. No magic, we'll all arrive by mortal means."

"But Bridget had no idea what is going on," she protested.

"She does now. Quinn opened her eyes last night. Not how he'd planned on telling her, but he and I had a little conversation. Eventually, he understood it had to be done."

"She had no idea he was a gryphon?" Her amazed stare shifted from Gavin to Tristian. "Bloody hell, she lived with the man."

Chapter Twenty-Five
Meeting in a Castle Ruins Takes an Unexpected Turn

She leaned forward fighting the wind as she walked up the winding trail to the castle ruins on the rocky cliffs. Pulling her coat close around her, she tugged her hat down over her ears. Gavin touched her on the shoulder and said something, but his words were lost in the strong gusts buffeting them rounding the bend.

"Bruce could've found a more out of the way meeting place, but I'm not sure how," she grumbled.

"Had his reasons," he yelled over the howl of the winds.

She stopped and stared at the crumbling stone castle and shook her head. A groan echoed through the stone structure when Gavin pushed open the heavy wooden door which barely hung on its hinges. Inside the castle at the far end of a huge room stood Bruce and Angie, Tiarnan and Erin, Hannah and Tristian, Bridget and Quinn warming themselves in front of a stone fireplace with steaming beverages in hand.

The roaring fire sent up orange and blue flames a couple feet high. Gale was snuggled down in a large overstuffed chair several feet back from the fire. Her feet were tucked beneath her.

"Guess we're the last to arrive," Gavin whispered.

She shot him an incredulous look and backed out the open door blinking up at the crumbling structure.

"Come on, Synn. You can admire the architecture—or lack thereof—later," he urged.

"B-but…" She paused and took two steps through the door and rubbed her eyes, not believing what she was seeing for the second time.

This time Bruce's booming voice echoed off the stone walls as he turned to face them. "Welcome. Come warm yourself by the fire before we proceed. You look absolutely frozen."

"The castle is enchanted." Gavin waved an arm in front of him. "I've heard stories about them, but never been inside one."

Her mouth formed an O, and her gaze flitted around the huge open room. Stone staircases hugged opposite sides of the walls towering up to what appeared to be second and third floors. Paintings on the walls depicted bloody battles on one side and a magical faerie land on the other. Portraits of Bruce and Angie, and Andre and Matiah hung on either side of the fireplace. "Is this your place?" Sidling next to the fireplace, she glanced in Bruce's direction. *Ohhh…it was so warm.*

"No… It belongs to my father. He prefers the tropical climate of Tahiti these days but keeps this for special occasions. It shields against prying eyes or magic of any creature. Consequently, the venue fit our needs today."

"I don't mean to be disrespectful, my lord, but this is my battle. Baltizar brought his minions here to disrupt the lives of innocents because of me. I can't allow anyone to become collateral damage because of me."

Bruce looked thoughtful, tented his fingers, and rocked back on his heels. "First, it's Bruce. Not my lord. You know better, Synn. Second, you may be his intended target for revenge. However, he's crossed the line once again regarding Brandy and Stefan. This time disrupting their wedding plans. I owe a debt to Stefan for saving Angie's life. Baltizar's behavior is traitorous. We're going to terminate him and anyone connected to him."

Heat rushed to her cheeks. "I see."

"I don't think you do, but here's what I have in mind." He took out a large rolled sheet of paper and spread it out on a massive wood table in the center of the room. With a nod from her husband, Hannah fired up her laptop and projected a grid on the stone wall along with a time line. They all gathered around to get a better vantage point.

****

In a star strewn night sky, a few wispy clouds floated across the full moon. She stood in the backyard watching Storm race around like a Tasmanian devil, squeaking a toy and enjoying freedom from the leash. Gavin came up behind her and wrapped an arm around her.

She'd felt him coming and leaned back against his broad chest, tilting her face up to his. "Is he really willing to annihilate a whole race of dark demons to eliminate Baltizar?"

He searched her eyes for a moment, brushed his lips over hers. "I don't think it will come to that, but to answer your question—yes. If they've acted on Baltizar's behalf, their days are numbered. It's not like they didn't know whose bidding they were doing—especially after he was banished to the seventh level of Hell."

"What if he's in their mind, controlling them?"

"As he did you? Breaking free is their only chance, as you did. No use rehashing this, it's not our decision to make. Bruce is determined to end him once and for all, including any followers who might rise up later and challenge. As Bruce stated in the castle, he's been in contact with commander Nathanial North of the elite legion of angel warriors. Commander North gave his go ahead with offers of assistance if needed. His legion stands at the ready. Baltizar's days are numbered, one way or the other."

Her eyes widened. "I guess I missed that briefing."

He shrugged. "I believe the final straw was his attempt to abduct you in a business establishment full of mortals. Under normal conditions, Tristian and his team would handle the assignment. Since you wield the sword, wear the gauntlets, and have made it clear you want to finish him—"

"How can I be expected to wield Fae magic of the Kilara when I've held the sword only once and kinda controlled the gauntlets last night. Yet, never felt their power together. The lives of my friends, family, and others depend on my ability to cause the fatal blow to Baltizar." She slumped against him. "This is a lot."

"Aye, it is, but you'll not be battling him alone. Tristian can end him and will if necessary. Be careful what you wish for—you're being given the chance." He took a couple of steps back, gently gripped her shoulders, and turned her to face him. "You got this."

I sure hope so. Living here had changed her. There

was a time when an assignment was given, she'd carry it out without a thought as to harm to herself or the intended victims. Her actions didn't have consequences, unless she failed—which never happened until Brandy and Stefan.

She rubbed the back of her neck. If she was honest, she'd always known her life in servitude to Baltizar went against something buried deep inside her. The others carried out his commands without consciences or remorse. Yet it seemed she was fighting against herself even though he assured her his bidding was what she was meant to do.

Now she knew why. Deep down, she wasn't a vicious demon, but half Fae and half demon. She straightened a little and squared her shoulders Her ancestors were members of the elite Guardians Guild protecting man and magic kind—not destroying them.

"Hey lass, where have you gone?" He waved a hand in front of her face then leaned down and kissed her nose. "Your dog is digging up me flower garden. Ma will not be pleased."

She blinked and searched the yard. Sure enough butt in the air, front paws throwing dirt everywhere was her pup. "Storm. Stop that right now." Sprinting out to the middle of the yard, she reached down, grabbed the pup by its mane, and shook once. "No. No. Bad dog." She snatched the pup up holding Storm so the flailing muddy paws faced away from her as chunks of mud went flying in every direction. She kicked the dirt clods into the foot-deep gaping hole. Staring guiltily at the mound of rich, black dirt piled up with bulbs and roots sticking out every which way, she turned to Gavin. "I'm soooo sorry."

He snickered. "In the grand scheme of things, that's minor." He knelt, scooped the dirt into the hole, placing the bulbs and plants upright then tamping the soil down. Pushing to his feet, he brushed his hands together in an attempt to dislodge most the dirt and mud from his fingers. "Let's get that mud ball in the house and cleaned up. Tomorrow, I'll replace the fence around the garden. I was going to clean it out anyway. The growing season is over."

She was silent for a couple of beats. "If we are going to have an on-going problem at the pub with his minions, I can quit."

"Don't be ridiculous. Your Overlord said business as usual until the veil thins around All Hallows' Eve and his plan is put into action."

Chapter Twenty-Six
An Uneasy Calm Settles in Until the All Hallow's Eve Celebration

It had been over a month since Bruce revealed his dangerous plan at the castle meeting. Since that time, it had been far too calm for Gavin's liking. On one hand it was good for Synn. Her lessons with Tristian were uninterrupted and met with success after success building her confidence and abilities.

She now wielded the Sword of Kilara and the silver gauntlets power as if she was born to both with only a few hiccups. Like the time she'd blindsided Tristian when he came in though the back door to the pub's kitchen in unfamiliar clothing and brandishing a warlock's dagger. She'd used the gauntlets protection with Fae magic and sent him flying back through the door. He was unceremoniously deposited in a bog one-half mile away. She shielded herself and the pub from his powerful magic. A test well completed.

He was so proud of her, but his feelings were tempered with what was to come.

Tourist season brought all kinds of new faces to the pub. The establishment was filled to capacity most nights making it hard to tell friend from foe. He'd allowed only a couple of out of town bands to play at the pub early on in the month. Quinn and his band were booked every weekend through mid-November. Cori did gigs on Wednesday night and joined his band on weekends.

Sometimes Quinn showed up during the week and accompanied her on the guitar or piano. Home life was a bit rough around the edges for Quinn since revealing his true nature to Bridget. He claimed she was taking it in stride, but…

The schedule kept the tourists entertained and coming back for more. However, the bookings were met with grumbles of favoritism from other out of town groups. In previous years, he'd usually booked different bands every weekend through the tourist season. He couldn't take the chance a new member of an out of town band was a plant.

Under normal conditions, he'd be ecstatic the pub was doing so well. However, unfamiliar faces in the pub set his nerves on edge these days, especially when he had to work the kitchen and couldn't keep an eye on things out in the pub. There was no doubt in his mind Synn could take care of herself—but still…

All Hallow's Eve was less than a week away. Bruce, Angie, and Tristian had planned a huge celebration that night at Andre's castle in hopes of luring Baltizar and his minions out into the open and away from the town. The knot in his stomach grew with each passing day until the night finally arrived.

He stowed the overnight bags in the back of the pickup, along with Storm's crate, and enough food until they returned. The pup would be spending the night with Katie and her family. Synn wasn't happy about being separated from Storm, but she didn't want her in harm's way either.

She boosted the pup into the back seat with a chew

stick, unclipped the leash, hooked Storm's harness to the seatbelt, closed the door, and climbed into the front seat. "All set," she said cheerfully dressed in her pixie costume.

He drove by Shaughnessy's pub which was staffed by mortals tonight with a planned celebration for All Hallow's Eve, featuring a well-known out of town band, since Quinn's band was playing at Bruce's Halloween bash at the castle. He had vetted the band himself. A few of Tristian's team were providing security. Nothing out of the ordinary here.

He'd been hesitant to include Quinn's band at the castle. But he and Quinn had grown up with the guys in the band who were all gryphons and one warlock. They knew the score. Besides the band would be gone before midnight.

Ma and Da were fit to be tied when Bruce told them his plan and why their presence was required at the castle. Staff from Bruce's estate in America and Andre's home in Tahiti were catering the soiree at the castle. With any luck it would all be over tomorrow and his sister's wedding could be the focus once again.

Next stop, he dropped off Storm and her crate. Synn left instructions for her care with Katie and explained the food, treats, and chewies. "Synn, come on." He wrapped an arm around her waist and tugged her toward the truck. "Katie knows how to take care of a dog. We're only gone one night."

She arched a brow but allowed him to lift her into the truck. Once settled in the seat, she rolled down the window and waved to Katie and her family. "Bye Storm, we'll be back tomorrow." She paused and under her breath said, "I hope."

"I heard that."

The cliff-side castle looked forlorn as he drove up the winding road. They followed the same foot path up to the ruins as before. The battered heavy wooden door stood formidably at the entrance. He pushed it open to dank and darkness.

Synn hesitated then stepping inside. "Are you sure—"

The minute the massive door closed with a groan, music, mouth-watering aromas, and laugher assaulted his senses. The enchanted castle was aglow with soft candle light from pumpkins and silver candelabras. A starlit night sky decorated the ceiling, complete with a full moon in the far corner.

"Gale has a way with magical decorations." Synn pirouetted in a full circle admiring the décor.

"Aye, she does." Gavin nodded.

Long wooden tables and chairs lined the edge of the dance floor. Quinn and his band played an Irish jig on stage in the middle of the dance floor. Suddenly, Cori breezed out onto center stage playing her fiddle in traditional Irish garb. Her bow was decorated with streamers of different colored ribbon flying about her head as she step-danced across the stage. Her solo lasted only a few minutes, but the performance was breathtaking to an Irishman who could step dance with the best of them.

The famous Irish dance troupe had nothing on Hannah, Gale, Bridget, Tiarnan, and Erin as their feet flew to the lively music. Tristian leaned against the bar beside Mary and Tim, talking to a young man. All were tapping their feet to the beat.

"Welcome," Bruce greeted him with a hearty clap

on the back. "Glad you could make it. Bar is to your left." He made a wide sweeping motion with his arm. "Buffet is to your right. The food will be ready shortly."

Angie hugged Synn first then him. "Bags still in the truck?"

He nodded. "I'll get them later."

She glanced toward the door and snapped her fingers. "They'll be in your room, up the stone steps to the second floor first door to your right." Angie grabbed Synn's hand and dragged her toward the dance floor. "Looks like fun."

Synn shook her head vigorously. "Never tried, wasn't able."

"Well...you are now. Come on. I'm of the understanding Gavin and his family can put all of us to shame. Besides the exercise will burn off the adrenalin that is rolling off you." Angie, dressed in a traditional witch's costume, complete with striped purple and black stockings, also reached for Gavin's hand. He danced away from them with a kick and a twirl and joined Hannah.

After two more traditional Irish Jigs and Reels, he was winded and searching for Synn. She was sitting with Bruce and Angie. He walked up behind her and wrapped his arms around her, then spirited her onto the dance floor for a slow dance before joining the other couples at the buffet.

Waiting for a slice of prime rib, he glanced at the lad dressed in full Scottish highlander regalia standing next to Gale, who was dressed as a faery princess, and extended his hand. "Gavin Shaughnessy. You're a brave man to come dressed as a Scotsman on Irish soil." He grinned. "Even on Halloween."

"Dillon Dunlop," the lad said with a smile, juggling his plate from one hand to the other and grasped the outstretched hand. "She insisted." He jerked his chin toward Gale. He recognized the Glasgow bur in the young man's voice. "Not from around here."

"Naw. Glasgow. Gale refuses to leave Ireland. I'm here to find us a place to live when we get married. The accommodations above her shop isn't my idea of a home. My family is not thrilled, but they love Gale—they'll adjust." Dillon took the tongs and put a slab of prime rib on his plate and picked up silverware.

"Oh, wow congratulations. Gale didn't share the good news." *No disguising spell. He's a warlock.*

"Been a little busy." She paused for a beat and flipped her hair to the side. "Besides, Gavin Shaughnessy, my personal life 'tis none of your business," Gale teased. "I was savoring the memory of his proposal, before everyone gets to telling us how to plan the wedding." She wound her arm around Dillion's waist. "Dillon, this is Synn, Gavin's lass." Holding out her plate, she waited until Dillon served a smaller piece of meat and added a roll.

One eyebrow winged up, but he reached out a hand to Synn. "Nice to meet you."

"Same here." She shook his hand then released it turning her attention to her friend and squeezed her arm. "Pretty big secret." Picking up the plate Gavin filled for her, she added a roll and glanced toward the table. "Where do you want to sit?"

"Don't feel bad. The only person that knew was my cousin Cori." Gale blushed. "No time to tell ya with all that has happened."

Synn heaved a heavy sigh. "You got that right. Cori is your cousin?"

"Yep."

"Dunlop. Huh?" Gavin rubbed his chin. "Any relation to Bessie Dunlop?"

"Aye, she was my great-great-great-great grandmother on my da's side." Dillon moved toward the chairs where Erin and Tiarnan sat dressed in their usual attire.

"Powerful line of witches," Synn chimed in. "Dark time in Scottish history." She followed Dillon and Gale leaving the chair at the end of the table for Gavin and took the one on the other side where Tristian and Hannah ended up.

"Aye, that it was," Gavin agreed wiping his brow. "That was quite a workout. Been a while since I've danced." He pulled Synn's chair out, waited for her to sit, and plopped into the chair at the head of the table, noting his da sat at the other end.

Andre breezed in with Matiah on his arm. "Sorry we're late. A disturbance in the time and space line delayed our port between." He waved a hand dismissively. "To be expected on this day. Almost didn't port but got the all clear from several sources."

Bruce stood. His chair made a scraping sound as he slid it back. "What can I get you and Mother to drink?" Waving an arm toward the buffet, he grinned. "Help yourself to the food." He paused. "I wasn't sure you were going to make it."

"Wouldn't miss the first party held here in over a century." He winked at his wife.

Angie jumped up nearly knocking over her chair in an effort to reach Bruce's parents and engulf them in a hug. "So glad you came."

"Son, sit down. I know my way around this place." Andre stopped and surveyed the room. "Like what you've done here."

Bruce nodded in acknowledgment and eased into his chair.

The conversation was light during dinner. No one wanted to discuss what they were expecting with the band members still there. The band members had all grown up with him and Quinn. They'd learned early on not to ask too many questions. Quinn had been read into the situation because of Bridget.

After dinner the band played a couple more sets. They were out of the castle an hour before midnight.

The knot in Gavin's stomach was still there, but no trepidation in his gut. *Was it going to happen tonight? Will Bruce follow through with his plan at the stroke of midnight?*

Almost as if Bruce had read his mind, he stood. "It's done. Now we wait. Tristian and I will take the first shift. If anyone wants to get a little shut eye, now may be a good time."

Chapter Twenty-Seven

All Hallow's Eve Came and Went Without the Expected Result—Now What?

By the next morning, there was no sign that Baltizar had breached the veil between Hell and the mortal world. Even though Synn understood Bruce had lifted the enchantments keeping Baltizar in the seventh level. Creatures with magic signatures were detected near the grounds of the castle, but they didn't venture inside the boundaries or near the building itself.

By the time she and Gavin descended the stone steps, the couples in attendance last night were in the main hall of the castle lined up in front of the breakfast buffet. She crossed the hall and picked up a plate. Last night her stomach was in knots anticipating the worse and hoping for the best to enjoy the fare provided.

This morning she was famished. Her mouth watered as she surveyed the set up with eggs, bacon, hash browns, various fruits, and veggies along with an assortment of meats. When she lifted one of the warming lids, a mouth-watering aroma of fresh-baked cinnamon rolls burst into the air. The rolls were huge, with melting creamy frosting. She licked her lips.

Angie thrust a piece of bread on her plate. "You'll love it. It's Maeva's world famous coconut bread. Go on, take a bite."

She looked longingly at the cinnamon rolls but tore

off a corner and nibbled on the bread. "Mmm… This is fantastic." She took another slice. "Is Maeva here?"

"No. She doesn't care for Ireland's climate. But she sent several loaves with us." Matiah smiled. "Never leave the island without it."

Glancing around, she arranged the bread on her plate making room for the cinnamon roll. Picking up the tongs, she plopped one on her plate. The gooey frosting puddled on the edge of her plate. "For later." She grinned and grabbed another plate for her eggs and bacon.

"Hungry?" Gavin chuckled heaping a variety of food on his own plate.

Tim filled his plate and turned to Bruce who stood next to him. "Where do we go from here. Mary and I have to return to the pub today, as well as the rest of our staff that were off yesterday." He glanced from Gavin to Bridget and then to Synn.

"I can stay at my cottage or Gavin's until the bastard shows himself. I promised to pick up Storm early from Katie's. Are we sure he knows? Why…" She was babbling, but she couldn't seem to help herself.

Bruce held up a hand. "Things didn't go as we thought last night. But we can't put individual lives on hold indefinitely." He paused and glanced at Tristian.

"We go on like nothing happened. Keep your guard up. It's a waiting game now. Hannah and I plan to stay through the wedding and probably until after the first of the year." Tristian balanced his plate on one hand while he poured a glass of orange juice.

"Angie and I have to return to DC but will be available at a moment's notice. I expect to be kept in the loop."

"Will do." Tristian leaned over and sipped his over full glass of orange juice.

Tiarnan, his plate piled full, eased down at the table. "Erin and I will go about our daily routine, ready and waiting." He picked up the glass of orange juice in front of him.

"We'll not be far," Andre said mysteriously. "Not going home until this is finished."

"What about Brandy's wedding?" Mary blurted. "I can't be expected to plan a joyous occasion while waiting for the devil himself to destroy all we hold dear."

There it was hanging out in the open. What everyone feared most. She paced around the table. The silverware rattling against the china plate she carried. "I could leave…disappear…"

"No," Gavin bellowed. "Not going to happen. You're not the only one on his radar. If you'll remember, this whole thing started because he programmed you to kill Brandy and Stefan in order to get back at Tristian."

"But I failed. He holds me accountable for his downfall and banishment." She licked her lips. A wane smile turned up the corners of her mouth. "I did defect to the light side."

Gavin groaned. "Aye, 'tis true, but you are only one piece of the puzzle. As long as you stay put, we'll have your back and stand a better chance of terminating his existence including his followers." Tawny feathers sprouted along his hair line and sticking out through his hair. "Eliminating future risk to Brandy and Stefan. You're not the only…"

The feathered effects of his temper were endearing. She'd never tell him that as she bit the side of her cheek in an effort not to smile. "I get it. But I'm still putting everyone in danger—even the innocents in our own little town." She shook her head. "I can't be responsible for... I don't deserve."

"Without you, the Sword and Gauntlets of Kilara won't be part of our arsenal," Erin pointed out. "A very important part."

"You mean if I leave, you still plan to confront Baltizar?" she asked incredulously.

"Of course." Tiarnan nodded.

Still chewing the last bite of bacon, Tristian's arm shot up. He took a swig of coffee, swallowed. "Enough! This is what will happen." The room quieted, and everyone stared at him. "Business as usual. Synn and Storm will stay at Gavin's." He glanced in Mary and Tim's direction. "I need Synn's schedule for the foreseeable future. Try not to deviate from that schedule. If you have to, notify me immediately. Understood?"

Mary nodded.

Tristian gave her a thumbs up. "Bridget, stick close to the magic people in your life. Quinn, no out of town gigs until the situation is terminated. The rest of you, stay alert and don't go out alone. Safety in numbers. Questions?"

"How do mere mortals contact you." Quinn's voice held a note of contempt.

"You don't need to worry about it since you're not a mere mortal. Bridget will need to stay close."

Bridget whirled around, hands on her hips and a gaze locked on Quinn.

There it was. Quinn had been outed to everyone. He ran his fingers through his hair before leaning down and whispering in Bridget's ear. Her eyes went wide.

Scrubbing his hand over his face, Tristian paused then pointed to Andre. "Sir, any chance you have a mobile version of your AI, Alish?"

"As a matter of fact, I have a beta version we are experimenting with. She doesn't have all the bells and whistles of Alish at home. But she's workable on my secure mobile phone and tablet. Why?"

"As a way of keeping track of the necessary players from one location. Can that be done in real time?"

"Possibly." He scraped the last bit of egg off his plate and slipped it in his mouth.

"Andre, I'll wager you and I can put our heads together and make it work. We could set up a command center in Ma and Da's house." Hannah's gaze switched to her parents who nodded in consent. "Ever been hacked?"

"Not so far. Magic and distance have kept her safe so far, but here— No guarantees, especially mobile." Andre leaned back in his chair and put his arm around Matiah's shoulders.

"Why don't you and Matiah plan on staying with us," Mary said. "We have plenty of room, and you'd be in close proximately to Tristian and Hannah." She grinned. "They're a bit overbearing, but they'll grow on you. Hannah is a whiz on the computer."

Hannah rolled her eyes at her ma. "It's a great idea."

"It's settled. We'll meet you there after we close up the castle. Don't want any undesirables taking up residence." Andre chuckled.

****

"I don't play the waiting game very well." Synn dressed in black jeans, a garnet sweater, and black ankle boots. She let Storm out of the crate, leaned down patting the pup's head, and scratching behind her ears. "It's off to the pub for us. Don't get into trouble. We've enough to go around as it is."

Storm cocked her head to one side, perked up an ear, and leaned into her. It was almost as if the pup was trying to understand what was being said and comfort her at the same time. "Woof, woof." The pup trotted out of the bedroom to the back door and waited patiently to be let out.

"What are you complaining to Storm about now?" Gavin sauntered into the kitchen behind her, wrapped an arm around her waist, and kissed her on the cheek. "Oh, you smell fantastic today."

"As opposed to what?" She turned in his arms.

"I merely meant that I like the fragrance you are wearing. That's all. You always smell delectable. Today you simply are wearing one of my favorites. Don't read more into that than there is." He grinned. "Wanta grab a bite at the pub, or fix something here? Larder is nearly empty. Need to stop at the market during our break and stock up."

"Any news from Brandy?" She glanced at him.

"Nothing new. Looks like she and Stefan will arrive the last week of December. Ma suggested your New Year's Eve wedding idea, and Brandy liked it. So that's how Ma is proceeding. Hannah will be tied up with the surveillance until all hell breaks loose." He snickered.

"It's not a laughing matter." She bristled.

"Aw come on. It's a little funny." He jiggled her arm and pulled her in for a more intimate kiss. "I've been thinking."

"Oh, now that's something different." She snickered.

He ignored her. "You share my house; why not share my bed? We've cleared the major hurdles that were in place when you moved into the cottage. Not to mention the unexpected ones. Face it. We're a couple, and everyone acknowledges it."

"Until I meet the bastard face to face and destroy him, I can't be sure he isn't able use the magic he inadvertently transferred to me to somehow control me."

"I'm sure enough for both of us."

"Impossible. You've never met him; you can't know…"

"The nightmares you were so kind to share were enough to convince me of what he's capable of. But you're stronger and smarter now. The awakening of ancient Fae Guardian blood pulsing through your veins, not to mention their awesome weapons at your disposal make you the winner in my book. That magic link to him that you fear is going to be his downfall. Mark my words."

"I'll do that." She glanced at her watch, then walked to the door, opened it, and called Storm in from the backyard. "Guess we're eating at the pub today."

"If we don't get to work, Ma is going to have both our hides, and that's something to worry about." He snagged their coats off the hooks inside the front door.

She grinned, clipped the leash on the pup, and

sprinted to the truck. "You got that right." She couldn't continue dreading each day and wondering if it would be her last or her friends or family…

From experience, she knew Baltizar would take his sweet time. He'd always told her revenge was a dish best served cold. She was sure he was aware he was no longer shackled to the seventh level of Hell. However, he'd realize it was some type of trap. *What was he up to?* She straightened her shoulders and climbed into the truck determined not to let thoughts of him consume her every waking minute.

****

Days stretched into weeks and into the month of December without a trace or sighting of Baltizar or his minions. Plans continued for the wedding without mention of the situation to Brandy or Stefan. She was surprised that Mary and Hannah were able to keep that information away from Brandy.

More and more of Bridget's responsibilities rested on her shoulders as her friend took over Mary's duties. Mary devoted most of her time to the wedding arrangements. The added work load helped keep her mind on her duties rather than an appearance by Baltizar. Being ever vigilant had its downfalls too. The full throttle adrenalin feeding her fight or flight response hindered rather than helped the situation.

Third week of December, Bruce and Tristian went on the offensive using magic in an attempt to flush the bastard out. As a result, rumblings surfaced of Baltizar's death at the hand of his own demons for putting their entire ranks at risk of annihilation.

That was pure unadulterated bullshit. Before she switched sides, there were always murmurs of mutiny in his ranks but were rarely acted upon. The few times that a plot was discovered, he terminated the individual leaders and everyone associated with them as an example to others. Knowing the Overlord of the Western hemisphere and his teams were gunning for them might have turned the tide. But she doubted it.

Chapter Twenty-Eight

When You Least Expect it—Are You Still Prepared?

Synn inhaled deeply enjoying the pine scent from the fresh cut Christmas tree, evergreen garland, and wreath mixed with the mouthwatering aromas wafting from the pub's kitchen. She sniffed, ohhhh—fresh baked bread and rolls. Mary must be here. She considered sneaking into the kitchen and snatching a few rolls from the warmers while Mary's back was turned. A trick Gavin used routinely but nearly always got caught.

Stopping to survey the sparkling holiday decorations, she smiled. Never had she had so much fun. Sunday before last, at Shaughnessy's, the pub staff and friends had put up Christmas decorations. When all the bows, lights, garland, and baubles were hung, they'd circled the piano and sang carols. Mary baked cookies. Gavin and Tim served stew and fresh soda bread. A far cry from her holiday's past. She smiled caressing the garland draped around the fireplace mantel.

The pub was quiet now, and she savored the silence. In the next couple hours, customers would fill the room shouting holiday greetings to each other as the band set up on stage. Cori would perform tonight. The establishment would be filled to the rafters.

Lifting the pass-through at the end of the bar, she dropped it back into place without a sound. She silently padded to the swinging kitchen door and peeked in. Mary was nowhere in sight. The back door was ajar. Cold air seeped in as she tiptoed her way across the floor to the warmers. She stuffed a fresh-out-of-the-oven roll in her pocket and took a bite out of the one in her hand that was nearly too hot to handle. *Heaven.*

The sound of footsteps on the porch had her whirling around and scooting out the swinging doors, careful to still their motion behind her.

"Synn—Bridget, is that you?" Mary called out as she bustled through the back door. "Katie called in sick."

"It's me," she said around a mouthful of bread. *Busted.* "Thought I'd see if you needed any help."

"And help yourself to the fresh bread, I'll wager." Mary waggled a finger at her.

"How'd you know?" She pushed into the kitchen.

"I didn't until now. At least not for sure." Mary chuckled and swatted her on the behind. "You're picking up bad habits from my son, you are."

"Storm is in the little corral Tim built for her in the storeroom. Gavin will be here shortly. Tim called and wanted him to stop by the house on his way. So the pup and I walked here. Good exercise."

Mary turned and eyed her carefully. "You okay?"

"Yep. Now what can I do?"

Gavin burst through the back door carrying a couple crates of cider and a paper bag. "Da said you were making hot spiced cider tonight, and we were low on cloves and cider." He swung the crate up on the counter then tossed the paper bag to her. A bottle of cloves rolled out of the bag and landed on the floor. "Where do you want it?"

Mary glanced at the crates. "You better have several more of those, boyo."

"Da's got the back end of the truck full." He strode out the back door.

Tim came in carrying two crates, sat them down on the floor, and brushed his hands together. "I'm off to pick up Brandy and Stefan in Dublin. See you in a few hours." He kissed Mary on the cheek. "Sure you don't want to come?"

"We're short-handed as it is. You go on and drive careful." She put her hands on either side of his face and kissed him full on the lips.

Tim pulled reluctantly away holding her hands in his. "Aye." He hurried out the door.

She looked over her shoulder at Synn. "You can start pouring the cider into the large kettles over there on the stove. We'll make the first couple batches now, let it simmer, then make another just before opening. The night specials are prepared. We're ready to go." Mary dusted her hand off and wiped them on the towel tucked in her waist.

She opened the bottles and began pouring. "Why didn't they fly into Cork Airport?"

"No connecting flights from Dublin to Cork tonight." Mary jumped as the door banged open.

"Something smells fantastic." Bridget sprinted through the door, took her hat and mittens off, and stuck them in her coat pocket. Then she hung the coat on the peg beside Synn's jacket.

****

Two hours later, true to her prediction, the pub was

standing room only. She and Bridget delivered food and drink to the tables. Gale and Dillon had arrived early to stake their claim on a corner booth and ordered. Later in the evening, Tristian and Hannah joined them as Quinn's band began to play.

Synn's feet were killing her as she ducked under the pass through and tapped Gavin on the shoulder. She pointed to the kitchen, then flew through the swinging door for the umpteenth time and skittered to a stop in front of Mary. "I'm going to take a quick break, catch a breath of fresh air out back on the porch, and check on Storm."

Mary gave her a thumbs up.

Two steps onto the porch, she heard screams followed by several loud crashes. The wind slammed the door to the storeroom shut. She raced across the porch and reached for the back door. The silver gauntlets sparkled under the porch light as they made their way up her forearm. "Shit" A weight on her back startled her as the sword of Kilara appeared in her hand, the scabbard weighing on her back. Tristian's voice in her head. *Think before you act.*

Forcing herself to pause, she peeked in the window. The kitchen was empty, but the swinging door was still moving back and forth banging against the wall. Once again making sure her magic was concealed, she crept inside and moved stealthy across the floor. Her breath caught in her throat, and her heart pounded in her chest as she peeked out the kitchen door to the scene in the middle of the pub floor.

A cloaked figure had Mary by the throat, holding a ball of fire in the other hand, while a dozen or more creatures circled around him. Baltizar? The figure hurtled the fire ball behind the bar. Something snuffed it out. Gavin popped up then disappeared again. A crack of light and the air sucked out of the room like a vacuum. The pub cleared out, leaving only magic kind. The corner booth was empty. Where were Tristian, Hannah, Dillion, and Gale?

Magic washed over her. She whirled around to see Angie standing in the middle of the kitchen. The witch crept closer. "Tristian transported the mortals out of harm's way. They won't remember a thing, except Bridget who is with Quinn overseeing them. You Ready? Gale, Dillion, Tristian, Hannah, and Bruce are positioned in the pub ready to strike. We're going to take out this joker's merry band of demons flanking him."

She nodded taking one more peek in the room planning her attack.

Angie slammed the swinging doors open drawing the hooded figure's attention. Synn squatted down, slipped out the doors, and moved sideways hugging the wall of the pub taking cover behind the other magic kind still in the room.

Mary struggled. The figure's hood slipped. His cracked lips pulled away from the yellowed teeth in a menacing grin as he pressed the knife harder to Mary's throat. A trickle of blood wound its way down her throat. Fury raged inside Synn as she recognized those features. The creature lobbed several more fire balls at the bar laughing maniacally. They exploded one after another.

A whoosh and intense heat followed as the flames licked the ancient wooden bar, flared in the corners, and spread across the floor. The mirrors behind the glass shelves shattered, bottles of liquid splattered coating the walls and floors feeding the flames.

She tamped down her temper. Emotions had no place in a battle. Especially during one she was determined to win. Making her way closer to the center of the room where the creature stood, she positioned herself to the side and slightly behind him. The other magic folk in the room continued to run interference. They took his followers out one by one until there was only a solitary creature left standing on the other side of the room.

Suddenly, she jumped up on the table, crouched and lunged, shoving Mary to the floor with her foot.

Baltizar howled and grabbed for Mary but was able to only catch hold of her skirt. The cloth tore, leaving him holding a piece of red plaid fabric. He ignited it and threw it on her back.

Mary rolled, got to her hands and knees scurrying across the floor out of harm's way. A booted foot stomped on the burning cloth and swept Mary off the floor. A quick glance, she recognized Gavin's head full of tawny feathers as he disappeared into the crowd with his ma in his arms.

Baltizar's mouth opened, and he roared. His eyes bugged out. She saw recognition there. He jerked the table out from under her and slammed it to the floor. Summersaulting backward, she landed on her feet with the sword held in front of her. He raised his arm and shot bolts of lightning toward her. She dodged right then left her sword deflecting the blows. The jagged shafts pierced the wooden floor, and flames erupted.

A dagger appeared in his right hand. He swung it wildly toward her. She sidled right, lobbing a fireball in his face. He howled in pain covering his face for a beat. Taking advantage of his momentary lapse of focus, she brought her sword up in an arc letting it cut through the air leaving a green phosphorescent trail and severing Baltizar's head neatly from his body. The gem in the hilt of her weapon pulsed red as his head flew across the room, hit the wall with a thud, and blood spatter coated the surfaces in close proximity.

With the next downward slice of her sword, she split him from throat to groin. Still he remained upright, though wobbling a bit. *What the hell does it take to kill the bastard?* She put all her weight and power behind the final slice, quartering his body, and it fell to the floor in pieces. *It's about damn time.* Tendrils of smoke curled from the edges of his flesh, as the flames flared and consumed its prey.

The stench of burning flesh filled her nostrils. She gagged, poking at the burning mass with the tip of Kilara. Stabbing the point in the wood floor, she leaned on the sword for a beat. Gavin's soot and blood smudged face appeared in her peripheral vision. For the first time, she noticed the battles winding down around her. They'd won. A pang of sadness tore at her heart as she surveyed the damage. She sucked in a breath at the devastation and coughed violently.

"We gotta get out of here." He grasped her arm and tugged. She was frozen in place. "Synn, come on." He scooped her up in his arms and carried her out front door. Sirens wailed in the distance. Flames shot higher and higher consuming the building that for centuries and generations had housed Shaughnessy's Pub. The burning wood crackled and popped, propelling red-hot cinders into the night sky.

Her body tensed as anger grew until it was like a living breathing thing. She screamed out. Her hands still fisted around her Kilara. He set her on her feet and backed away. "Darlin', put the sword down. It's just stuff. We're all safe. A bit battle worn, but safe. You did a spectacular job in there."

"Bastard! He's burnt your family's legacy to the ground." She paused, her shoulders sagged, and head leaning to the side. *It's all my fault.*

"No, we—you—were prepared. He was consumed by rage, which as you know, has no place on the battle field. In the end it cost him and his follower's their lives."

"And your family—it's wonderful, loving legacy—destroyed." She stared sadly at the building engulfed in flames, beams crashing to the floor, embers floating across the night sky. Suddenly she straightened. "Where's Mary?" Panic seized her, and her gaze searched the chaotic scene. "Where's Mary?" she wailed. "Mary? Mary? Oh God, where's Storm?"

Blue and amber lights of emergency vehicles flooded the night. He pulled her to him, holding her firm as she tried to break free. "Ma's fine. A few cuts, scratches, and bruises, but she'll be fine. You saved her life, you know." He paused, cupping her face in his hands. "Storm is waiting for you in the truck. Hannah had just arrived and came running after the first explosion, saw Storm rush toward the building, and grabbed her."

She slumped against him. Battle fatigue hit her hard.

He stroked her hair. "There's going to be a lot of questions. We better get our stories straight for the authorities." A soft rain fell and sizzled against the scorched timbers. The mist settled in obscuring everything but the burning building.

She stiffened. "What about Bridget and Quinn and their charges."

"Tristian instructed them to make sure all the mortals got home safe then meet back here, or where ever we rendezvous to make sure everyone is accounted for."

Tim's vehicle came to a screeching halt in front of the pub. He, Brandy, and Stefan jumped out of the car and rushed over.

"What the hell happened? Where's Mary?" Tim looked frantically around the area.

"I'm here. I'm fine." Mary pushed through the crowd charging toward him followed by medical personal. She turned and shoved at them. "I told you I'm not going nowhere."

Tim enveloped her in his arms. "Thank God." He focused a stern glance in Gavin's direction. "I leave you in charge for a few hours." Tim spread his arms wide. "And I come back to this?"

Synn felt Brandy's hot stare on her and turned to face her. "It's all my fault. I'm so sorry."

Brandy swiped at her. Gavin positioned himself between the two. "Sis, before you go jumping to conclusions, you should know that she saved Ma's life. Without her actions, Ma would be dead. A causality of Baltizar's fury and revenge. We been dealing with this for months, but Ma and Da didn't want to worry you."

Brandy's eyes widened, her mouth opened and shut like a codfish, but no sound came out.

The group of friends gathered around the couples

nodding in agreement.

Tristian strode up with Hannah right behind him. "The good news—all the wedding stuff, including your gown is at the house, safe and sound. The bad news, we'll have to find an alternate venue for the reception." He glanced at the smolders mass in front of them. "I believe the pub will be under renovations for a while."

Bruce ambled into the crowd his arm around Angie. Both their faces smudged with soot. Their clothing was torn and bloody. "I have several venues in the area appropriate for both your wedding and reception, complete with staff, and can be ready at a moment's notice. You're welcome to use any one."

"Now that it appears we're all together and accounted for, why don't we adjourn to Ma and Da's house and gather our wits." Hannah reached an arm around Brandy and hugged her tightly, then included Stefan in the hug. "Sorry about all this. But think of the stories you can tell about the events leading up to your wedding."

Brandy burst into tears. "I'm so glad you're all okay."

"No one is going anywhere until we get your statements." A police officer muscled his way through the crowd. A unified sigh came from the group.

"Can't we return to our house? You can interview all of us there out of the rain. It's been a bloody hell of a night, and I for one want to go somewhere I don't have to stare at my family legacy and livelihood in shambles." Tim took his coat off and wrapped it around Mary.

Stefan stared at the police officer. "Hell man, we weren't even here for any of the action. We just arrived a few minutes ago. What can it hurt to interview them all in a warm comfortable home? It's not like you don't know where the Shaughnessy family can be found."

The officer blinked and looked confused. "I guess it would be all right." He motioned another officer over. "I'm going to allow these people to go over to the Shaughnessy's house. We can interview them there."

The group scattered into various vehicles and caravanned to Tim and Mary's home. Last to leave the area, Synn and Gavin shuffled to his truck. She paused at the door as he gazed at the pile of burning rubble.

To her surprise, he wiped his eyes, turned around to face her and bend down on one knee. "I know this is not very romantic."

Scrunching up her face, she wrinkled her nose. "You got that right." For the first time since leaving the building, she noticed that the sword and gauntlets were gone. A little sigh of relief left her lips. She turned her attention to him.

"Would you let me finish. I've something important to say."

"Well, it's about time." She smirked.

"Anyway, as I was saying—with this bunch of renegades, you never know what will happen next. Baltizar is dead as well as most of the bad guys. That being his entire inner circle." He grinned up at her. "I've waited long enough..." He cleared his throat. "We've waited long enough. I love you. Will you marry me?"

"Well—they say for better or worse. Right?" She paused staring down at him. "I'd say it's not going to get much worse than this." She reached down and yanked him to his feet, kissed him soundly, then gazed up at him. "Yes. I'll marry you."

He kissed her hand. Bringing his lips to hers, he traced her lips with his tongue as she parted them and poured all his feelings into the kiss. The warmth careened all the way to her toes. A zing of desire shot to her center, and she returned the kiss with reckless abandon. Eventually, she became aware of a crowd gathering around them and insistent barking. They broke apart. She clambered into the truck. Storm, her whole body wiggling with joy, licked her face in greeting.

"I'm glad to see you too, girl."

"We're going; we're going." Gavin vaulted over the truck's hood, scrambled into the driver's seat, and grabbed her left hand. "By the way, I'll put a ring on that finger as soon as we make it home."

"I'll hold you to it." She laughed. "We better get to the house before trouble finds us again."

"Oh, I believe Brandy aka trouble will have her hands full with Ma, Hannah, and the rest of her friends." He snickered, leaned over and kissed her again.

When they reached his parents' home, lights were a blaze in every window. Reflections from the porch light pooled in yellow puddles on the ground. If a house could be considered happy, this one was. She grinned, scooted over, reached an arm around his neck, and kissed him tenderly on the cheek.

A look of surprise spread across his face in the pale moonlight streaming through the truck window. "What was that for?"

"For believing in me and showing me it was possible to have a normal life with friends and family."

She sat back against the seat and sighed.

Gavin snorted. "This says the woman that slayed the demon, burnt down the pub, and …"

"I didn't burn down the pub. Baltizar and his minions did." She protested reaching for the door handle.

He snapped his fingers. "Just a minute." Digging through the glove box, he cursed under his breath, then opened the console between the front seats and smiled wide. She leaned over to see what he was doing. He closed his hand over something. "Got it." When he opened his hand, in the palm was a blue velvet box. He flipped the lid open.

Her breath caught as she gingerly took the box. Inside a ring with a marquise diamond surrounded by tiny emeralds sparkled in the moonlight. "For me?"

"You're the only one I asked to marry me." He took the ring out of the box and slid it onto her finger. "Perfect."

Holding her hand so the ring caught the light, she gazed at it for several minutes, then folded her hand to her heart. *It's really happening. I can't believe it.* When she brought her gaze to meet his, tears rolled down her cheeks.

"Now there, lassie. You're supposed to be happy, not crying. At least that's what I've heard." He tipped her chin up, brushed the tears away with his thumbs, and kissed the corner of her lips. With his mouth over hers, he showered kisses over her lips and along her jaw line.

She quivered at the sweet tenderness of his touch. Her lips found their way instinctively to his, she lingered, savoring every moment with her arms wrapped around his neck.

Suddenly the front door banged open, and Tristian called out, "Come on. We're all waiting on you. The food's getting cold."

Her stomach gurgled loudly. She released him with a shy smile. "Guess we better get in there, or they'll be out here dragging us in.

"Aye, you got that right."

Once inside, they were greeted by friends and family. A complete smorgasbord was set up in the dining room.

"Where'd all the food come from?" Gavin grabbed a plate. "I know you keep stuff on hand but not this much."

Mary beamed spreading her arms wide and motioning to the table. "Courtesy of Bruce and Angie." She reached out and pulled Synn into a hug. "Welcome to the family."

"Wait. What? How did you know? He only—" she stammered.

Brandy, her hands wrapped around a mug of steaming liquid sauntered over to her ma. "Did I miss something?"

Chapter Twenty-Nine

Change of Venue, Change of Heart, and an Engagement

Hannah joined the group holding a plate heaped with food. Her eyes rounded and her mouth formed an O before she found her voice. "Wow, would you look at that rock on her hand. Way to go little brother."

He grinned like a Cheshire cat. "Go big or go home we Shaughnessy's always say." He turned to his blushing bride-to-be.

She put her hands to her cheeks where red patches bloomed then spread over her entire face.

Brandy followed her sister's gaze. The mug slid out of her hand and crashed to the floor. She immediately stooped to pick up the broken glass. Mary rushed over with a mop.

Angie waved her hand, and the mess disappeared along with the mop from Mary's hand. "This is a celebration. We don't have time for menial tasks." The rest of the women hurried over to garner a peek at Synn's ring.

"It's about time." Tim wandered over and slapped his son on the back. "Congratulations."

"Have you set a date?" Mary glanced at the ring.

"Nooo…" Synn stammered. "Its all happened so fast."

"As far as I'm concerned, the sooner the better."

Gavin grinned.

"Speaking of weddings." Brandy sighed. "Unless I'm mistaken, our reception venue just went up in flames."

"Aye, it did." Tim rubbed the top of his thinning hair, then scrubbed a hand over his face. "Won't be available—may never be…"

Tristian rested a hand on his father-in-law's shoulder. "Do you have blueprints of the place?"

"Aye, in me office here at the house. Glad I didn't leave them in the pub. Why?" Tim picked up his glass and downed what was left of his whiskey. He held his glass out for a refill.

"I've an idea." Tristian shot a glance at Bruce who gave a slight nod. "Could you bring them up here? I'll clear off the kitchen table so we can spread the plans out."

"Sure. But I don't know what good it'll do." Tim set the glass down and disappeared down the hall.

"What do you two have in mind?" He left Synn with the knot of women fussing over her ring and moved into the kitchen. Tristian handed him the Christmas center piece from the table.

"Don't get his hopes up. It's going to take a long time and financing to set things right." Grabbing a mug from the cupboard, he filled it with coffee and took a gulp.

"Hear us out. Before you go all dooms day on us." Tristian took the pot of coffee off the warmer, poured a mug, and rinsed the pot. "Need a new pot. Where do you keep the fresh ground again?"

Mary bustled into the kitchen. "Here let me take care of that before you break something." She opened the cupboard door and stood on tiptoe reaching the canister on the top shelf. It bobbled in her hand and fell. Tristian reached out and caught the tin.

"You were saying?"

"Oh, get out of my way." She grinned up at him.

"May I continue? Magic destroyed it... Magic can rebuild it." Bruce held his hand up as Gavin opened his mouth to protest. "Using mortal crews during the day will keep up an appearance of normalcy, and magic personnel will work during the night." Bruce paused looking at his brother-in-law. "What do you think a week or two tops?"

Tristian nodded. "Easily."

"A week or two for what?" Tim entered the kitchen with a set of rolled up plans. "This is blueprints from the remodel a few years ago." He paused. "The original hand drawn one isn't legible anymore."

"To rebuild the pub in time for Brandy's wedding reception. She's rescheduled the ceremony to December 31st." He glanced into the dining area in time to see Hannah headed their way.

"At the stroke of midnight," Hannah chimed in making her way to the table. "What are you guys plotting?"

Quinn, Stefan, Dillon, and Andre backed away from the table and held their hands up feigning innocence.

"A venue for Brandy and Stefan's reception." Tristian winked at her. "Including one hell of a New Year's Grand re-opening bash. The whole town will be at the reception, so..."

"I like it. But I don't see how that is possible." Tim scratched the top of his head. "You were there—you saw." He took the new bottle of good whiskey, poured three fingers, and downed half of it. "Helluva night."

"Like I told Gavin. Magic destroyed the pub. Magic will rebuild it." He held up a hand. "Before you argue appearances. Let me set out our plans."

****

Though she'd eaten half of the food on her plate, her head pounded, peripheral vision faded in and out as the women clamored around, asking questions, and admiring her ring. Their faces blurred, voices faded, and her legs buckled. A strong hand at her elbow and Angie's soft voice whispered. "I think you better sit down. The magic aftermath is hitting you." Angie guided her to the recliner in front of the fireplace. "Could I get a glass of water over here and a blanket?"

Synn turned her head toward the tinkling sound of ice in water. Matiah grabbed the pitcher of ice water from the dining table and poured it into a tumbler on the end of the table. She carried the glass over to her. "Here you go, darlin'."

She took several sips. The room quit spinning and her vision started to come back into focus. "What was that... Never felt like that."

"Wielding too much magic, power, and Fae weapons all at the same time." Gale touched her on the knee. "You'll be fine. And you'll get used to it." She paused. "At least that's what Tiarnan said before he and Erin left. Said they'd be around. Wouldn't miss Brandy's wedding for anything."

She glanced around for Gavin, finding him with his head bent over the kitchen table with the rest of the men. She pushed up from the chair. Dizziness still had her in its grips, but she leaned on the chair and centered herself. "Storm is still in the truck. We weren't planning to stay long. I gotta let her out. Don't want an accident in Gavin's truck."

"I'll get her," Brandy offered.

"Thanks, but she doesn't know you...and it's been quite a night for her too. Besides, I could use a little fresh air." She gulped down the rest of her water and took a carrot from her plate and bit into it.

"Then I'll walk out with you." Brandy caught Stefan's attention in the kitchen, nodded toward the door, then continued eye contact for a minute or two more.

Brandy grabbed her coat and picked up Synn's off the back of the couch. Once out the door, Brandy followed her toward the truck. A black nose was pressed against the steamed-up passenger window. Storm began to bark the closer they got to the truck.

"It's okay, Storm. Friend." She patted Brandy on the arm. *Now that's something I never thought I'd be sayin'.* Opening the door, she clipped the leash on. The pup jumped out of the truck and tugged on the leash toward the house. "No, we're not going in there. Around back." Storm altered her course.

In the back yard, she let the pup off leash and waited.

"Any idea how soon—soon is for Gavin? I mean about the wedding?"

"Not really. Tomorrow, if it was up to him. But we won't interfere with your wedding festivities. May just have Bruce or Andre officiate the bond, that's all I—we need. No big deal."

"Oh, that's where you're wrong. Gavin is the only son and Irish marriages are a big deal. Ma and Da will have a fit if you do that. I have a better idea."

Chapter Thirty

Two Weeks Later—A New Year's Eve Celebration—A New Beginning

Gavin waited in the living room in front of the massive stone fireplace. Stefan stood a few feet from him. Bruce and Tristian lounged at either end of the hearth talking in hushed tones to their mates. His parents' home had been turned into a magical faerie land of twinkling multi-colored lights, fragrant scents of candles, and flower arrangements filled the air.

Katie's daughters skipped into the room. Carefully lit each candle and hurried back to the kitchen. The candles' flames danced to their own beat, casting shadows on the walls. Red roses and white carnations decorated the room. Brandy and Synn had different ideas about the flowers, but in the end agreed there was room for both ideas.

Unable to stand still any longer, he paced to where Stefan stood examining something on his suit coat. "You ready for this?" He stopped beside Stefan for a moment.

"You bet. It's been a long time coming." Stefan shifted nervously from foot to foot. "What I'm really looking forward to is the honeymoon. Tristian is letting us use his beach house in Hawaii for a couple of weeks." The vampire straightened his suit jacket, checked the red carnation in his lapel, and grinned.

"I'm glad the girls worked it out. Family is so important. It's something you realize when you don't have one."

"Synn said the same thing." He checked his carnation and moved back to his assigned spot.

Mary hustled down the makeshift aisle with Storm short leashed and plopped down in the front row positioning the wiggling pup between her feet. She gave Storm a chew stick to keep her quiet and busy.

Over the last couple of weeks, it was satisfying to watch Brandy, Hannah, and Synn working, laughing, and even arguing in a sisterly manner, something he'd had his doubts about even though he never let on.

It had been a whirlwind of activity since the night Baltizar, his followers, and the pub were destroyed. The resurrection of Shaughnessy's Pub out of the smoking pile of ruins was no small feat. Destroyed by magic, and rebuilt by magic, turned out to be by the blood, sweat, and hard work of several individuals. Long time patrons of the pub and local contractors worked on the pub by day. At night a whole different team of workers turned on the magic.

His da and ma kept busy with Brandy's wedding plan adjustments. Red roses, white carnations, and baby's breath went into the bridal bouquets. Smelled heavenly, but he stayed out of the way for fear of being put to work. Overseeing the restoration of the pub overnights had his sleep schedule completely discombobulated. When the sun peeked over the horizon, his eyelids drooped. Yet, when darkness fell, well—he was still tired.

The pub had never looked better. A new bigger state of the art kitchen had his ma beaming. She had plans to overhaul the menu, which sounded like a lot more work for him. Da and Ma decided to semi retire once the pub was open for business, working only when they felt like it or on busy weekends. They signed the whole shebang over to him as an early wedding present, which suited him just fine.

Tiarnan and Erin had checked in periodically usually during his shift. They made suggestions to add a few Fae touches. Some of their family recipes were added to the drink list in the new pub. Tristian had used magic to refurbish the wooden and brass bar from the old pub. Though he'd had his doubts, the results were outstanding. Extending the dance floor and stage was his idea. After consulting with Quinn, several modifications to the sound and electrical systems on stage made a huge difference.

More booths, tables, and chairs in an extended main room of the pub would mean bigger crowds but easier cleanup due to the extra room to move around. Plush pit style seating around the new massive moss rock fireplace area would be a popular addition. Tonight—all the changes would be on display at the New Year's Eve and wedding reception celebration in Shaughnessy's Pub.

Strains of organ music penetrated his consciousness. He glanced around. The folding chairs that replaced the regular furniture were filled with smiling people dressed in their Sunday best. A few stragglers hurried to find a seat as the first chords of the wedding march echoed through the room.

His gaze shifted to the entrance from the kitchen where the bridesmaids waited to begin the procession. Katie's youngest, bounced down the makeshift aisle, pigtails swaying, tossing rose petals in the air, rather than dropping them on the ground as she'd been shown at the rehearsal. He smiled.

Ian, one of the long-time regulars volunteered his great-grandson, Angus, to be a ring bearer. He wasn't sure who the other little boy was walking beside Angus.

The procession began. He looked over the heads of the bridesmaids and sucked in a breath. She was breath-taking, in a long shimmering gown that shifted as if a trick of light between aqua and emerald green. The dress hugged her curves and accentuated her sparkling aqua eyes. He recalled something Synn had said about Molly adding a touch of magic to the bridesmaid dress that she'd loved, making it work for her wedding dress. On her head a crown of flowers with multi-color ribbons streamed down her long raven hair. His bride-to-be was all he'd ever wanted. He glanced at his sister on the arm of his da and smiled. Brandy didn't look bad either in her white lace gown with train and veil.

Brandy's offer to share her wedding date with them making it a double wedding had shocked not only Synn but him, and his parents as well. Angie jumped all over the idea and helped make those arrangements, since her own wedding to Bruce had been a double wedding with her childhood best friend, Willow.

****

The first strains of the Wedding March hung in the air, a bead of sweat trickled down the side of her face. Her heart thundered in her chest as she drew in a breath. Bruce stood at her side, dressed in a suit and tie, looking relaxed and a small smile on his face. He turned to look at her and squeezed her hand resting on his arm. "Ready?"

"Hold that thought." Glancing out the windows toward the ocean, she quick stepped to the double glass door and stared out at the misty landscape. Her parents had been in her thoughts in the past weeks. "Well, Mom and Dad—I believe—I'm going to be all right." She paused, turned the handle on the door, stepped out on the porch, and wiped tears off her cheeks. Notes of the harp music and the sound of faraway heels clicking on the hardwood floor followed her.

She sucked in a breath as shapes formed in the mist that now settled as thick as pea soup around the house. "Mom? Dad?" Her gaze transfixed on their faces. Was she dreaming? "How is this possible?" Reaching out a hand, she leaned toward the images, and her mom raised a hand. She tried to touch it, but her fingers went right through the image with a frigid sensation.

"It's a special day of celebration. We've only a moment, but we always knew you'd make your way." Her father's image wavered a bit but smiled. "We're sorry we failed to keep you safe and your powers hidden. But sometimes fate has the upper hand. Your guardian blood was meant for greater things. We're so proud of you—our Fae warrior. You have a family now, and they'll be good to you. Be happy." The words faded away as the ice crystals danced on the railing. Her parents waved one last time before their images faded into the fog.

Tears streamed down her face. She didn't care. Over the course of the last few months, she'd cried more than she had in her entire life. She scrubbed her hands over her face. Angie's beautiful makeup job would be smudged—ruined—her eyes red and puffy. She blinked. Some beautiful bride she'd make. *Not*. She shrugged. *I'll leave that to Brandy*. The clicking heels grew louder then stopped right behind her. She whirled around almost running smack dab into Angie.

"Girl, you're holding up the wedding. Let's have a look at you." Angie shook her head make a clicking sound with her tongue. "Oh, my, this will never do." Angie gave a gentle wave of her hand over Synn's face then nodded. "Much better." Angie gave her a quick hug and shoved her toward the front room. "Off with you."

She inhaled letting it out slowly. Calming herself, she walked to where Bruce, Brandy, and Tim waited to walk down the aisle. She slipped her hand though Bruce's crooked elbow, gave a nod, and mouthed sorry to Brandy. They took the first step together toward the loves of their lives waiting for them.

Bruce paused beside Gavin. The Overlord offered Synn's hand to him.

"She's your responsibility now. Treat her well, or you'll answer to me." Bruce turned and joined the groomsmen to his right.

"I will." He licked his lips and barely got the words out.

Tim turned Brandy over to Stefan and sat down in the front row with Mary. Storm made a soft woof. Mary quieted her.

Andre conducted the ceremony, which was mostly a blur in her mind. At the first stroke of midnight, they finished reciting the vows they'd written. Gavin nearly dropped her ring, but she'd quickly snagged it with her finger. As the twelfth chime sounded from the grandfather clock in the room, Andre introduced them as husband and wife to a standing ovation from the family and close friends gathered to witness this joyous occasion.

Gavin took her in his arms, touched his lips to hers and she lost herself in the kiss. A few clearing throats and chuckles brought her back seconds later. She hurried to keep up with his long strides back down the aisle.

"It's time to party!" Gavin loosened his tie, grasped her around the waist and hoisted her over his head.

She giggled. "Put me down. You're embarrassing me."

He lowered her until her feet touched the ground and brushed his lips over hers. Standing on tiptoe, she caressed his cheek as his lips slowly descended to meet hers. She slipped her arms around his neck and quivered at the sweet tenderness of his kiss. Shivers of desire raced through her.

Raising his mouth from hers, he gazed into her eyes. "Well, how's it feel to be Mrs. Gavin Shaughnessy?" He grinned, his face still flushed with excitement.

"About like it did when I was plain Synn—only with a longer, harder name to spell." She snickered.

His crestfallen expression lasted only a beat, then he roared with laughter. "Never know what's going to come out of your mouth."

Storm bounced over to her, all wiggles, snuffles and finally barked.

She bent down and rubbed her ears. "You were a good girl."

Gavin reached in his pocket and took out two treats. "I was prepared should she cause a commotion during the ceremony." He tossed the treats to the pup.

"Always prepared, that's my man."

Hand in hand they sprinted out of the house amid a shower of birdseed and bubbles to an awaiting carriage along with Storm, Brandy, and Stefan. Big storybook snowflakes fell as the horses made their way to the pub where the New Year's Eve celebration and reception would be held.

When they arrived, Mary greeted them. "I'll put Storm in her new accommodations in the storeroom. She has her own play yard, you know."

****

He whisked her out on the dance floor for their first dance as husband and wife, sharing the floor with only Brandy and Stefan. As the last notes of their slow dance sounded, Quinn stepped to the microphone. "Do I have the bride's and groom's permission to liven things up?" He looked expectantly to the couples.

He nodded in unison with Brandy, Stefan, and Synn. Cori stepped out of the shadows and began an Irish jig on her fiddle. Quinn's band accompanied her as her feet danced in time. The guests flooded the dance floor. After a few more dances, Angie grabbed the couples.

"Time to cut the cake." She led them over to a large table covered with a red and green lace. A five-tier wedding cake frosted in white with red roses sat atop the table at the end of the bar.

Bridget stood behind the cake, cutting the first layer into pieces and putting them on plates. Four plates with cake sat in front. She pointed to the pieces of cake. "Those are for the brides and grooms. Now give each other a bite, so the rest of us can enjoy a piece too."

Stefan's eyes twinkled with mischief as he nuzzled

Brandy's neck. When he raised his head, she met his mouth with a kiss and a big piece of cake, smearing it all over his face as she laughed. He grinned and returned the favor as Brandy tried to duck but wasn't fast enough. A photographer snapped a picture.

"Don't you dare," Synn warned him holding a neatly cut piece of wedding cake on a fork up to his lips.

Warily he opened his mouth and took the bite. "Ummmm. This is delicious. Who created this confectionery work of art?"

"Brenda from the bakery down the street," Hannah volunteered.

He offered up a bite of cake for Synn, as carefully as she had his. She took the bite, smiled and… He never saw it coming. Whap. She smushed a small piece of cake into his mouth. After smearing it on his cheek, she disappeared under the pass through and into the kitchen laughing outrageously.

Licking the frosting off his lips, he took a napkin and cleaned his face off. "You are so busted, Synn." He laughed thinking back to the woman lacking confidence and direction, who made the decision to make Ireland her home, and adjusted to her new life. She was a far cry from the woman he'd just married, and he couldn't be more proud.

"I got some great shots." The photographer chuckled.

"Oh, just wait there's more opportunities coming up." Gavin grinned and glanced around for his bride.

Andre tapped him on the shoulder. "So where are you spending your honeymoon?"

"Some place out of the way here in Ireland. Synn

doesn't want to…"

"I may have changed my mind. What did you have in mind." She popped up behind them, resting her hand on her husband's shoulder.

"Been talking to Matiah in the kitchen—huh?" Andre smiled as his wife made her way through the crowd to him.

"Sort of."

"Okay is someone going to tell me what's going on?" He glanced at the faces gathered around them.

"Since Matiah and I are going to spend the next couple of weeks with my son and daughter-in-law, we thought we'd offer our villa and staff in Tahiti for your honeymoon." He caught Synn's gaze and held it. "There is no place safer. And we don't like to leave it unattended for long."

Synn's eyes widened, and she blinked several times.

"Oh—Synn—there is this cute little cottage right next to the huge waterfall you'd just love." Hannah sighed. "Tristian and I stayed there for Bruce and Angie's wedding. It's right next to the main house, but so cozy. There's a path to the beach lit with tiki torches."

"We're taking Storm with us." She hesitated. "Will that be a problem? We'll watch her constantly and clean up after her, of course. She's still a puppy, you know."

"So we've heard." Andre glanced at Matiah, who nodded. "Not a problem. So is that a yes?"

Synn bobbed her head up and down. Matiah took an emerald encrusted comb out of her hair and handed it to Synn. "This will help guide you to our home.

You'll have to port there."

She took the comb and smiled wide. "Thank you so much."

"Aye, you don't have to do this—but…" He looked at Synn wondering what had changed her mind. "We accept your offer. Thank you so much."

A wistful expression crossed Matiah's face. "It's been a long time since a Fae Warrior with Guardian blood visited our place."

"I don't believe we've ever had a Demon-Fae Warrior visit our place. It's about time." Andre chuckled, correcting his mate.

A New Year, a new beginning, and a celebration in the newly re-opened Shaughnessy's Pub, he couldn't think of a better way to start their life together. Snapping his fingers, he turned to his ma and da standing behind the bar. "Think you and Ma can take care of things while we're gone?"

His ma reached over the bar and slapped at him. "We've been taking care of things long before you kids were a twinkle in your da's eye. Believe we can handle it." She laughed and slung an arm around her husband. The celebration lasted into the wee hours of the morning.

He and Synn stood in front of the pub waving to Brandy and Stefan as they climbed into the cab taking them to the airport headed to Tristian's beach house in Hawaii.

An hour later, he and Synn stood on the porch with Storm prepared to depart for the cottage in Tahiti. Synn held the emerald comb up as the air swirled around them in colors of green and blue. The cold damp atmosphere around them changed to a warm, floral scented breeze with birds singing and sounds of a water fall crashing over rocks nearby.

His fingers twined with hers, they sauntered across the lush grasses edged with colorful foliage and tropical flowers to the little cottage beside the massive waterfall. Different sizes and shapes of crystals hung from the porch bouncing rainbows in the air as the sun beams glittered through the mist of the falls. Trotting beside Synn, Storm was short leashed, her nose pointed toward the sky sniffing all the new scents.

"What made you change your mind about leaving Ireland?" He paused to glance over at her.

"My parents."

He raised a brow. "I thought…"

"My parents were dead. True. Something magical happened." She told him about seeing her parents just before the wedding, about their conversation, and their last words to her. "Be Happy." She reached up, caressed his cheek, and smiled. "Our goal going forward."

"Works for me." Turning the door handle to the cottage, he pushed it open, swept her up in his arms, and carried her over the threshold.

A word about the author…

Tena Stetler is a best-selling author of award-winning paranormal romance. She has an over-active imagination, which led to writing her first vampire romance as a tween to the chagrin of her mother and delight of her friends. After many years as a paralegal, then an IT Manager, she decided to live out her dream of pursuing a publishing career.

With the Rocky Mountains outside her window, she sits at her computer surrounded by a wide array of witches, shapeshifters, demons, faeries, and gryphons, with a Navy SEAL or two mixed in telling their tales. Her books tell stories of magical kick-ass women and mystical alpha males that dare to love them. Well, okay there are a few companion animals to round out the tales.

Colorado is home; shared with her husband of many moons, a brilliant Chow Chow, a spoiled parrot, and a forty-five-year-old box turtle. When she's not writing, her time is spent kayaking, camping, hiking, biking, or just relaxing in the great Colorado outdoors. During the winter you can find her curled up in front of a crackling fire with a good book, a mug of hot chocolate and a big bowl of popcorn.

http://www.tenastetler.com

Thank you for purchasing
this publication of The Wild Rose Press, Inc.

For questions or more information
contact us at
info@thewildrosepress.com.

The Wild Rose Press, Inc.
www.thewildrosepress.com

To visit with authors of
The Wild Rose Press, Inc.
join our yahoo loop at
http://groups.yahoo.com/group/thewildrosepress/